TOUCHING THE HERO'S HEART

Taken by Destiny, Book 3

By Aurrora St. James

ARE YOU SIGNED UP FOR DRAGONBLADE'S BLOG?

You'll get the latest news and information on exclusive giveaways, exclusive excerpts, coming releases, sales, free books, cover reveals and more.

Check out our complete list of authors, too!

No spam, no junk. That's a promise!

Sign Up Here

www.dragonbladepublishing.com

Dearest Reader;

Thank you for your support of a small press. At Dragonblade Publishing, we strive to bring you the highest quality Historical Romance from some of the best authors in the business. Without your support, there is no 'us', so we sincerely hope you adore these stories and find some new favorite authors along the way.

Happy Reading!

CEO, Dragonblade Publishing

**Additional Dragonblade books by
Author Aurrora St. James**

Taken by Destiny Series
The Earl's Timely Wallflower (Book 1)
Tempting the Reclusive Earl (Book 2)
Touching the Hero's Heart (Book 3)

CHAPTER ONE

Present Day
Corbin, Kentucky

WHAT THE HELL *have you gotten us into, Lily?*

Archer Bennett's fingers clenched around the steering wheel of his Jeep and the hair on the back of his neck prickled. He'd seen nicer apartment complexes than this in Afghanistan, so why the hell was his sister living here?

The sign on the two-story roach motel advertised clean apartments and cheap rates with instant availability. He snorted. They were available because people didn't appreciate having to wear a hazmat suit in their own apartment. What a joke.

Almost a week earlier, his little sister Bellamy had called him up in a panic because she couldn't reach their other sister. He'd been sure Lily was fine. Bellamy tended to get a little wound up and she'd tried to get him to come out to this tiny town with her. It had seemed like a waste of time, so he hadn't.

His stomach gave an uncomfortable lurch. Truth was, he hadn't wanted to leave his house if he didn't have to. Some days, it was just too painful.

Bellamy had called again three days later from Lily's apartment but this time her voice was thick with worry. Their sister wasn't there, but her phone and purse were, and no one had notified the police. He'd been concerned. Of course, he had. But what could he do from Colorado that she couldn't do there? Or that's what he'd told himself. Any excuse, right? Anything to avoid facing his sisters and answering their questions about his injury. And his team.

When she hadn't called back by the next day, he'd finally called her and received her voicemail. Four hours later, he left another. Unease had set in. Bells wanted his help with Lily; she wouldn't avoid him. When he couldn't reach her the next day, or the next, the fear—and guilt—finally punched through his walls. He'd grabbed some gear and got his ass to Kentucky. To this run-down place, his sisters shouldn't have been anywhere near.

Archer kicked open the door to his Jeep, checked his knife, and grabbed his cane, locking the vehicle behind him. At least three cars had missing wheels, one had a smashed-in window and graffiti covered another. He had no intention of letting his Jeep become the fourth. He was getting his sisters and getting out of this dump.

A chilly breeze blew, sending brown leaves scattering over the cracked pavement. They crunched under his boots as he limped toward the apartment office. He pulled his jacket closer and focused on his objective: Find Lily and Bellamy, then go home where he could rest in peace. Oh, and give them hell for worrying him and dragging him out here to begin with.

He scanned the area again. Piles of mechanical parts were stacked against the sides of apartment buildings that looked like they'd been painted roughly forty years ago, by toddlers. Bellamy had said it was bad, but he hadn't imagined *this*.

The glass door to the apartment office had a large crack running down the center and was covered in black metal bars. A dented, black garbage can sat by the door, with dozens of cigarette butts on the ground around it. Archer yanked the door open and stepped inside the dingy, small space. The overwhelming smell of cigarette smoke choked him and forced him to take shallow breaths.

A man in his thirties sat behind an old desk with his feet kicked up, and a cigarette clamped in his lips. Smoke curled in the air, creating a cloud that drifted along the ceiling. Piles of paper, ratty chairs, and bookshelves cluttered the rest of the room. The only item of any value seemed to be a red-enameled egg with gold filigree that looked like one of those fancy Fabergé eggs. It sat atop one of the bookshelves, looking like the crown jewels in the middle of a sewer.

The man ran a hand through his thinning brown hair when he spotted Archer, then rubbed it on his dirty white tank top.

"Help you?" he rasped.

"Which apartment is Lily Bennett's?"

"Who are you?"

Archer shifted his weight off his injured leg. "The man looking for Lily's apartment."

The guy grinned and stabbed his cigarette out in an overflowing ashtray. "Gotta be more specific, buddy." He pointed at a nameplate that read *Dennis Rogers, Manager*. "I'm the apartment manager. I take care of this place and the people who live here. Can't let just anyone in to see one of the residents."

"You take care of the residents. That's why you haven't notified the police that she went missing?" Archer flexed his hand on the cane handle.

Dennis crossed his arms over his chest and leaned farther back in his chair. "Who says she is missing?"

Shit. He'd dealt with too many men like this during his time in the SEALs. He didn't have the time or the patience for Dennis, and he was in too much pain to be polite. He leaned in so he was at eye level with the man. The smell of nicotine and sweat stung his nose. "I do. Give me the key to her apartment or take me there. Either way, I'm getting into her apartment now."

"Who the fu—"

Fear for his sisters overrode any courtesy he might have summoned. It churned his stomach and threatened to bring up memories he'd locked away a long time ago. Archer strode around the desk, grabbed a fistful of Dennis's shirt, and jerked him to his feet. "I said *now*." He shoved Dennis toward the door. "If she's in trouble, your delaying won't do her—or you—any favors."

The man stumbled forward, then turned and glared at Archer. He must have realized that it was a fight he wouldn't win because he muttered a few curses and slammed through the door.

Archer followed. Dennis led him to a ratty building and up the exterior stairs. There were no light bulbs in the stairway lights and more cigarette butts littered the steps.

"Damn, it's cold. You should have let me grab my jacket, dude," Dennis muttered. They stopped at a door near the stairwell, and he fished a ring of keys out of his dirty pants. "That other chick that came here a couple days ago never returned my original key. Had to have a locksmith make a new one. If Lily comes back, tell her she owes me the four hundred seventy it cost to get the new key."

Archer wasn't listening. He was looking at the dozens more cigarette butts clumped in little piles far too near Lily's door. The same brand Dennis smoked. He narrowed his eyes at the man. This was the guy that Bellamy said had been too busy going through Lily's apartment to call the police. Looked like he'd been spending a lot of time outside of it as well.

A chill slid down his spine as a new thought took root. Was the guy stalking Lily? Was he responsible for her and Bellamy's disappearances? What if they'd been taken and he could have prevented it by leaving his fucking house? A tight knot formed in his gut and his heart pounded. Archer forced himself to control his breathing. His nightmares were getting to him. That was all it was. Even so… he speared Dennis with a hard look and pointed at the butts. "If I find out you had anything to do with their disappearances, you'll *beg* to go to jail."

Dennis's throat bobbed. He shrugged as if unconcerned, but the movement was stiff, and his shoulders remained hunched up by his ears. "Wasn't me, man. And who says they're missing anyway? You know women. They probably went shopping or some shit and didn't tell their guard dog. Not that I blame 'em. I wouldn't want to hang with you either."

"Just open the door."

Dennis unlocked the door with a shaky hand and pushed it open. "There ya go. I ain't leaving my key this time. If you find Lily or that other chick that looks just like Bellamy—you know that hot supermodel? Tell them to return my key and pay the rent. If it's not paid by tomorrow, then I'm boxing the place up and putting it in storage. I've got a list of people waiting to rent here. Can't keep the good places open for flighty tenants."

Fucker was delusional. He shoved past Dennis, then shut the door in his face.

"You must be related to that bitch. She always shut the door in my face too," Dennis called from the other side.

Archer swung the door back open and grabbed the man's shirt, dragging him an inch closer. "Talk about my sister that way again and it'll be the last time you speak with all of your teeth."

"You can't show up here threatening people. I'll have the cops here before—"

Archer shut the door in his face again.

Dennis swore. "Lily's car is still here, in case you're interested, asshole. So's the blonde's." He stomped away.

Archer scrubbed a hand down his face and looked around the efficiency apartment. "Dammit, Lily," he muttered. The place was no bigger than a shoebox. The cottage he rented was bigger than this place.

A fold-out bed, a bookcase, and a table with some tools on it were surrounded by a couple of beat-up chairs. She didn't even have a kitchen. It was a half-step up from a beer fridge and a camp stove. The only personal item of Lily's that he could see was a photo of the three of them. Their mom had taken it on their last camping trip before he left for boot camp. He looked happy and carefree, with an arm around each of his sisters, holding up two-fingered bunny ears behind Bells.

I don't know that man anymore.

He couldn't remember being that carefree. It felt like looking at a picture of someone else. Archer shook his head and did a sweep. Lily's phone was plugged in by her purse, with her driver's license and debit card inside, but no cash. He also found what he thought was Bellamy's phone on the bed. The battery was dead, but the pink case had a sparkly butterfly on the back which was something Bells would've loved.

The tools on the table were small, more for making jewelry or something. Hadn't Lily said something about making bracelets a couple of months back? Not like he'd planned to buy one. Who the hell would he give it to? He couldn't remember the last date he'd been on. Hell, he couldn't remember the last time he'd had sex. He'd been happily married to his SEAL team until he'd fucked up.

He pushed the thoughts away before he fell into a hole he couldn't climb out of. Bells and Lily needed him.

Something had gone down here. He was sure of it. The dried brown spot on the corner of the bookcase was clearly blood. But whose? If it was one of his sisters'…

Shit. He should have come with Bellamy. He closed his eyes and drew in a hard breath. Didn't matter. He hadn't and he knew better than anyone that you couldn't change the past. Sure as hell couldn't time travel back to fix your mistakes.

Archer turned for the door, intent to go check out the vehicles Dennis had mentioned when something gold glinted in his peripheral vision. He gripped his cane and gingerly squatted to look. Fire burned from his calf to his thigh as his left knee bent and the muscles strained. The physical therapist said with exercise and work, it would get better. He'd heard her say that to a guy that lost a limb though, so he wasn't putting a lot of stock in it. If this was as good as his leg was going to get, he'd have to live with the pain and weakness. Because he sure hadn't died from it.

Once he was kneeling, he scanned the floor. Beneath the table, tucked against the leg, was a piece of metal. He reached for it and turned it over in his palm. The little piece of gold filigree looked delicate and out of place. He looked around Lily's apartment but didn't see anything it might have broken off of. The intricate gold swirls belonged on something fancy. Something he'd seen recently.

Like the little Fabergé red-enameled and gold-filigreed egg in Dennis's office.

A hard knot settled in his stomach as he pushed to his feet. His left leg protested, and he had to lean on his cane for a moment until the muscles loosened up. Then he limped toward the door. That egg had been in this apartment and Dennis was going to answer some questions. Starting with how he got that egg and where the hell his sisters were.

May 1814
London, England

"MY BROTHER IS impossible. He promised that he would help me make a match this Season, and all he's done is introduce me to the worst boors imaginable." Violet Hawthorne threw her hands up in the air as she paced the drawing room in their family townhouse. Because it was unseasonably cool out, the windows were closed, and the room felt stuffy. She had a mind to open them anyway to air out the room and maybe get a whiff of the roses in the garden below. Anything would be better than a stuffy drawing room furnished by a stuffy brother.

"Oh Vi, if that were true, he would have agreed to meet with Lord Comlyn last week when he expressed interest in you," Lily replied.

"Lord Comlyn is older than the archbishop!" Violet stopped pacing and glared at her sister-in-law. Lily had come into their life quite unexpectedly when she time-traveled to a street in the village near their country estate and had almost been run over by

Violet's carriage. She'd done the proper thing of course. She'd taken Lily home and called a doctor. Her brother, Gabriel, had seen Lily and been smitten. How could he not with Lily's beautiful, dark hair with its caramel streaks and her bright, blue-green eyes? Her figure hadn't been a deterrent either. Violet envied her full bosom and curved waist, all achieved without stays—though Lily mentioned something called a "bra." She didn't know where one would purchase something like that, especially in this era.

She looked down at her breasts. They were smaller than Lily's, but not quite as small as Lily's sister, Bellamy's, breasts. How important were breasts when it came to attracting the right man?

"Violet?"

"Hmm?" Maybe she should purchase a smaller set of stays that might enhance them under her ballgowns. Men *did* seem to appreciate a woman with a full bosom.

"I said that Gabriel is trying to find a match that will not only provide for you but also be someone you will care for." Lily's voice sounded somewhat strained.

Though really, how strained could she be? *She* was married to a man she loved—Violet's irascible brother. "How will he find one when he growls at them like a rabid wolf when they inquire about me?" She plucked at a thread on the cuff of her sleeve, trying to keep her face blank when she added, "Last night I overheard Lady Parling gossiping with *glee* that I'd be on the shelf within the month."

Lily sighed and set her teacup down on the table by the chaise she sat on. She patted the cushion. "Come sit."

Violet shuffled over and sat. "I don't understand why Lord Taylor wasn't suitable."

Lily reached over to tuck one of Violet's curls behind her ear. "Because Zeph said the man spent more time in the gaming hells than he did. Gabriel was concerned Taylor would lose the whole of his fortune before you stepped foot down the aisle."

She frowned. Zeph Lael was one of Gabriel's closest friends. and she adored him. If he'd seen Taylor at the hells, then Violet wanted nothing to do with the man. *Only…* "How is a woman to know the measure of a man, then? If Zeph hadn't known about Taylor, we might even now be out for a ride in Hyde Park."

Lily put her arm around Violet and laid her head on her shoulder. "I don't know. Although I suspect this is why so many men have mistresses in this time. Neither party knows each other well enough to know if their marriage will work for life."

"You and Gabriel didn't have such an issue. My brother is so smitten that he'll still be in love with you in the next life."

Lily chuckled. "I certainly hope so. Otherwise, I will have to track him down and force him to love me all over again."

Violet smiled at that. She truly was happy for Gabriel. He'd worked so hard to build their family fortunes back up after their father had squandered them. He deserved a love as true as the great romances.

"I don't know how we'll ever come to an agreement, Lily. I don't want a man in his dotage who won't be able to father children."

"I'll make certain he excludes men old enough to be your grandfather."

"And my father," Violet added.

"So a man younger than the Archbishop of Canterbury. What else is on this expansive list of wants in a husband?"

She raised a hand and began to tick off her fingers. "One, he must be kind and a gentleman. I don't want a grouch like my brother."

Lily snorted a laugh.

"Two, he must be hale. I can't take a man to my bed who won't survive the night."

"Violet! I will not be sharing that with Gabriel. He'd lose his mind."

She pressed on, cheeks flaming a bit at having shocked her sister-in-law. But really, was that such an unreasonable request?

Besides, she loved some of those odd phrases that Lily used when Violet said something that surprised her. *Lose his mind! Perfect.* "He must also have his own home. Preferably an estate with a title and land. And, of course, be financially sound. I won't live in a shack even if I love him."

"No shacks. Anything else?"

"Only one. He must love me as much as Gabriel loves you."

Lily hugged her again. "That's the easy part of the list, Vi. Who wouldn't love you?"

Her eyes misted a little. What had they done before sweet Lily came into their lives? And now that Lily's sister Bellamy had come through time and decided to stay as well? Her family was almost complete. She just needed to find her own match.

"Are we having a cuddle?" Bellamy asked as she entered the drawing room. She squeezed her thin frame onto the chaise on the other side of Violet and put her arms around her, mashing her between the two sisters.

Violet laughed, her frustrations from earlier gone. She'd never had a sister, only a vexing older brother. Lily and Bellamy were what she always thought having sisters would be like. Bellamy had arrived almost a month ago. She'd time-traveled using the same automaton clock that Gabriel's friend Christian had created the previous year. Instead of appearing at their country estate as Lily had, she'd arrived outside the townhouse door. Fortunately, Christian had found her and brought her inside where she and Lily reunited. Their relationship had been strained for years in their time, which meant they continued to bicker a bit in this era. But that made them all the more like real sisters. After all, she and Gabriel bickered all the time. *Well, less now since he married Lily.*

"Could I persuade either of you to go shopping with me?" Bellamy asked. "I heard that Southard's on Oxford just received a new shipment of silks."

Violet perked up. "New silks? I'd love a new dress before the end of the Season."

Lily yawned and laid a hand on her stomach. "This baby makes me tired. I think I'll take a nap while you enjoy your outing."

Bellamy waggled her eyebrows. "Does this nap include Gabriel? Shall we save supper for you or just expect to see you tomorrow?"

Lily flushed and a small smile touched her lips. "He does enjoy our naps."

Violet envied that secret smile and the knowing look in Bellamy's eyes. She wanted that with her own husband.

"Come on, Vi. Let's go shopping and leave the two love birds alone. That way Lily can scream as loud as she wants without disturbing anyone."

Her sister groaned and covered her face with her hands. "Bells!"

"What of Christian?" Violet asked quickly, hoping to divert the conversation away from her brother in any sort of amorous situation. In the months since Gabriel had married, her brother seemed to take every opportunity to steal kisses from his wife. "Will he join us?"

"He's in his workshop working on a new automaton." Bellamy chuckled. "He gets so involved in his projects that I doubt he'd hear them if they were in the same room."

The love on her face sent a small pang through Violet's heart. Was there anyone out there for her? Was she truly meant to spend the rest of her life on the shelf like Lady Parling had said? The thought distressed her. More than anything, Violet wanted love and her own family. The more time that passed, the less that seemed likely to happen. She'd turn nineteen in a few months. Most of her friends were already married. She didn't think she'd be able to face a third Season on the marriage mart. At that point, the gossips would wonder what was wrong with her that the Earl of Rothden's sister couldn't find a match. A sense of helplessness settled over her. Gabriel *had* to accept one of her suitors this Season. If he didn't, she'd be a spinster for life.

Bellamy stood and took her hand, pulling her to her feet. "Let's go see if they have any new colors of silk in."

Violet smiled and let Bellamy lead her from the room. She welcomed the distraction. Besides, who knew if she might meet someone new on their outing? Someone that Gabriel couldn't say no to because he was perfect?

CHAPTER TWO

Present Day
Corbin, Kentucky

Archer stared at Lily's car and felt sick. Rust held the Honda together. She lived in the worst neighborhood and drove a car that was guaranteed to fall apart the next time she hit a pothole. He scratched at the scruff on his chin and swore. None of this made a damn bit of sense.

When their parents had died, he'd been deep into a mission and didn't get the news for two weeks. He'd started sending home money for Lily and Bellamy to help with the expenses. With his help, Lily kept the family home until Bells graduated high school and went to college. Then she'd sold everything and split the money between them. He'd continued to help with Bellamy's college after that, telling himself that he was doing what he could since he couldn't be there for them in person. The times he'd been stateside, he'd purposely avoided the past and his sisters. Seeing them was a painful reminder of losing his parents so suddenly. Of the intense regret he felt at not being able to go to their funerals.

Then four years ago, Lily told him to stop sending money because Bellamy had left school to start a modeling career. He'd assumed that both of his sisters were doing well. Bellamy was splashed across the cover of magazines all over the world. Shit, he couldn't count the number of times he'd seen her as a pin-up on some guy's wall or how many times he'd physically reminded someone not to talk about her within earshot. So yeah, he knew she was doing well.

Lily never complained about money. She had her share of the sale of their parents' house and she'd always been happy to talk to him and hear any of the travel adventures that he was able to share. She'd rarely shared anything about her life.

She kept the conversations on me.

Why hadn't he realized that earlier? Had she even told him that she'd moved here, or had it been Bellamy who'd shared that? Dammit, he knew she moved around a bit, but he had no idea… As the oldest, it was his responsibility to protect the girls. How could he have let this happen?

You didn't want to know. You purposely kept them at a distance, even before you got injured because seeing them reminded you of things that no longer existed. The good times before you left for basic training. You didn't want to know because it hurt.

Archer stifled a growl. He felt like shit. Bellamy called it right during their last conversation while she'd stood in Lily's apartment, devastated because their sister was missing. They were the worst siblings in the world. They hadn't made an effort to keep up with each other, or their middle sister. Maybe if they had, she wouldn't have been living like this.

As soon as he found Lily, he was going to hug her. Then he was going to demand some answers.

He limped back to the apartment office and opened the door. A fresh cloud of nicotine hit him like a fogbank, leaving a bitter taste in his mouth.

Dennis scowled at him, tapping his cigarette against the ashtray, and ran a hand through his dirty brown hair, tugging it forward to conceal his receding hairline. "Well? Did you find Lily hiding under the bed?" He smiled, displaying yellowed teeth, amused by his own wit.

Archer fished the piece of gold filigree out of his pocket and tossed it on a stack of papers on the man's desk. "No, but I found this. Look familiar?"

Dennis shook his head. "Nope. Never seen it." He crossed his arms over his stained white shirt and leaned back in his chair. It creaked under his weight.

Dammit, he didn't have time for this asshole. His sisters were missing, and he needed answers *now*. He stomped around the desk, shoved Dennis's feet off the stack of papers, causing the man to teeter in the chair, then pointed at the gold fragment. "So if I put it up against that fancy egg on your shelf, it's not going to perfectly match and fill in an empty spot where it broke off?"

Dennis's eyes widened and he shot a panicked look at the egg before looking back at Archer, blinking rapidly. "A-a-all right, l-look. Yeah, it was in her apartment. When that blonde didn't return the key, I thought she ran off. But her car was still outside. S-so I went up there, only no one answered. I'm the manager here. I-I've got the right to look around."

Archer leaned down until they were at eye level and gave him a hard look. "Since when does *that* give you the right to take things that don't belong to you?"

The man jerked back at his softly spoken words and almost toppled out of the chair.

Archer stood straight and gripped the head of his cane. "Thought you had to have a new key made."

Dennis paled and wiped a bead of sweat off his forehead. "I had an… I mean, I found one after. The point is, all of Lily's stuff was still there, man. So was the blonde's. Nothing in her car but her clothes and wallet." He tilted his chin up. "I ain't a thief, you know. I don't take people's credit cards."

Archer ground his teeth together. He just admitted to breaking into Lily's apartment and Bellamy's rental to go through their belongings but could boast that he wasn't a thief?

"I saw the fancy egg and took it as collateral for the rent. Figured that if Lily never showed, I'd sell it to make back what she owed and put her stuff in storage until someone came to collect it."

"You're a regular white knight, but that's still stealing."

Archer walked around the desk to inspect the egg.

"Screw you, man. You don't know how tough it—"

"Shut up, or I'll report you to the police when I file the missing person's report that you failed to do after not one, but *two* women went missing on the property that you 'manage.'"

Dennis pushed out of his chair and edged toward the door. He shook his head, frantic in his denial. "How the hell was I supposed to know that they didn't just move on? They're adults. It ain't my responsibility to keep track of them." His voice rose with each sentence until he sounded like a choir boy.

Archer ignored him, picked up the egg, and inspected it carefully. As he'd thought, the gold filigree overlaid the red enamel, but a piece was missing, a piece that exactly matched the bit of gold lying on Dennis's desk.

The egg was heavier than he expected. It looked quite a bit like the famous Fabergé eggs, although smaller. This one easily fit in the palm of his hand. Tiny gold hinges on either side hinted that there was more within.

"What's inside?" he asked.

"Inside?"

Archer slanted him a look. "You break into Lily's apartment and take this, and expect me to believe that you didn't open it?"

"I… huh. It opens? How? I didn't see anything." Dennis stared hard at the egg from across the room. Then he glared at Archer. "Are you screwing with me? Trying to make me admit to something that I didn't do?"

His confusion appeared sincere, but Archer didn't trust him. He wasn't sure he could trust his *own* instincts anymore.

He looked back down at the fragile egg in his hand. Lily and Bellamy were missing, and this item appeared to have been the only item of value in Lily's possession. He didn't come all the way to fucking Kentucky just to leave what could be an important clue to their whereabouts sitting on some guy's shelf.

Archer hooked his cane on his forearm so he could hold the egg in one hand and open it with the other. Two little doors parted. Inside lay a clock with the hands set to twelve and beneath, two little dancers.

The clock began to chime. The dancers spun as if on a ballroom floor.

"What the…" Dennis mumbled.

He didn't hear if the man said anything else because, at that moment, white light burst out of the clock and blinded him, making his lungs lock up. *A bomb!* The world tilted heavily to one side and tingles raced through his veins.

He was back in the sands. The noise of the vehicle mixed with the laughter of his team members as they joked about Kodiak's failed pass at the chick in the bar the night before. The loud whistle and the roar of an explosion that sent shockwaves through his body.

No. Not again.

Archer gasped and clenched his hands. Something cut into his palm.

Then the world went silent. He blinked and black spots flickered in front of his eyes. He blinked several more times until they cleared.

A shout rang out and a horse whinnied. When his brain registered what his eyes were seeing, Archer gripped his cane and ran as fast as his injured leg would allow.

May 1814
London, England

VIOLET LOVED THE shops in Cheapside. Linen drapers and milliners, haberdashers, cobblers, jewelers… any merchant a woman could want lined the wide thoroughfare. Fashionable women and finely dressed men wandered along the walk while carriages and buggies trundled by on the wide road.

"What a lovely day," Bellamy said as she stepped out of the haberdashers behind Violet. She adjusted the blue bow of her bonnet which matched her sapphire eyes and the lovely blue muslin walking dress she wore. "It almost feels like spring."

Violet laughed and pulled her shawl tighter. Thick gray clouds obscured the sun and threatened a rain shower at any moment. It was the end of May, and the weather should have been quite warm. However, the winter had been the coldest she'd ever experienced, followed by an almost equally cold spring. "Every day is a lovely day when one is shopping." The footman loaded down with purchases behind them gave a barely audible groan. She stifled a laugh and pretended not to notice.

In some households, an audible reaction such as that could be cause for dismissal, but Gabriel always said that an attendant's performance far outweighed any more untoward attitudes. Although she suspected that had far more to do with his steward, Reginald. The man seemed to enjoy matching wits with Gabriel and Violet could admit to encouraging him on occasion just to see her brother's reaction.

"I saw you speaking to that young woman while I was browsing the buttons," she said to Bellamy. "She did appear to be overwhelmed by the selections available."

Bellamy smiled wide. "She was. The poor girl's mother had been trying to make her purchase a green ribbon to go with red satin and gold lace. She would have looked like a Christmas package at her ball."

"You seem to enjoy helping others with fashion."

"I do." Bellamy linked their arms as they walked toward the next shop. "For instance, bright yellow is in fashion right now, but if you ever decide to wear it, I won't let you leave the house. I realize that we've only just met, but I can't in good conscience let you make such a terrible mistake that could jeopardize your future. It's all wrong for your coloring."

"I'd look like an unattractive lemon. Whatever would I do without you?" Violet grinned. She loved having Bellamy and Lily around. When her dear friend Patience could join them, it was even better. "Shall we stop at the jeweler's before returning home? I'd like to find a gift for Lily's birthday."

"Yes, but I think we should let this poor man put some of the packages in the carriage before his legs buckle under the weight." Bellamy turned back to the footman and gave him a warm smile. "Evan, really, there's no need to carry all of that. Why not put it in the carriage and meet us at the next shop?"

His cheeks turned scarlet, and he ducked his head behind the top of the packages in his arms. The poor man had a fair complexion that showed his every emotion. "I shouldn't leave you unattended."

"It's only for a few minutes," Bellamy said. "What could happen? We'll be right up the street at the jewelers. Drop those off and come meet us there."

He glanced between them both, eyebrows winging up.

"Go on, Evan," Violet added. "I promise to protect Bellamy with my life."

Bellamy lightly pushed her arm. "I don't think that will make him feel more secure," she whispered.

"Why not? Are you implying that I couldn't protect you?"

The footman cleared his throat. "Perhaps if you would wait here? I shall hurry these over and return quickly."

Violet nodded. "We'll stay right here."

He hurried away, boxes of silks, muslins, and hats piled high in his arms. Violet admired his fine form. Had she put a strong body on her list of attributes needed in a husband? She turned to ask Bellamy when someone jostled her.

"Pardon, mum," a man said as he walked by. He tipped his hat, and she caught a glimpse of dark hair and eyes under a beaver hat. At the same moment, the weight of her reticule around her wrist gave way. She spun just as a younger man grabbed the silk purse and tucked his knife away. He flashed her a smile, then tried to dash by.

"Stop!" she cried, grabbing fistfuls of his jacket. That horrid rat! How dare he steal her reticule and smile as he did it!

"Violet, don't!" Bellamy tugged on her arm. "You could be hurt!"

She shrugged off Bellamy and grabbed her reticule, trying to tug it out of his hands. "Give that back at once!"

Her thief grinned and held tight. He looked no older than herself with his sandy hair and freckles. "You have spirit, I'll warrant. But this is mine now."

Violet gripped her reticule tighter and tried to wrestle it from him. "Give it back, you beastly man."

Bellamy grabbed one sleeve of the man's coat and turned, calling for Evan.

The three of them spun around, knocking into several women who'd stopped to stare at the spectacle. One cried out as if she'd been attacked instead.

"Come now, love. Don't you want to help the needy?" His eyes twinkled. The wretch was enjoying their tussle!

"Your needy family of thieves?" She put all her weight into her tug. Their squabble finally garnered attention from several men passing by.

"Here now, let the lady go." A man stepped up and grabbed the thief's rough coat.

Violet yanked hard on the reticule at the same moment the thief let go. An undignified shriek flew out of her mouth as she stumbled back. She tripped on the hem of her dress, arms windmilling as she fell backward.

Someone shouted and a horse whinnied nearly in her ear. Violet's heart clenched, then began to pound, hard. She was too close to the road but couldn't stop her fall. Her eyes went wide as two horses thundered toward her, so close they filled her vision.

Oh no! She didn't want to die. She'd never even been kissed!

Time slowed. She heard Bellamy's frightened voice call out, but she couldn't respond. Couldn't breathe. All she could see were the horses' flashing hooves and churning legs as she fell in front of them.

But then strong arms latched around her and pulled her up at the last second. Sound rushed back to her ears, deafening her. She clutched the shirt of the person who held her, holding tight. Air sawed in and out of her lungs and yet, she felt like she couldn't breathe. Couldn't stop the trembling of her body as the cold air seemed to seep through to her bones.

The arms around her were muscled and pulled her closer to a hard chest. She breathed in a clean, woodsy scent that helped to clear her mind a little. A gentleman held her. His body radiated a wondrous heat that had Violet leaning into him, soaking up the heat.

"Are you okay?" he asked in a smokey growl.

The sound of his voice drew her in, making her press closer when she should have separated herself from him to save her reputation. Something hard pressed against her arm as she nestled against him. A wooden cane was hooked over his forearm.

Strong hands moved to grip her upper arms. "Are you okay?" he repeated.

Violet dragged her gaze away from the cane, up a wide chest, over the bronze skin of his throat, to the handsome face above. He wasn't handsome in the classical sense, or with the gentlemanly refinement she was used to. Scruffy dark hair covered his jaw and highlighted his mouth with its full lower lip. But he had a fine nose and green eyes, the exact shade of the leaves in a forest.

She blinked.

His eyebrows rose.

Violet, you ninny, quit staring.

She couldn't. He was handsome and strong, and he'd *saved* her. She was spellbound.

"Violet!"

Bellamy's voice sounded far closer now. It jolted her out of the daze.

"I... I am fine. Thanks to you, Mr...?" Her words were shaky, and she still trembled. She should step out of his arms, but he felt so warm and safe. Very safe. The kind of safe a woman could feel knowing that no one would steal her reticule and horses wouldn't run her down.

He looked down at her, eyes roaming her face. His arms tightened the slightest bit, pulling her closer to his chest.

She'd never been this close to a man, pressed up against him, full body. Even Gabriel's hugs were looser than this. It was *delightful*. He looked quite rugged, she decided. Probably due to the scar that ran from his ear down the side of his neck, partially hidden by the hair on his jaw. It would give him a formidable air if he weren't holding her so gently.

He must have noticed her looking at his scars, because his throat bobbed, and he stepped back, making sure that she was standing upright on the sidewalk before letting her go.

She still hadn't looked away. Violet flushed. *Don't be rude. You've better manners than that.* She reached for her shawl only to find it gone. She must have lost it struggling with that thief. Violet peered around the formidable frame of the man who'd rescued her, but the young thief was nowhere in sight. At least she'd retrieved her reticule. *Ha!* Let that teach him not to steal from a lady.

"Violet. Oh my God, are you okay?" Bellamy said as she reached them and pulled Violet into a hug. "I saw you fall, and I was…" She froze then as her gaze turned to Violet's rescuer. "Archer?" she asked in a breathy whisper.

Archer? Violet looked up at the man again.

His dark eyebrows pinched together. "Bellamy?"

"What the hell are you doing here?" they asked in unison.

Oh. Oh my. Her handsome rescuer was Archer Bennett. Lily and Bellamy's older brother. From the future!

CHAPTER THREE

ARCHER SCRUBBED A hand over his face and angled the scars visible on his face and neck away from the beautiful young woman he'd just yanked out of danger. She'd stared a little too long at them, making him uncomfortable. He'd never been that pretty-boy handsome women seemed to favor, but damn, now he looked rough. The beard could only hide so much. The poor woman was already shaken from her ordeal; he didn't want to make it worse by scaring her.

If he'd been a split second longer, the horses and carriage would have trampled her. And what the fuck was a carriage doing on the road anyway? It hadn't looked like one of those open carriages you found at tourist destinations that slowly plodded along with some beleaguered tour guide rambling on in a monotone.

He turned, meaning to get a better look at it and scan for threats when his odd surroundings sunk in. The men wore suits with long overcoats and top hats, while the women wore long gowns and bonnets. Carriages toured up and down the dirt road, sometimes passed by men on horseback. He frowned at that, but more importantly, his neck no longer tingled with danger. The people around them paid no attention as they went about their business. He looked back at the young woman.

She wore a long, fussy pink dress with embroidered flowers.

A bonnet covered most of her hair, but some chocolate brown curls framed a face with the most striking amber eyes he'd ever seen. With her creamy skin and trim figure, she looked young. Maybe eighteen.

Too young for you, Bennett.

Way too young. He was only thirty-one, but with all that he'd seen and done, he felt closer to fifty standing next to her. Not that a pretty woman like her would be interested in a scarred, older warrior like him, anyway.

He shook his head at himself. Why was he even thinking about this nonsense? His love life was the least of his concerns at this point. He needed to figure out where the hell he was and find his sisters.

Two minutes ago, he'd been standing in that scumbag Dennis's office holding that egg, and then—

A familiar voice broke through his thoughts—thankfully—and forced his attention from the woman.

A tall, thin, *familiar* blonde barreled toward them.

"Violet. Oh my God, are you okay?" His sister Bellamy said as she reached them and hugged the woman. "I saw you fall, but I was…"

Seeing his missing sister there brought a nearly staggering flood of emotions, paramount of which was intense relief. She looked like an actress in a period drama with her fancy dress and blonde ringlets tucked under a bonnet but didn't seem to be injured or in danger. A bit of fear loosened in his chest. It wouldn't fully dissipate until he found Lily, but having Bellamy in his sights was a welcome start.

Bellamy's gaze swung to him, and she froze, mouth dropping open. "Archer?" she asked in a breathy whisper.

"What the hell are you doing here?" he demanded, waving an arm at their surroundings. Furthermore, where was here and how did he get there?

Her eyes misted, and then she launched herself into his arms.

He stumbled back a step, his injured leg protesting. "Easy," he said.

"I… I can't believe you're here. I hoped you'd come but I didn't actually think it was possible. Although it shouldn't even be possible that I'm here, so that's sort of silly, but oh my God. You're here." Her words ran together in a jumble, and she wiped a tear off her cheek. Then she hugged him again.

"You're not making any sense, Bells." He patted her back, then gently set her away so he could lean on his cane to take some weight off his leg. Heat climbed up the back of his neck as he did, terribly aware of the beautiful young woman still standing beside them. He'd never really been vain, but damn. No man wanted to be seen as an unattractive invalid when standing by a woman like her.

"Sorry," his sister said. "Of course, I'm not. You don't know what's happened."

"You're damn right, I don't." Archer clenched his jaw. Same old Bells. She didn't seem the least bit concerned that he'd been worried. It pissed him off. "Why the hell didn't you answer my calls, Bellamy? Let me know you were okay? Last time we spoke, you were going to file a missing person's report on Lily. Then *you* disappeared." He dragged in a breath, trying to calm down. Making a scene in public drew too much attention to them. He felt too exposed here. They needed to get somewhere safer. "When I couldn't reach you, I thought something terrible had happened to you both. I thought you'd been kidnapped. Or *worse*. Jesus, I went to *Kentucky* to find you."

At least she looked contrite at his admonishment. "I'm sorry, Archer. We couldn't…" She looked around and then lowered her voice, "call you."

"Why not?" he asked. Then, as he comprehended what she'd said, he frowned. "Wait. *We?*"

"I'll explain everything. I promise." She turned to the woman. "Violet, are you okay? You scared me to death fighting off that mugger."

His eyebrows shot up. This young woman—Violet—fought a

mugger? The top of her head barely reached his chin, and she couldn't weigh more than one hundred twenty pounds.

Violet's cheeks turned a light pink, and she twisted the silk bag in her hands. "I wasn't going to let that thief steal my reticule. You… you won't tell Gabriel, will you? He won't let me out of the house for the rest of the Season. If that happens, I'll be so far on the shelf that I may as well become a nun."

Bellamy's lips twisted like she was fighting a grin. She nudged Violet with her elbow. "Okay, but you owe me."

They shared a smile. One Archer had seen all too often right before a seven-year-old Bellamy did something she wasn't supposed to. He cleared his throat.

"Archer, this is my friend Violet. Vi, this is my brother Archer."

Violet smiled up at him, avoiding looking at his scars he noted, and held out her gloved hand in a way that made him think of the Pope waiting for his ring to be kissed.

He shook her hand instead. "Nice to meet you." If he'd expected her to be offended at the more casual greeting, he was mistaken. She practically lit up and pumped his hand a little too rough in return.

"How delightful! I've never had an American handshake. Is this how it's done?" She worked his arm up and down again.

"Not so exaggerated." He showed her again, lips twitching as she mimicked him with intense concentration. He shouldn't find it adorable, but he did.

"What happened, Violet? I called for help and suddenly you were falling into the path of the carriage. I couldn't get to you in time." Bellamy's voice shook a little and she reached out to squeeze Violet's hand.

"Oh, I was pulling on my reticule when the thief released it and I stumbled backward." She looked his way. "That's when your brother arrived out of nowhere to catch me from falling. Thank you, Mr. Bennett," she added. "If you hadn't rescued me…"

Those amber eyes softened, drawing him in. His chest hitched and warmth stirred within. Something about her seemed almost magnetic, like he couldn't look away.

He'd seen a lot of beautiful women all over the world, not all of whom were good people, so beauty wasn't usually enough to attract him to a woman. Violet piqued his interest, and he didn't know why.

"It's just Archer," he said, voice gruff because he was still irritated at Bellamy. "I'm glad you're not hurt." Her fingers tightened in the silk bag she held. "Fought a thief, huh?" He knew grown men who wouldn't have been so bold.

"It was very foolish," Bellamy said.

Violet's chin went up a notch. "You wouldn't say that if it were Christian who struggled with the thief. Why should I be any different? Besides, Gabriel taught me to protect myself."

Who were Christian and Gabriel? "Bells—"

A man in a dark blue uniform interrupted when he jogged up to them, panting.

Archer stepped in front of Bells and Violet to protect them in the event that the man proved a threat. His hand rested on his hip, close to where the knife was sheathed under his shirt.

The man halted in surprise, twisting to peer at the women behind Archer. "Your pardon, Lady Violet. Lady Bellamy. When I finished with the packages and didn't find you at the jeweler's…" He cleared his throat. "Is all well?"

Bellamy stepped up beside Archer and looped her arm through his. "Quite well. Evan, this is my brother, Archer Bennett. He'll be joining us."

Lady Bellamy? Archer studied his surroundings again. Shops lined this side of the street, their windows full of old-fashioned clothes, shoes, and other accessories. The people walking past them wore the same style of colorful clothes and spoke in English accents. Add in the horses and carriages and it looked like a movie set from the eighteen hundreds. Although he didn't see any cameras or a director. *Where the hell am I?* England? Was he hallucinating? The shrinks at the VA had warned him that hallucinations were a potential symptom of PTSD, but they'd never mentioned a complete change of *era*. If that was the case, he was seriously messed up.

"Evan is one of the Rothden footmen," Bellamy said.

"Footman?" The term rang a bell, but he couldn't place it. History was Church's forte. His best friend and platoon leader had spent every moment he could studying different periods and often regaling their team with fascinating bits he'd found. Like Faberge eggs, for example. He never would have known—or cared—about the jeweled treasures if it weren't for Church.

"I think I'd like to return home if you don't mind," Violet said. "We can find a gift for Lily's birthday tomorrow."

"Wait, Lily is here?"

Bells laughed. "She is." To Evan, she asked, "Could you bring the carriage for us?" He nodded and disappeared back into the crowd of shoppers.

Archer rounded on his sister. "Dammit, Bellamy. Answers. Now."

She crossed her arms over her chest and glared back. "Not here. Not in public."

He knew the stubborn tilt of that jaw well. "Fine." He wanted to get them off the street anyway. There were too many people for his comfort.

Her posture relaxed and she pulled him into a hug. "You're really here." Her tone was a mixture of excitement and awe.

"Obviously." Although he still didn't know where "here" was. He definitely wasn't in a dirty apartment office anymore.

"You found the clock."

He didn't follow. "Clock?"

"The red enamel egg. You must have opened it, right?" Bellamy clutched his arm.

The Fabergé-type egg that Dennis stole from Lily. "Yes. The apartment manager had it. Why?"

Violet leaned closer. "You found it also? How exciting. What happened?"

Exciting? What was so exciting about… memories resurfaced from the few minutes he'd been in that cramped, smoke-filled office. Opening the little doors, hearing a tinny chime, and seeing a bright white light. He'd thought it was a bomb at first, but he was here in a place that looked like something out of a Sherlock Holmes movie.

His breath stalled. Was he… was he dead? He looked down at his hand. His palm was imprinted with a swirled pattern, the skin around it flushed red. He remembered the gold filigree biting into his skin when the world went white. If he were dead, would he still have the mark?

There had to be some other explanation. Was he in a coma? Was he going to come to in a hospital bed? Had someone drugged him?

"Archer?" Bellamy laid a palm on his forearm.

"I took the little egg from the apartment manager. I had it in my hand when there was a blinding light. Next thing I know, I'm standing on this street. I must have dropped it." He peered over his shoulder at the spot.

Her fingers dug in, her nails leaving little half-moons on his arm beneath his short sleeve. He frowned at her. "What?"

"Was the clock with you when you arrived?"

"I think so. I don't—I can't see it over there, unless…did it roll?"

Violet gasped and covered her mouth with a gloved hand. He couldn't read her expression, which struck him as odd. Every emotion she experienced seemed to cross her face. There was too much there to interpret. "Where did you drop it?" she asked, her voice a little breathy.

Why did he find that so sexy?

Bells tugged on his sleeve, dragging his gaze off of Violet. "Please, Archer. We need to know."

He remembered opening his eyes and then taking a half dozen steps to catch Violet. "There," he said, pointing to a spot at the edge of the walk.

Bellamy hurried over and searched the ground. Her shoulders slumped.

Archer limped over to her, still aware of Violet right behind him. The clock lay crushed in the dirt. He must have dropped it and then it had rolled into the lane where carriages and horses ran over it.

"Do you think we should take it back to Christian anyway?" Violet asked. "Maybe he can use this one to figure out how to make his work?"

Archer turned sharply. "There are *two*?"

Violet chewed her lower lip, drawing his gaze to her white teeth and that plump lip. "In a manner of speaking."

His eyebrows knotted together. What the hell did that mean?

"Good thinking, Violet. I'll just… put them in my reticule." Bellamy watched the steady stream of carriages and horses. "We can't leave it here but getting it will be dangerous."

"There's our carriage. Let's have the driver stop right in front of it to block the way," Violet said.

Smart. He liked a woman who used her head.

Too young! he reminded himself. "I'll gather the pieces. No need for you ladies to get dirty." He gave her his best attempt at a smile, but it felt strange. He didn't smile much anymore, he realized, especially not at someone in an attempt to be… polite.

Violet stared at him, her gaze lingering. He felt it like a physical caress and his body responded, heating his blood. She studied his face, even the scars on his neck, and then offered a tentative smile.

Maybe she didn't find him hard to look at. Something sparked in his chest, making his heart beat a little harder. Her lips were pink and plump, drawing his gaze again as she licked her lower lip. He dragged his attention off her, not willing to admit to himself how challenging it was, and found his sister motioning for a carriage to stop.

The man in the uniform—Evan—hopped down from beside

the driver.

"My lady," Evan said as he opened the carriage door and offered his hand to Bellamy.

"Gather everything you can find, Arch," she said, then took Evan's hand.

He stepped into the road and, using his cane for balance, slowly lowered himself to his knees. Sometimes his left leg stiffened up so badly that bending his knee felt almost impossible. He was nearing that now. He blocked out as much of the pain as he could and reached for the clock wreckage. Half of the egg remained mostly intact. A number of tiny gears had spilled out of it and were ground into the dirt amid a horse hoof print. He cleaned them off on the edge of his shirt and stowed them in the pocket of his jeans. One of the little gold dancers had broken as well.

Archer brushed aside more dirt, digging out the remaining pieces. A fine, shimmery white powder covered some of the gears and made the dirt on one side glitter. *Odd.*

Once he felt confident that he'd gathered what remained of the clock, he pushed himself to his feet and bit back a groan.

Violet leaned out of the carriage. "Did you find it all?"

"I think so."

She grinned. "I can't wait to hear what Christian says." She waved him closer.

Bellamy appeared beside her. "Let's go see Lily."

He nodded and brushed the dirt from his hands and pants. Ignoring Evan's offer of assistance, climbed into the carriage.

He wasn't sure what he expected, but it wasn't this plush interior with glowing candlelight and tufted seats. Archer took the empty bench facing Bells and Violet and rested his cane against the seat. He stretched his left leg, grimacing as it cramped. The movement sent shards of pain up his thigh and into his groin. He squeezed his eyes and breathed through the pain. When he opened them, both women stared.

"I'm fine," he said in a gruff tone because he didn't want to talk about it. He didn't want to answer questions about the injury, especially where and how it had happened. He couldn't. The mission was still classified, regardless of the fact that he was no longer in the Navy.

Bellamy's brow furrowed and she opened her mouth to respond.

"Bellamy, would you hand me that blanket? I'm quite chilled from standing outside so long." Violet glanced at him from under her lashes as she spoke.

A surge of gratitude rose in his chest. She'd distracted his sister from the barrage of questions he could read in her eyes.

"Of course. Here you are. We'll have some tea brought in when we arrive," Bellamy said as she arranged the lap blanket over herself and Violet.

Which reminded him. "Where are we? And where are we going?"

"Uh, about that…" Bellamy rubbed her thumb over a loose piece of thread on the blanket. "There's a reason we couldn't call you, Arch." She glanced at Violet, then faced him. "You see… we're in London. But not the London you know. The clock… it brought you—and Lily and me—back in time. It's 1814. May 1814."

That… didn't make sense. He had to be in a coma. Or hallucinating.

Bellamy met his gaze, showing no guile or any hint that she was teasing. He slowly opened the velvet curtain covering the window and looked out. They'd probably traveled a few blocks in the time they'd been in the carriage, yet the scene outside remained the same. The people all wore formal suits and dresses. Ladies carried parasols or wore bonnets as they strolled the streets. There wasn't a car or phone pole in sight. He should have at least been able to see something in the distance. A plane, a tower. Anything but blue skies tinged a bit brown from smog and chimneys puffing black smoke into the air. "You're saying we what? Time traveled?"

"Exactly." Bellamy leaned forward. "I know it's hard to believe, but if you look around, you won't see any cars or people rushing to work while staring at their phones. No modern clothes."

Archer tried to absorb what she implied. Time travel. Once, he would have thought it impossible, but he knew scientists were trying to prove it was possible. Hell, even the government had experimented with things like mind control. Who was to say that someone hadn't finally figured out a way to make it work?

But if that were true, he didn't think the operational device would be in a gilded egg the size of his palm. For one thing, how would you determine where and when you wanted to go? That meant he'd either cracked his skull somewhere, Dennis had killed him, or the egg warped time and space. He snorted. No way that creep Dennis got the upper hand on him. He probed his scalp but didn't find any tender spots.

"You're not in a coma," Bellamy said, reading his actions. "It's real. I wouldn't lie to you about this."

Violet nodded. "We don't know how the clock works, but somehow it brought all three of you to us. Bellamy and Lily belong here, so…"

She trailed off, saying without words that she thought he might belong there also.

Archer watched the buildings go by, still looking for anything familiar. Violet was wrong. He didn't belong there. He wasn't sure where he belonged anymore. Reintegrating with society after the attack had been difficult at the best of times. Becoming comfortable in a place and time he knew nothing about? Not likely, if he were really in the past.

He touched the windowpane. The glass felt cool and hard beneath his fingertips, as real as any other window. He thought back to the dark temple hidden in a jungle that his team sheltered near one night with its shimmering walls and moving shadows. Creepiest fucking night he'd ever had. "I've seen some strange stuff. Anything is possible, I suppose."

Bellamy's eyebrows shot up. "You believe me?"

He shrugged. "I don't know."

"You'll believe us when you see Lily," Bellamy said. Then she laughed. "Or the first time you have to use a chamber pot."

She said it as if it were the worst thing in the world, but he'd been in so many places where bathrooms were a luxury that it didn't even faze him anymore.

They traveled for another few minutes, during which Archer felt every pothole. Whether this was a dream or a coma, it still hurt like hell. There didn't seem to be a paved road in the entire city. It helped keep his mind off his spinning thoughts, which were starting to give him a headache.

"Archer, I've been here about a month," Bellamy said as she worried the loose thread on the blanket again.

He narrowed his eyes at the nervous habit. Bells was afraid to tell him something. Beside her, Violet looked at her hands resting in her lap.

"You couldn't return home?" For that matter, why didn't Lily come back?

"I intended to come home, but, then I met Christian, and we've become close."

"The man that you said made the clocks?"

"Clock," Violet amended. "There's only one."

He stared at her, mind working through the information. "The one from the past and the one in the future are the same."

She nodded.

"Why not use the one from—" this was weird to say—"*this* time to return home?"

"I fell in love with Christian before I could. Then," she cleared her throat, "then we discovered that the clock we have doesn't transport anyone through time."

Archer brushed his fingers over the fragments in his pocket. "Sometime between now and when Lily got it, it was altered to manipulate time." That meant that, if he really *had* time traveled, he couldn't go home right away.

He scowled as the carriage hit another bump and massaged his thigh. He didn't have his pain medication or muscle relaxers on him. They were in his bag back at Lily's apartment. Dennis was probably already selling them to an addict.

But more concerning, he didn't know anything about medicine. How would he manage his injury? They weren't still using leeches to bleed people, right? Anyone trying to get near him with those slimy, squirmy things was going to find his fist in their face.

"So I'm stuck here until this Christian figures out how to make the clock do its thing." *Or until I wake from this coma.*

Bellamy took his hand. Her skin was warm and soft against his. "You could stay. Lily and I have missed you. We've been so worried."

He pulled his hand from hers and tried not to look at Violet, whose presence he was achingly aware of. He couldn't stay here. Not only because he needed the proper medication and physical therapy, but because there were too many dark shadows in his soul. What would Bellamy think if he told her he woke from nightmares every single night? Or that it had been his fault...

His throat closed. Archer shook his head. "Sorry, Bells. I don't belong here."

I don't belong anywhere. Not anymore.

WHEN DRAFTING A list for the perfect husband, Violet had one requirement at the top that was most important: the gentleman in question shouldn't have the same temperament as her brother. Archer Bennett seemed as gruff and demanding as Gabriel, yet one moment in his warm arms and he was all she could think about.

Violet, he's not the one for you. She didn't know much about him, but she *did* know that he had no intention of staying in this time and he certainly wasn't titled. Those were two excellent reasons to not even consider him as a prospective husband.

She snuck another glance at him as the carriage arrived at the family townhouse in Mayfair. The red shirt he wore molded to his wide shoulders and chest, skimming a flat stomach. She'd never seen a man's chest before. Not even Gabriel's. What did Archer's look like? When he'd held her to his chest, his body was solid beneath her hands. Not like the softness she saw in many of the men of her acquaintance. More like Christian and Zeph who often went to the boxing saloon.

Now, Archer stared out the window at the people and buildings they passed. His dark eyebrows were pinched together, and he turned the cane between his hands without seeming to be aware of it.

With his head turned toward the window, she had a better view of his scars. He'd seemed embarrassed about them earlier, and she suspected he wasn't aware that he displayed them now. Thin pink lines ran from behind his ear to his jaw and down his neck to disappear beneath the collar of his shirt. How much farther did they go down? All the way to the leg he favored? She wanted very much to know how he'd received such a terrible wound.

Bellamy and Lily had both said that he had been a soldier in the military. He'd been forced to leave his unit because of the injury, but neither of them knew what happened.

The carriage slowed to a stop and Archer turned his head from the window. Violet dropped her gaze quickly so he wouldn't catch her staring.

"Here we are," Bellamy said to her brother. "Lily is going to be so excited to see you. She never thought she'd see you again. Neither did I, actually."

He grunted a response.

If Violet hadn't been watching his face again, she wouldn't have seen the small lines that formed around his eyes and the look of regret.

Evan opened the door and offered his hand to Bellamy. She stepped out, allowing Violet to slide across the bench and accept his hand next.

Archer descended behind them, ignoring Evan's offered hand. He looked at the red brick row houses, with their iron fences and arched doors, then the houses across the street.

As he turned, his shirt stretched across his chest, drawing her gaze once more. She felt her cheeks heat as she admired the way his blue trousers molded to his legs and backside. The fabric, similar to what Lily had worn when she'd arrived, was faded and worn thin over the pockets, and a ragged hole was beginning to form in one knee.

What would he look like in the tailored clothing of a gentleman? His dark hair would brush against his white cravat and the coat would emphasize his wide shoulders. He would be very fine indeed.

Archer turned then, his gaze moving over her face.

Her cheeks burned hotter, and her stomach swooped at the dark intensity she saw there. When his gaze fell to her mouth, he looked as if he thought about kissing her, and it surprised her how much she hoped that he would. What would a kiss—his kiss—be like?

"I'm so excited for Lily to see that you're here," Bellamy said. She led the way up the steps to the front door. Henry, their butler, opened it before she could reach for the handle.

Violet felt something warm on the small of her back as she followed, and realized with a little surge of pleasure that it was Archer's hand. She smiled at him. He was quite a bit taller than her as the top of her head only reached his chin.

Archer looked away and a bit of pink dusted his cheeks above his beard.

"Thank you," she said. "For everything."

He jerked his head in a nod but didn't look at her again.

She followed Bellamy into the hall and removed her shawl and bonnet, handing them to Henry. The man didn't show a bit of surprise that Archer accompanied them, with his strange manner of dress and no coat. By this time, she supposed, he was used to family members appearing with oddly dressed and somewhat flummoxed strangers in their wake.

Beside her, she saw Archer take in the marble floors and large, gilded mirror. Two doors led off the hall to the dining room and drawing room, and a set of stairs gave access to the rest of the house. Did he like her home? She couldn't tell. Many people who visited appreciated the grandness of the townhouse. Gabriel was an earl after all, and their family held wealth and lands. Especially since Gabriel had rescued them from the brink of utter ruin after their father died.

"Where's Lady Rothden?" Bellamy asked Henry.

Henry had the same reddish-blond hair and kind disposition as his father, who'd previously worked as their butler until his retirement. "My lady is in the drawing room with Lord Rothden and Lady Bancroft," he replied.

Lily and Gabriel were entertaining Aunt Josephine? Perhaps now was a good time to take a walk. The weather wasn't *that* gloomy. Or maybe it would be better to find a book to read in her room. Aunt Josephine was supposed to chaperone Violet during the Season, but she spent most of her time hovering around the punch table gossiping with her dowager friends. Violet could be kidnapped by some blackguard in the middle of a ball and Aunt Josephine would never be the wiser. She had no wish to spend any more time with the woman than was necessary.

"Excellent." Bellamy grinned at Archer. "Let's surprise Lily." She grabbed his wrist and tugged him after her.

He stumbled a step on his left leg, leaned on his cane to steady himself, and followed.

Violet opened her mouth to chastise Bellamy to be more careful, then bit her lower lip. If he was anything like Gabriel, Archer would be embarrassed and angry at her for calling out a weakness.

She followed behind, twisting the silk of her reticule in her hands. Would their lives change now that the three siblings were together? Lily couldn't possibly leave. She'd married Gabriel, and

Bellamy was besotted with Christian. Violet expected that they would announce their engagement soon. What would happen now that Archer was here?

When they entered the drawing room, Lily squealed. She shot out of her chair, almost dumping her tea on Aunt Josephine, and threw her arms around Archer's waist to hug him close.

He ruffled her caramel curls and returned her hug. Violet stepped aside, giving them space.

Gabriel's eyebrows rose as he set his teacup aside and stood. He had similar coloring to Archer, although his hair was a shade or two darker and his eyes sometimes looked more brown than green. Both men were tall and muscular, though Archer was larger in both height and in the width of his chest and shoulders.

"Good heavens, what a racket," Aunt Josephine muttered from her seat. She dusted crumbs off her bosom from the lemon cake in her other hand, dyed red curls bouncing around her face.

"Archer, what are you doing here?" Lily asked.

"Looking for you and Bells," he answered, managing to sound gruff and yet somehow pleased all at the same time.

"Really? You left your house?"

Bellamy tried to cover her laugh with a cough. "I was just as surprised."

"Do you really think that I'd sit around when my sisters went missing? Especially after…" Archer's jaw worked, and he scowled.

Bellamy crossed her arms over her chest.

Violet almost stomped her foot in frustration, curious to know what he meant to say.

"Did you really just say that when I *begged* you to help me search for Lily?" Bellamy demanded.

Lily put a hand on her sister's arm. "Don't."

Bellamy bristled but let the moment pass.

Gabriel stepped up beside Lily and laid a hand on her lower back. "You must be Archer Bennett. Lily and Bellamy have spoken of you often. Welcome to our home."

Archer nodded. He looked her brother over until his gaze

snagged on Gabriel's familiar touch and shifted closer to Lily. "And you are...?" his low voice held an edge that sent a shiver down Violet's spine.

"You didn't tell him?" Lily asked Bellamy.

"I told him where we are." Bellamy shot a quick glance at Aunt Josephine. "But not much more."

Lily's hand went to her belly, where her pregnancy was just beginning to show.

Violet watched Archer. He seemed to catalog every detail around him, from the furniture, to the people, to the doorways. His gaze lingered on Lily's hand and Gabriel's touch and his forehead furrowed.

Gabriel seemed aware of Archer's protectiveness but met his gaze evenly and held out his hand. "I'm Gabriel Hawthorne. The Earl of Rothden. Lily is my wife."

That got Archer's attention. He studied her brother again, then took his hand in a firm, possibly crushing, grip. "Archer Bennett."

Violet could see the questions forming in his eyes. Lily and Bellamy had much to tell him. As much as she wanted to linger, listening to them tell their stories and watching Archer's reaction, Aunt Josephine wasn't aware that the women—and now, Archer—had time-traveled from some distant future that Violet couldn't even imagine.

"Aunt Josephine," she began, hoping to encourage the woman to go to her room to lie down before dinner. But before she could, a soft snore greeted her. Aunt Josephine had fallen asleep in her armchair.

Gabriel chuckled as he joined Violet. "It never ceases to surprise me how quickly she drops off. She should sleep through their conversation." To Lily, he said, "We will let you speak in private."

"But..." Violet protested.

He took her elbow and gently led her toward the hall. "Lily has told me a great deal of their history, and her worries for

Archer," he murmured. "She may say things to him that he would prefer we not be in attendance for."

She nodded. There were many things she would rather Gabriel not say to her in front of anyone else. Violet looked back at Archer one last time before they left the room.

His gaze was on her. Heat swirled in her belly, and she fought the urge to clamp her hand over the flutters there.

He dipped his head in silent acknowledgment, then turned his attention to his sisters.

"What do you think of the eldest Bennett?" Gabriel asked as he led her up the stairs to his study at the back of the townhouse. This was Gabriel's favorite room, probably because it was decorated almost the same as his study at Hawthorne Hall, their country estate. The light-yellow walls brightened up the dark wainscoting and solid wood furniture in the room. In some ways, it was a reflection of Gabriel himself. Dark and brooding at times, and bright with laughter in others. The thought made her smile. While they often fought of late, especially over her choices for a good match, she loved him dearly.

"Vi?"

What had he asked? Her thoughts had been on Archer. She pressed her lips together and took the seat across from him at his desk, busying herself with arranging her skirts. She wasn't sure what she thought about Archer Bennett. Her thoughts about the width of his shoulders and his muscular chest were not suitable to share with Gabriel, however.

"He seems noble," she said.

"Noble?" Gabriel looked at her as if she'd sprouted feathers from her ears. "Violet, I cannot in memory ever recall you describing someone as *noble*."

She shrugged and brushed at her skirts again. "He is."

Gabriel pierced her with a look she knew well. *Oh, blast.* She'd erred by keeping her comment indifferent and aroused his suspicions.

She crossed her arms over her chest. "I was being generous. I find him to be gruff and annoying like you." *Ha!* That would teach him to snoop for more than she wanted to reveal. It wasn't entirely true of course. She didn't find Archer annoying.

Gabriel chuckled. "The curse of the elder brother. Dashing the dreams and plans of the younger sister."

"At least you're aware of your shortcomings," she said with a sniff.

"And you wonder why I am not eager to marry you off to the first eligible man." He shook his head. "Who else will remind me of my imperfections?"

"Isn't that what your friends are for?" She gave him a pointed look. She wanted much more from life than to exist solely to remind her brother of his shortcomings.

"Little imp." His eyes softened. "If I could keep you with us forever, I would, Vi. But I know that is not what you want. You want a husband and family of your own. Now that I have Lily, I understand why."

Her heart twisted in her chest. She hadn't meant to prod him. "It's not that I don't want to stay with you and Lily. It's that I *want* what you have. What Mum and Dad never had. You love Lily so much. You'd never consider a mistress."

"She is everything to me," he said, a hint of a smile playing on his lips. "I could never want for the love of another."

"I want a man who looks at me the same way you look at Lily."

"Have you met such a man these last two Seasons?" Gabriel asked.

Violet's thoughts immediately turned to Archer. She swallowed. "No."

He searched her face as if he didn't quite believe her.

Please don't pry.

"In that case, there is someone that I'd like you to meet."

That was unexpected. Despite the sinking feeling in her stomach, Violet sat forward. "Who?"

"There is a gentleman who has inquired about courting you.

Viscount Mansfield. He has a solid income and an estate only a few hours from Hawthorne Hall." Gabriel smirked. "He's even younger than the archbishop."

Violet laughed. "Lily promised she would add that to the list." She cocked her head. "I don't think I've heard of him."

"He's just returned from Scotland. He managed the family estates there until the passing of his father."

Estates in Scotland could be exciting. She'd always wanted to visit there and see the men some of her acquaintances considered barbarians. Was he a barbarian? Surely not. He was English. English people couldn't breed the uncouth.

"How does he know of me?" she asked.

"Vi, when a man is in want of a beautiful wife of good breeding, with a good disposition, and a sizeable dowry, you are at the top of the list."

"And if such a woman has a gargoyle for a brother?" she teased.

"She moves to about the middle of the list. However, I consider that a positive. Any man willing to face a gargoyle for a woman is worth consideration, wouldn't you agree?"

She grinned. "You make an excellent argument, dear brother."

"Does he meet enough of your conditions to make an introduction?"

He did meet most of her requirements. "Is he a good man? Not one that spends his time at brothels and gaming hells?"

"He seemed friendly. Zeph was unaware of any vices. However, since he is new to Town, I think it best that we make our own judgments when meeting him."

Her thoughts wandered back to Archer. *It's just because he rescued me. In a few days, this fascination will be over, and he will be looking for a way home. I must think of my future.* She met Gabriel's concerned eyes and replied. "I will meet him."

"Excellent. He intends to be at Lady Kensington's dinner. I shall make the introduction then."

She nodded. "What if I do not like Lord Mansfield?"

"Then I suppose I shall have to reconsider your previous proposal to lock you in your room and brick over the doorway."

Her mouth dropped open. She made that comment in anger months ago. However, did he remember these things? "I believe I said you would lock me in a tower or brick me into the wall."

Gabriel grinned. "Ah, quite correct. It is good to have choices. However, since I don't have a tower in the townhouse, I suppose it'll be the wall. I hope that meets with your approval."

She couldn't hold back her smile. "It does. I suppose I shall have to try very hard to like Lord Mansfield then."

He laughed. "In the event that you don't suit, I leave it up to you to let me know when to order the brick."

Violet settled back in her chair. She adored Gabriel. When he wasn't being overbearing, he was the best brother a woman could ask for. She wondered if Lily and Bellamy thought the same of Archer.

"You didn't say what you thought of Archer Bennett," she said.

Gabriel's eyebrows rose at her sudden shift in conversation. "That is because I have not had more than an introduction. I hope to spend more time with him this evening after dinner while you ladies retire to the drawing room."

She hadn't meant to ask anyway. What difference did it make if Archer liked… that is, if *Gabriel* liked Archer.

She rose. "I think I should freshen up prior to dinner."

Gabriel sat back in his chair.

Violet spun on her heel and strode to the door. Any more time spent in his presence, and he would ask her something she didn't want to answer.

"I think we are all keen to learn more about the elder Bennett. Wouldn't you agree?"

She paused at the door, cursing his astute sense of observation. "Yes. Of course. Lily and Bellamy must be so excited. I shouldn't want to miss out."

"Indeed."

Ugh. His look said he wouldn't rest until he uncovered all her secrets. She hurried out the door.

Henry was climbing the stairs as she exited. The butler bowed when he saw her. "Lady Violet, a delivery has arrived for you." He held out an envelope.

"A delivery?"

"Yes, my lady. Flowers. This card arrived with them."

Someone had sent her flowers? Violet took the card with shaking fingers. What color were they? What kind? Who would be so bold?

Evening shadows gathered in the hall. Violet stepped closer to the candlelit sconce, eager to read the note. Her brows drew together at the single line scrawled in a messy hand.

Your faithful admirer.

"Henry, did you see who delivered the flowers?"

"Yes, my lady. A delivery boy."

She nodded her thanks, then descended to the hall. On the table below the gilded mirror, sat a crystal vase filled with pink and white peonies. They were beautiful.

Violet took a deep breath of their sweet fragrance and admired them. A smile tugged at her lips. The sender might wish to remain anonymous, but Violet loved the adventure of a mystery. She couldn't wait to discover the sender's identity. Was it someone she was well acquainted with? Someone not yet ready to face her brother, but who'd taken a fancy to her?

Mind spinning with possibilities, she didn't hear the soft footsteps exit the drawing room.

CHAPTER FOUR

"Y OU'RE GOING TO be an uncle," Lily said with a smile that made her face light up.

Not words Archer had expected to hear from the sister he'd heard from two weeks ago, who hadn't even had a boyfriend. Now, Lily was married and expecting. Time travel—if this wasn't a coma-induced dream that felt incredibly real—messed with a man's head worse than the pain medications he'd been on while in the hospital. He shifted on the uncomfortable chair and kneaded his left thigh, trying not to draw too much attention to the movement. He sat near the fireplace in what Bells called the drawing room with his sisters. Sweat beaded between his shoulder blades and he wished he'd taken a seat farther away. No doubt the heat had lulled the elderly lady in the chair opposite him to sleep.

The room was formal in a way that reminded him of a museum or an old manor that people toured. Embroidered fabric covered the chairs and paintings of horses and the countryside hung on the walls. Oil lamps lit the room against the darkening skies and there wasn't a single power outlet or electronic device in sight. His best friend Church would have loved it.

After Violet and her brother left the room, a maid came in with a fresh pot of tea, which Bellamy poured into a dainty china cup that seemed absurdly fragile in his hand. His sisters took turns telling him stories of finding themselves in a strange new world and trying to acclimate.

As Bellamy talked, he noted that her face looked softer, as did her shoulders and arms. She was still too thin after years in the modeling industry, but the little bit of added weight gave her a healthy glow.

Lily looked radiant in her old-fashioned dress as if she belonged here. She laughed easily and the teasing banter with Bellamy held none of their previous animosity. He'd never seen her this happy. Not since before their folks died. She'd shouldered so much of the burden for their family after the car crash: arranging the funerals, taking care of Bellamy, settling the debts left behind… Lily deserved happiness. God knew one of them did, and it sure as hell wasn't him.

He mustered up a small smile for her. "I'm happy for you, Lils. You'll be a wonderful mother, no matter what Bellamy says." He winked at her.

"Hey!" Bells grumbled. She glanced at the slumbering older woman, then grabbed the pillow behind her and whacked him with it. "We're getting along now. Don't ruin it."

Lily laughed. "Don't worry, Bells. I'll stick him with babysitting duty as often as possible."

"Hell no. First of all, I'll be gone by then, and second, I'm no good with kids. I'd be a drill sergeant instead of a father."

Both women sobered at that.

"I'd hoped you'd consider staying," Lily said. "Now that we're all here, back together after so many years, you'll leave?"

Her pleading tone cut into him like a serrated blade. Bellamy's eyes misted. *Dammit.* He waved at his injured leg, "I'm still seeing the physical therapist a few times a week." He didn't mention the regular therapist he was also forced to see. "Unless I'm really off of my history lessons, they don't have what I need here."

Lily's eyes narrowed. "What exactly is it that you need, Archer?" Beside her, his little sister cocked an eyebrow and crossed her arms over her chest.

He rubbed a hand over his knee. The look on Lily's face said they were no longer talking about doctors. He played dumb anyway. "Pain medication to start. The exercise machines to rebuild my muscles and flexibility…"

Lily waved his words away. "I'm certain we can find ways for you to manage while you heal. But unless your doctor ordered an isolation chamber, there's no reason for you to rush home. We just got you back."

"Not to mention… you can't go home. Not until Christian finds a way to make the clock work," Bellamy added.

He grimaced, still not entirely convinced he was *here*. "When can he get started?"

"Maybe you should wait to put the man I'm going to marry to work until after I introduce you to him?" Bellamy glared at him. "Or did the military train the manners out of you?"

Special operations trained him to deal with almost any situation, including hostage negotiation, which he was starting to think that he might need when it came time to leave his sisters. "Fine. When can I meet him?"

"At dinner tonight. And not a moment before."

He grunted. "Fine."

"What's the real reason you're so desperate to return?" Lily pressed.

He leaned back in his chair. "What do you mean?"

She rolled her eyes. "I mean that we haven't seen you in years and you can't wait to leave. That has nothing to do with your pain. You're either trying to avoid us, you have something you must return for, or both. And don't think you're getting away from that drill sergeant comment."

Archer gripped the back of his neck and stared at the ceiling. "Why couldn't I have had brothers?"

"Because they wouldn't challenge you to be honest, which you clearly need," Bellamy replied.

He huffed out a frustrated breath. "There's something I have to do."

"What is more important than being with your family?" Lily asked.

Archer pushed out of his chair, grabbed his cane, and went to the window. Rain fell in sheets, making the unpaved streets a muddy mess, just like his life. He'd made so many poor choices. How could he begin to explain his need to do *something* to make up for it? There was nothing he could do for his teammates or for Church. He'd decided months ago that maybe finding Amanda's killer would provide a bit of redemption. "I want the man who took Amanda to go to jail." She'd been his best friend in middle school until she disappeared.

"That wasn't your fault," Lily said softly.

Regardless, it was something he had to do, for her, and himself. He turned away from the window to where his sisters sat. "Okay then. If I'm here for now, where can I bunk?"

"There is a guest room on the same floor as Violet and Aunt Josephine, although she may protest."

"Who, Violet?" he asked.

Bellamy snorted and nodded toward the woman who still slept in the chair near the fire, then glanced at Lily. "Although maybe you should remind her that she's supposed to be the chaperone, instead of sleeping or drinking through each function."

Lily laughed and a sparkle of mischief danced in her eyes. "Excellent idea. I'll have Gabriel tell her."

Archer leaned on his cane. His leg ached and the heat of the room was making the sweat and the dirt on his clothes and hands feel grimy. "If someone would show me the way? I want to clean up." He'd have to put his dirty clothes back on. Wouldn't be the first time. Probably not even the fiftieth.

"I'll have a bath sent up," Lily said. She eyed his clothing. "You're about the same size as Gabriel. I'll fetch some clothing for you. The people here change several times a day. They dress up for dinner."

Great. What the hell did that mean? A suit and tie? "Thanks."

Bellamy rose and touched his arm. "I'm so glad you're here, Arch. I know you don't want to stay, but I hope we can make enough memories while you're here for all of us to last a lifetime."

His heart thudded harder at her words as they sunk in. When he left, he'd be leaving his sisters behind forever. They'd be dead and buried in the past and an ocean away.

He'd truly be alone in the world. Despite how often he'd felt that way, he'd always had his sisters to go back to. All he had to do was reach out. Once he left here, he'd sever those ties permanently. Was that what he wanted?

Lily woke up the woman she called Aunt Josephine and suggested she change for dinner. The woman rose and cracked a wide yawn, then took a few unsteady steps toward the door. Archer took her arm, so she didn't fall though, he realized bitterly, that if she *did* fall he might go down with her.

"Thank you, young man. My, you are a handsome one. Have you met Lady Violet? She would give you nice babies."

Archer cleared his throat, while his sisters barely contained their laughter as they slipped out the door. *Traitors.* Aunt Josephine seemed not to be expecting an answer, however, and leaned on him as they left the drawing room.

Movement in the hall drew his attention. Violet held a small envelope in her hand as she bent over to smell a large bouquet of pink flowers that sat on the side table. A small smile played on her lips.

Her beauty hit him like a sucker punch. Archer tried to shake it off. He didn't know this woman. She could be vain and mean for all he knew. His fingers clenched around his cane, the wood digging into his palm.

She didn't seem vain or mean though. More like a good whiskey. Dark with amber undertones. Sweet with a hint of fire.

Damn, he loved that combination. His gaze snagged on her plump lower lip. Would she taste like whiskey? Dark and delicious? His cock stirred at the tempting image of spreading Violet out beneath him, lowering his head to taste her. The sensation shocked him out of the daydream. It had been months since he'd felt this level of desire. Since before he'd been medically discharged from the service.

Why now? With such a young woman, no less.

Get it together, Bennett.

"That's her," Aunt Josephine said. "That's Lady Violet. You should court her." She patted his arm before she left his side and then slowly climbed the stairs.

"What lovely peonies, Violet. Who are they from?" Lily leaned forward to smell the blossoms. The vase contained at least a dozen fragrant flowers.

"Aren't they beautiful?" Violet gestured to the vase. Her other hand dropped to her side, trying to tuck the envelope into the folds of her skirt.

Bellamy made a noise of appreciation and joined Lily in admiring the bouquet.

Archer moved beside Violet. He lowered his head to whisper in her ear, "What's the note say?" The scent of cinnamon teased him. He breathed the sweet and spicy scent in from her hair and skin, and his thoughts once more turned carnal.

Her amber eyes widened, and she shuffled her hand deeper into the folds of her skirt. "What note?" she whispered back.

"The one you're hiding from my sisters." Did she taste like cinnamon too?

Violet's chin rose a notch. "Nothing that concerns you."

Something dark churned in his chest, instantly banking his desire. "Do you have a secret lover, Violet?"

She rounded on him and slapped the envelope against his chest. He rocked back a step in surprise.

"I would never! It would ruin my reputation. You're as impertinent as they are. See for yourself, since you're so inquisitive of my affairs."

Lily turned at Violet's outburst. "Is that the note that came with the flowers?"

Violet narrowed her eyes at him as if to imply that this was *his* fault.

The relief he felt, combined with her small burst of temper, made him grin. It tugged at his scar running along his jaw in an uncomfortable way, reminding him that he hadn't smiled in a while. He took the envelope from Violet and opened it to reveal a single piece of paper.

"Your faithful admirer" was scrawled on it. The handwriting looked too sloppy to be female, and there was no signature.

Archer froze. His childhood friend, Amanda, had received notes from an admirer before she disappeared. The memory, coupled with his fear from earlier about his sisters, sent a chill down his spine and made his tone harsh. "Who sent it?"

Violet shrugged and looked away.

Bellamy took the paper from him so she and Lily could look.

He focused on Violet. "You don't know?" he asked.

She shook her head, a small smile on her lips. "No, but isn't it sweet? I've never received flowers before. The mystery of it makes it more exciting!"

He frowned. "Have you received anything else from this 'faithful admirer'?

Violet planted her hands on her hips. "What concern is it of yours?"

"Vi, he's just being protective," Lily said as she slipped her arm around the young woman's waist. "It's who Archer is."

"Well, there's simply no need," Violet sniffed, nose tilting into the air.

Archer gripped his cane and gritted his teeth. "Whoever sent those might not have good intentions."

"There's nothing ignoble about sending flowers to a woman that you like," Violet hissed back. "Is it so wrong for a woman to have an admirer? Am I too unattractive to have one?"

Bellamy coughed to cover a laugh.

He glared at his sister, then Violet. "You're damn beautiful and you know it." He sucked in a breath to calm his temper. "I'm only saying that this may be more than it seems. You need to be careful. This man might want more than you're willing to give."

"Well, I think it's nice for whoever it is to send such a lovely gift *and* quite clever. If I knew who sent them, I would have to decline the gift. Since I do not, they are mine to keep. It's rather nice to be wanted by a suitor."

Lily cleared her throat. "Archer, let me show you to your room and call for that bath. Violet, maybe you should talk to Gabriel about the flowers and anything else you've received."

"Maybe everyone should stop meddling in what is not their concern." Violet took the note from Bellamy and stomped up the stairs.

Archer glared after her.

Bellamy laughed. "She's a handful."

"Like you when you were young," Lily replied.

Violet was right about one thing. This wasn't his concern. The woman could do what she wished. He needed to focus on getting home.

THE NUMBER OF curses coming from Archer's room through the open doorway was scandalous. Violet tiptoed closer so she could peek inside to see what had the man flustered.

He stood in front of the full-length mirror dressed in tan trousers, a basil green waistcoat, and a black tailcoat. He tied his cravat in a bow, pulled it loose, and retied it twice more. With another curse, he yanked it off and tossed it on the bed behind him. "I'll go without," he grumbled.

Violet couldn't contain the giggle that escaped her when he gave the offending fabric a grumpy glare.

His head snapped up and met her eyes in the mirror's reflection.

She stepped into the doorway and pressed her back against it. "Having difficulty?"

"There's a reason that men no longer wear them in my time. No one has three hours to put one on."

Violet scanned the hallway behind her, listening for Aunt Josephine or Bellamy. She didn't hear either. Aunt Josephine had probably gone downstairs for a glass of wine. Bellamy would be helping Christian tie his own cravat. The man often looked disheveled unless Bellamy helped him. She suspected that Archer would be the same.

Since no one was about to see her ruinous behavior, she entered his bed chamber and closed the door. "Will you allow me to help?" She lifted the length of starched muslin up. A clean, woodsy fragrance wafted from the fabric, warming her insides. Archer's scent. She recognized it from when he'd caught her and held her tightly to his chest. A shiver of awareness stirred in her belly and shot lower to a more intimate area that stole her breath.

Archer eyed the cravat with distaste. "Lily says it's required for dinner. Guess we're not having pizza and beer."

"I don't know what pizza is. Gabriel has mentioned beer, although I don't know how often he drinks it." Violet approached him, hardly believing her own daring to be here in his chamber. Her brother would be incensed.

She laid the middle of the folded muslin against his throat and wrapped the ends around his neck. His hair was still damp from his bath and the wet strands teased her fingers. He was a good height, she decided. Her head came up to his chin and she imagined that if she lifted her face and stood on her toes, she... *a woman* could easily kiss him.

Violet flushed at the thought. What would that sort of kiss be like? Would kissing Archer be different from kissing another man? She'd meant to ask Lily or Bellamy about that. How different could kisses be from one man to another?

Lord Musgrave had wanted to kiss her at Gabriel's ball last year. She'd been agreeable to his suit, even though he was one of

Gabriel's friends, whom her brother deemed unfit. They'd lingered at the edge of the terrace, talking and flirting, when Lord Musgrave stepped closer, the intent to kiss her in his expression. When he'd wrapped his arms about her, she'd panicked and pushed him away. Her behavior had understandably confused him. Violet was confused herself. She thought she'd wanted to kiss him until the moment came, and then she'd shied away from his affections with uncertainty. When he tried for a second kiss... She overreacted a little in her effort to push him off.

At least she hadn't been the one to break his nose. That had been Gabriel's doing when he ordered Musgrave to leave. Violet regretted the entire incident. Not only had she crushed any future hopes for a kiss or a match with Musgrave, but it had also ended his friendship with Gabriel. What a ninny she'd been. Who knew when she'd have another opportunity to experience a kiss?

She stared at Archer's mouth. What would it be like to kiss a man with a beard versus a clean-shaven jaw like Musgrave's? Would the bristles be pleasant or rough?

"Violet?" Archer's voice sounded strained.

She blinked and realized that she was running her hands up and down the trailing ends of the cravat over his chest, biting her lip. *How mortifying!*

Should she step away and have him forgo the cravat? Continue on as if nothing untoward happened? Move to Scotland immediately?

Don't be irrational, Vi. He couldn't go to dinner without a cravat. What would Gabriel think of Archer then? She must continue as if she hadn't been stroking his chest and thinking of kissing him while alone with him in his room. It was the only sensible thing to do, and she prided herself on her sensibility.

Violet smiled and took up the ends of the muslin. She tied two quick knots, smoothed the ends, then crossed them in front. "Do you have a cravat pin?"

"How the hell did you do that so fast?"

"I've had a lot of practice with Gabriel. He used to fire his valet every week. A few days later, he'd hire the man back, and they'd begin their arguments anew. In the intervening days, I learned how to tie several styles. The Earl of Rothden can't be seen in public with a terrible cravat. What would the gossips say?"

"That he had better things to do with his time?" Archer fetched a gold cravat pin topped with a small emerald off the dresser and handed it to her.

Violet laughed. "I don't think they would be that kind." She tucked the pin through the knots to hold them in place. "There. You are now presentable for dinner."

Archer turned back to the mirror. He pulled the cuffs of his coat down and straightened his waistcoat. "I look…"

"Dashing?" He had such wide shoulders. Why had she not run her hands across them while she had the opportunity?

"I was going to say *different*. Formal."

She saw his eyes move over his neck in his reflection. Looking for his scars? With the starched high collar of his shirt and the beard, she couldn't see them at all.

"Perhaps there are advantages," he murmured.

"It is fashionable to be clean shaven," she said. "If you would like to shave…"

"No. Thank you." He traced the back of his fingers over his jaw. "They're… not pretty. And before you ask… don't."

Violet knew that he'd had a terrible accident. Lily and Bellamy said as much. What no one knew besides Archer was what occurred. She sensed that his scars ran far deeper than what could be seen. It made her want to wrap him in a hug and place a kiss over his scars. "Shall we go down for supper?"

Archer nodded and retrieved his cane. "Violet?" When she turned back to him, he said, "Thank you. For helping with the cravat."

She smiled. "If you must tell people that I assisted, please do not tell them where. If it's discovered that I was in your bedchamber alone, I'd be ruined. Then you would have to stay because you'd be forced to marry me."

His eyes widened. "Jesus. Okay, I'll pretend that I mastered this damn thing on my own, which I'm certain everyone will believe."

She laughed at his mocking tone. "Or that I was forced to correct your horrid attempt when I found you in the hall."

"More likely that you rescued me from hanging myself with it."

He was so handsome when a teasing light lingered in his eyes and the corner of his lip curled up in a half smile. Her gaze dropped to his mouth.

Archer swallowed and she tracked the movement as his throat bobbed. "Let's go down to dinner," he rasped.

It took effort to look away. His voice, his scent, the different way he spoke… all drew her to him.

He's leaving, Vi. As soon as Christian fixes the clock. Your future is here. Not with Archer Bennett.

She strode to the door and cracked it open. A quick peek showed the hall was still empty. Violet slipped out, feeling a little thrill at doing something scandalous and not being caught.

Archer stopped at her side. He scanned the length of her body, lingering on her hips and her breasts only a moment longer than the rest before meeting her eyes. He cleared his throat. "You look beautiful, Violet. The blue dress is pretty."

"Thank you." Heat swept over her face. She'd chosen a sapphire blue gown with lace trim that flattered her figure. One should always look their best. Especially when joined for dinner by new guests. Very handsome new guests who pulled her out of danger without any thought to themselves. Violet gestured toward the stairs. "Shall we?"

Archer followed her down the two flights to the dining room. The muffled thump of his cane on the stair runner seemed somehow comforting, adding life to the townhouse in a way that the chime of a clock or the clink of silverware did.

They met Bellamy and Christian in the hall.

"Lily and Gabriel went into the dining room. It should just be us tonight. It seems Zeph was called out of town," Bellamy said.

That was unfortunate. Violet enjoyed Zeph's company. Zeph Lael and Christian were Gabriel's dearest friends and had been since they'd schooled together at Eton. Lily said she found him quite mysterious, and Violet loved that about him. "I hope he'll return soon."

"You know he can't stay away for long." Bellamy turned to her brother. "Arch, this is Christian Albury, the Earl of Huntington. He's..." She smiled up at Christian. "He's mine."

Christian trailed his fingers over her cheek, then extended his hand toward Archer. "A pleasure. Your sisters have told us much about you."

Violet stifled a smile. Christian was still dreadfully shy, but since meeting Bellamy, he could manage introductions with ease.

Archer seemed stiff beside her as he shook Christian's hand. "Yeah. Nice to meet you. She said you invented the clock that," he twirled a finger in the air, "did all of this?"

Christian flushed. "It seems so. I hope to look at the clock that you brought with you."

Archer nodded and reached into his coat pocket. He removed a linen handkerchief and opened it enough to show the bits of gears and enamel.

Christian accepted the bundle, eyebrows slanting down. "It looks as if a carriage ran it over."

"It did," Archer replied.

Christian cast a side look at Violet.

"Not mine this time," she replied with a tilt of her chin. At Archer's quizzical look, she explained, "Lily arrived much as you did, except she appeared in front of my carriage." The woman had stepped into the street, quite disoriented.

Christian's lips pursed as he considered the fragments. "I think if I can reassemble the gears and adjust the—"

"Later, love," Bellamy said. "I'm famished." She tugged him toward the dining room.

"That's new," Archer said as they fell into step behind the

other couple and entered the dining room.

"What is?" Violet asked.

"Bellamy being hungry. With her modeling job, she never ate enough because she had to remain the ideal size."

The ideal size? Violet looked at Bellamy's tall, lithe form, with her smaller bosom and graceful walk. Her own body was somewhere in between the two sisters. She was taller than Lily with less of a bosom and smaller hips, but far shorter and nowhere near as thin as Bellamy. Is that what men wanted in a woman in his time?

"I think she's gained weight since I last saw her, but she's still too thin," Archer murmured.

"When you say she is the ideal size, did you mean her height?"

He shook his head. "In our society, great emphasis is put on a woman's figure. Magazines and advertisements show tall, thin, beautiful women like Bellamy to say that is what true beauty looks like. What all women should aspire to."

She nodded and they took seats opposite Christian and Bellamy. Gabriel sat at the head of the table with Lily on his left and Aunt Josephine on his right. Somehow Bellamy always had the seat beside Aunt Josephine, which Violet secretly felt glad for.

"Our society emphasizes fair skin and a lithe form," she said. "Women ought to always wear a bonnet when out in the sun or carry a parasol to keep our skin fair. We also should not stuff ourselves at meals lest we become too plump."

"Seems things haven't changed much."

Violet bit her bottom lip, debating on asking the next question. Once the others were suitably ensconced in their own conversations, she asked, "Do the men where you are from desire only that type of beauty? Is that what they want in a wife?"

Archer met her gaze. His eyes traveled over her face and settled on her mouth. When they flicked back up to hers, she saw something she'd never seen before in a man's eyes. She couldn't quite describe it, but it gave her insides that fluttery, warm feeling again.

"Only the most superficial of men." He looked away and reached for his wine glass. "Sometimes outer beauty can harbor an evil, twisted heart, and mind." He paused and twisted the stem of the glass through his fingers. "And not as much emphasis is put on marriage."

Violet wanted to ask more about his society, but their conversation wasn't private and Aunt Josephine, who wasn't aware that he came from another time, could easily overhear them. Instead, she asked, "What does a man call true beauty then, if not beauty in face and form?"

"I can't speak for anyone else," he said, still studying the wine glass.

He was quiet for so long, that Violet thought their conversation over. But then he put his glass down and murmured, "A man sees true beauty in a woman who is kind to others, and who loves her family. In her, he can find someone to be his partner in life. Who supports his endeavors while he supports hers... someone he can share anything with." He paused and lifted his eyes to hers. "Even things he can't tell others."

Violet could barely breathe. "Have *you* found such a woman?" she whispered. Did he have someone waiting for him in his time? The thought made her heart squeeze like it was being crushed in some phantom fist. She swallowed.

Archer's dark gaze intensified.

She felt warm and flushed like she couldn't draw enough air. His woodsy scent filled every breath. She couldn't seem to get enough of it, and she couldn't look away from his dark green eyes that glittered in the candlelight.

Then the moment was broken as Christian announced, "Archer, I believe I will need at least two days to repair the clock. After that, I hope to have an idea as to what was different. What caused the ah, aberration."

Archer seemed to collect himself before he turned to respond to Christian.

Violet's heart hammered in her chest, and with a start, she realized that her nipples had hardened. She shifted in her chair, hoping that no one noticed.

"Looks like you'll be with us for at least a week, Arch," Bellamy said.

"If not longer." Christian rubbed his thumb over the linen tablecloth and glanced at Aunt Josephine. "It's possible that it was not I that added the special… element to the clock. Perhaps that was added later."

Archer went still. Several long moments passed, and then he nodded. "I'll help."

"There is not much you can do until I reassemble the clock. For that, I need time and concentration." He gave Bellamy the kind of smile that Violet sometimes saw Lily and Gabriel exchange, and she sighed. *That's* what she wanted. That kind of love.

"We will have to get you some more clothes, and anything else that you will need for the time being," Lily said to Archer.

Shopping? Violet sat up. "I will go with him. I know *all* the best tailor shops."

Gabriel nodded. "Thank you, Violet. I'm afraid I will be tied up with business. Don't forget that we have Lord and Lady Kensington's ball, as well as Lady Milne's dinner party."

She nodded, then turned to Archer. "We must get you ready for your debut into society."

"Good heavens, Gabriel. You cannot clothe everyone in Town. You've already spent a fortune on gowns, and I cannot be expected to chaperone the girl to men's tailors," Aunt Josephine said, her unnatural red ringlets bouncing as she shook her head in disapproval. "You must have a care. The Rothden Estate cannot suffer losses like it did under your father."

Gabriel reached for the crystal decanter and filled the older woman's glass. "Allow me, Aunt Josephine. Your glass looked nearly empty."

"Oh, thank you, dear boy." She patted his hand a few times

which were closer to slaps under the pressure.

"Not to worry, Aunt. Everything is well taken care of. The Rothden Estate need not worry about money in my lifetime," Gabriel added. He winked at Violet.

Aunt Josephine smiled and drank half of her wine in one gulp.

Bellamy stifled a laugh behind a cough. "I would be happy to accompany you both."

But then Archer shook his head. "No need. I don't plan to go to your events. I don't belong there."

CHAPTER FIVE

TWO DAYS LATER, Archer leaned heavily on his cane as he walked behind his sister and Violet toward a tailor's shop. He ground his teeth against the pain that throbbed in his thigh and radiated down his calf in what felt like bolts of lightning.

At thirty-one and a former Navy SEAL, he was no stranger to pain. But *fuck*, this hurt. He hadn't realized until this morning how dependent he'd been on the medications the doctors had given him to manage the pain while his wounds healed.

He hated it. Hated that he had to take the medication and hated that he didn't have the relief of it now because he was in the fucking nineteenth century. His nightmares weren't helping his mood either. They'd plagued his sleep every night since he woke up in the hospital with memories of those final moments before the blast.

Last night had been the worst. Interspersed with the memories were visions of his sisters and Violet riding in the Humvee with him, their eyes wide as the *rap-rap-rap* of gunfire erupted nearby. He'd awoken in a sweat with a shout lodged in his throat and hadn't been able to find sleep after.

"Archer, you're like a bad-tempered bear this afternoon," Bellamy said when she looked at him over her shoulder. "Your scowl is going to frighten the poor tailor."

Violet half-turned to him, worrying her lower lip between her teeth as she looked him over.

Archer tugged at the cravat around his neck. Was that concern or pity on her face? Either way, he didn't want to see it. He focused on his sister and narrowed his eyes. "Then let's go back to the townhouse."

"Nope. It's a miracle we got you to leave in the first place." Bellamy gave him her signature blinding smile that usually got her what she wanted. "Do you really want to spend your time in someone else's clothes?"

Dammit. No, he didn't. That's the only reason he'd come out with the women, to begin with. Bellamy's grin widened when he scowled. She had him with that argument and she knew it.

Violet slowed her steps to match his uneven gate. "Are you well, Mr. Bennett?"

Mr. Bennett. He huffed in irritation. This time's propriety grated on his nerves, but he needed to blend in, so he'd spent the last two days learning etiquette and societal expectations from Violet and his sisters. "No. And it's *Archer.*"

Her eyebrows rose at his gruff tone.

Goddammit, now he felt like an ass for barking at her. He dragged a somewhat calming breath into his lungs. *Don't take it out on her, asshole. It's not her fault.* "Sorry." He winced. "I'm... hurting."

"Your leg?" Violet asked in a lowered voice.

He nodded once.

"The shop is one block up. When we get there, I'll talk with the tailor and Bellamy about the designs so you can sit and rest. If that would help?"

The tide of irritation in his chest softened. Archer mustered up a nod of appreciation. He didn't want to be treated like an invalid, but her thoughtfulness was nice. It was easy to snap at his sister, but he couldn't keep up his grumpiness with Violet.

His gaze wandered over the young woman. She barely came up to his chin, but with her white bonnet on, she seemed taller today. Archer had never really paid attention to what a woman wore unless it was next to nothing—which tended to get any man's attention—but her dresses flattered her figure and brought out the color in her cheeks. Today's green dress with embroidered flowers made her dark chocolate curls and those gorgeous amber eyes look even prettier. Add the spark of mischief he'd seen in her a couple of times since they'd met, and it was a miracle he could look away.

Violet looked up and flashed him that too innocent smile as they walked. It charmed him and made him feel old at the same time. Yeah, he'd seen way too much of the ugliness this world had to offer. He wouldn't tarnish her bright, vibrant outlook on life by pursuing anything, no matter how attractive he found her. He knew better than anyone that sometimes darkness suffocated the light. He'd just have to avoid her as much as possible.

Whether he liked it or not, he couldn't go home yet. Any lingering doubts about whether he was really in nineteenth-century London had been laid to rest on the carriage ride here. They'd passed the Egyptian Museum, which, thanks to Church's love of history, he knew no longer existed. It'd been torn down in favor of apartments. That, combined with the lack of all of the twenty-first century's conveniences, made him a believer.

This time period wasn't convenient, but it was relatively comfortable. He could deal with it. There had been plenty of times when his team had found themselves in a spot they hadn't anticipated. They'd been trained to adapt, adjust, and move forward with a new plan. The same applied here. He had to see to his body's physical and mental needs and be prepared when the time came to return home.

He had shelter and food, thanks to his sisters and Hawthorne. Clean clothing would be welcome. If he could sort out something in this time to dull a bit of his pain, that would be ideal. If not, he'd survive.

As if thinking about his situation had summoned a flashback, he suddenly heard automatic weapon fire, explosions, and screams. White light filled his head for a split second until he forced it all away with some breathing exercises. Yeah, he'd survived far worse. The only easy day was yesterday.

Bellamy stopped at a storefront with mullioned windows. A simple sign above the door read *A. Rowe*. "Christian says that Mr. Rowe is one of the best tailors in Town."

Violet nodded. "Gabriel uses him almost exclusively—Oh!" She took a step back as the door to the tailor's shop flew open and a man stepped out with a servant in tow. Archer stepped forward as Violet tottered; he reached for her elbow just as the man appeared to notice her.

He swept his top hat off his head and gave the ladies a low bow. "I beg pardon! A gentleman should be more careful in the presence of ladies."

Damn straight. Archer frowned. The man was about his height, with light brown hair and a lean build. The knot on his nose said it had been broken once. In an accident or a fight? The man gave Archer a cursory glance, then swept his gaze down Violet's figure and back up.

"A man mustn't trample such a lovely flower, after all," he said.

Archer checked his eye roll and locked down the irritation at this smarmy dude. He moved around him to reopen the shop door since the guy was too busy fawning over Violet to hold it open.

"No apologies necessary," Violet said with a bright smile. She tucked her arm through Bellamy's. "Thank you."

The man tipped his hat and strolled away. Archer held the door for the ladies and kept an eye on the man's retreating figure. At the next store, he looked back, ignoring Archer in favor of a lingering gaze after the ladies.

What man wouldn't look at two of the most beautiful women in this damn town? His actions were justified. So why was the back of Archer's neck tingling with an awareness he'd honed for years in the SEALs?

The man turned the corner and Archer entered the shop. The

space was larger than he expected, with ample space and several floor-length mirrors. Large tables lined one wall, draped in fabric. An alcove led to the back, through which he spotted several people with their heads bent, sewing garments. Violet and Bellamy were speaking with a young man who looked to be in his mid-twenties. When Archer approached, all three turned toward him.

Bellamy made the introductions.

The tailor, Mr. Rowe, eyed him critically. "You're wearing my work, but it was not made for you. Let's get you into something better fitting, shall we?"

"He needs a full wardrobe," Bellamy said.

Rowe eyed him again, then nodded. "I think I have some pieces that can be quickly adjusted. The steel-cut cloth would look dashing. Mr. Bennett, if you'll stand here please." The tailor directed him to a long table.

"Oh, but first Lady Bennett and I wanted to see the silk waistcoats you have available," Violet said.

"I would be delighted. Ah, Mr. Bennett, if you could wait a moment, I shall be with you shortly."

Violet winked at him over the tailor's shoulder.

His lips twitched. "That's fine." Once the three began browsing fabric and clothing designs, he sank onto a nearby chair. Archer stretched out his left leg, grinding his teeth against the pain.

He felt someone watching him and looked up to see Violet, watching him with a concerned face. She sent him a soft smile, then turned back to the tailor.

Since he'd met her, she'd been thoughtful of him, and unlike Bellamy, seemed to notice when he was hurting. He'd walked far longer on his injured leg today than he had in a couple of months.

The physical therapist would be happy at least. She'd been on him to walk more and had told him that it would help the muscles reacclimate to movement and hurt less. To Archer, it was more about rebuilding the mental fortitude. Walking and moving his leg—*healing*—meant admitting that he was the only one on his team left. He wasn't ready.

He'd fucked up, he'd lived, and walking symbolized moving on. He wasn't sure he could.

The throbbing in his leg had settled into a sharp ache by the time the tailor returned.

"If you'll stand here, Mr. Bennett." The tailor indicated a spot before one of the mirrors.

Archer let the cane take most of his weight as he climbed to his feet. Flickers of pain shot through the nerves in his thighs. He clamped his teeth together and moved into position. In the mirror, he saw his sister and Violet perusing different trimmings.

Rowe stood behind him with a long ribbon, making notes as he measured. "Have you tried white willow bark for the pain?"

Archer grimaced. He thought he'd done a better job at hiding the aches. "I haven't."

"It may help. It's better than laudanum, anyway. Nasty stuff. Too many of my clients rely upon it." When Archer didn't reply, the tailor said, "Your sister and Lady Violet have a fine eye for a man's wardrobe."

"Hm."

The tailor smiled at that. "Lady Bennett said you were a man of few words. You are new here? Just in from the colonies?"

The colonies? He hadn't heard America called that since high school history class. "Yes."

"What happened to the clothes you traveled with?"

Archer blew out a breath and rested his cane against the long worktable near his hip. "My sisters decided they were unsuitable."

Rowe's lips twitched. "I admire a woman so keen on fashion."

"You'd be good friends with Lady Violet then. I get the sense that she would throw those old clothes in the closest fire if she could."

"Indeed. She brightens up my store whenever she visits with Lord Rothden."

Archer eyed him. Did this man also want Violet? Did everyone?

Rowe caught his gaze in the mirror. "She is lovely, is she not? That spirit sparkles. She would make a fine wife to the right man."

"You?"

Rowe belted out a rich laugh. "No. She is… much too far above my station."

The man swallowed and his gaze flitted over Archer's shoulders. He remeasured them.

Oh. Archer ran through the past few minutes with Rowe in his head and realized that the man hadn't ogled either woman. It could be a matter of professionalism, but he sensed the man's preferences lay elsewhere. That had to be tough at this time.

When their eyes met again in the mirror, Rowe's hand stilled on his shoulder. His eyes widened at the understanding on Archer's face and his mouth opened. Nothing came out.

Archer gave a slight shake of his head. "Not my business, man."

Rowe studied the floor, pretending to straighten Archer's tailcoat. "You won't… speak of your suppositions, will you?"

"No." He thought of the men, the brothers that he'd lost. "You never know how much time you have in this world. A man should grab whatever happiness he can find." His gaze unwittingly drew to Violet. She stood nearby, viewing a case of stick pins and watch fobs.

"Even when that love seems impossible?" Rowe murmured.

Archer looked away from Violet to tug on the cuffs of his sleeves. He didn't have an answer for that. She was too young, and he was too damaged. His brow furrowed. Staying away was the right thing to do. Wasn't it?

He met Rowe's gaze in the mirror once more.

Whatever he read in Archer's expression made the tense set of his shoulders loosen and a tiny smile form. "The desire and the courage are two different things, are they not?" Rowe kept his voice low. "Thank you, Mr. Bennett. I will think about your words. I hope you consider them as well. Lady Violet is worthy of a good man."

Archer cleared his throat. "About that suit…"

Rowe chuckled. "Let's remove this ill-fitting clothing and see what I have to work with." He directed Archer behind a curtain into a small room to remove his tailcoat and waistcoat. "Even an American must know it is inappropriate to go to your shirtsleeves in front of ladies," Rowe said at Archer's questioning look.

Right. He stepped behind the curtain and removed his garments.

Rowe took them from him but didn't move. He stared at Archer's back. "Most gentlemen keep their knife in their boot."

"It's not as easy to access in a boot." He'd tried his own belt, but the waistcoat wasn't long enough to cover it, so he'd been forced to carry the knife at the small of his back. It was an old WW2 KA-BAR that had belonged to Church's grandfather, and he'd given it to Archer for his last birthday. Just two weeks before Church was gone forever. "I'm never without it," he said, voice raspy from the heartache.

The tailor considered it. "I believe I can add an area to your new trousers to keep it in. For now, I have several suitable waistcoats and perhaps one or two tailcoats that are ready for adjustment." He disappeared and returned with an armload of colorful fabrics.

Archer groaned.

"Fear not, Mr. Bennett. I am adept at quick fittings," Rowe said. He helped Archer into a midnight-blue waistcoat with steel-cut buttons. The cloth of the black jacket shimmered in the candlelight. The garment wasn't fully constructed, allowing Rowe to adjust the fit with his straight pins until he was satisfied.

Archer had to admit that he'd never had a tailored suit before. It fit his chest to perfection, showing off his wide shoulders and upper torso, which he was damn proud of. His leg might be damaged but everything above it he kept in shape.

A light pink rode the edge of Rowe's cheeks when he stepped away to study his work. "You will have the ladies in a queue at the ball," he said.

"Good thing I'm not going then."

Rowe's eyebrows shot up beneath the lock of light brown hair that waved over his forehead. He stepped back into the interior of the shop and called for Violet and Bellamy.

Moments later, the curtain swept wide.

"Dearest Lady Bellamy and Lady Violet, your Mr. Bennett has just informed me that he has no intention of going to events this Season despite my labor to make him look like *this*."

Bellamy's mouth dropped open. "Archer, you look amazing. Mr. Rowe, you are a genius with a needle. I hadn't realized how ill-fitting Lord Rothden's suit was until this moment. Doesn't he look handsome, Violet?"

Archer swallowed, uncomfortable with the flattery.

"Quite," Violet said. She fussed with the opening to her silk purse instead of looking at him.

"Lady Bellamy, I wonder if I might show you a new hat that I received that might be perfect for your Lord Huntington?" Rowe guided her away, leaving Archer and Violet behind.

He shifted the weight off his left leg and took in the lovely woman standing in front of him. "Do I make you uncomfortable?" He lowered his voice so the other patrons wouldn't hear his question.

Violet's amber eyes finally met his. She scanned his face, down to his neck, and his chest. "As Bellamy said, you look very handsome."

"It's just clothing, Violet."

She shook her head. With a quick glance around, she stepped closer. "Clothing is what you wore before we entered the shop. Mr. Rowe's tailoring makes you stand apart from any other man in London." Her cheeks flushed a lovely pink. "I shouldn't say this," she muttered, then, "I have never seen a man look so fine."

Pleasure curled in his chest. Knowing that she liked the way he looked pleased him. It shouldn't matter, but dammit, it did.

He edged closer to her until he could smell the sweet cinnamon of her scent. "I've never worn anything that fit like this." His dress blues didn't fit this well.

Violet reached up to straighten his cravat. "You look quite elegant."

He caught her wrist. "Violet, I…" God, he had no idea what he meant to say. She stood there in her pretty bonnet and green dress, with those eyes the color of warm honey in a flawless face, with lips that begged to be kissed. Every breath he drew filled his head with the scent of cinnamon. He shifted closer. The small move put his weight back on his left side and sent pain shards up his thigh. It severed the spell she cast on him.

Archer sucked in a breath. *What part of* off limits *don't you get, Bennett?*

He released her wrist and took an unsteady step back. The heat of her body fled, leaving a slight chill in its wake. He couldn't rely on himself to keep her at a distance. He had to make her see that he wasn't a good fit. Had to push her away. "Violet, you need to stay away from me. I can't marry you, so you shouldn't risk your reputation."

Violet straightened. She looked at him for a long moment, searching his face. She nodded once. "I'll fetch your cane." She turned in a swirl of skirts and fled to the other side of the shop.

To get his cane so he wouldn't be in so much pain. Archer ran a hand through his hair and tugged at the strands. He was an ass.

⇶⫷

"HE'S INSUFFERABLE," VIOLET said to her dearest friend, Patience Cradock, as the two sat in Violet's carriage on the ride back from Bond Street. Rain poured in thick sheets outside and the dark gray clouds indicated that it wouldn't let up anytime soon. She pulled the wool lap blanket closer about their legs and hips even as a shiver slid down her spine. It felt more like February than late May.

"Is that why you purchased the willow bark root for him?" Patience asked as she tucked a damp brown curl back into her bonnet.

Though she was only a year older, Patience had married Gabriel's friend, Noah Cradock, at the end of her first Season, and the two were quite in love. Lord Cradock had taken a single look at her sweet face and gray eyes and pursued a courtship the following day. Violet couldn't be happier for her friend. She was not at all jealous. Jealousy was unbecoming of a lady and Violet would never resort to being unbecoming.

"Just because he's perfectly boorish doesn't mean that I must be. Besides, if he is in less pain then maybe he will find it in himself to be civil," she said with a sniff.

"Hm."

"What does that mean?" Violet asked.

"It doesn't mean anything," Patience replied.

"Patience Cradock, I have known you for four years and the only time you 'hm' is when you disagree but have not decided quite how to tell me."

"Hm." Patience failed to hide her grin.

"I realize that it is rather disagreeable to smother one's friend in a carriage, but I am certain that I could form a reasonable explanation that even Gabriel would believe."

Patience laughed. "Violet, you like Archer Bennett."

She gasped. "I most certainly do not."

"You *do*. Otherwise, we wouldn't have braved this horrid weather to visit the chemist for the willow bark."

"He is Lily's brother and staying in our home. It falls on me to be hospitable, just as I will when I am the lady of my own house."

Patience eyed her with a look that said she didn't believe Violet in the slightest. Violet tried another tack. "Furthermore, I *cannot* like him. He doesn't meet the requirements on my list for a suitable husband."

Her friend gave a soft snort. "Violet, *no one* can meet the requirements on your list. I thought you wanted a husband, not a fantasy."

"My list is perfectly reasonable. Aside from that, if I don't know what I want, then how will I ever know when I find it?"

"*Pish*. Each item by itself is reasonable. Together, they set a standard no man can aspire to. He could be titled but have no money or land. He could be handsome but spends all his time at White's gambling away his fortune. He could be kind, but not as attractive as you would prefer. Don't you see? If you wait for a man to meet every aspect of your list, you will be on the shelf before long."

Violet picked at the blanket as she considered Patience's words. "I suppose it will be quite difficult to find all those qualities in a single man. Especially since Gabriel has declared his friends as unsuitable."

"If he hadn't, would there be one that you would consider?" Patience asked gently.

"No."

"Not even Zeph?"

Violet chuckled. "I fear we would find far too much trouble together. Can you imagine?" Zeph Lael was one of her brother's closest friends. His spirit for mischief and tricks was greater than Violet's. She adored him for it. Yet she didn't feel the attraction to him that she would expect for a man she wanted to marry.

Patience laughed. "London might not survive. However, that does not address the matter at hand. You *like* Mr. Bennett."

She shook her head. "He ordered me to stay away from him and said quite plainly that he can't marry me. Whyever would I like a man who doesn't want me around?"

Her friend eyed her with speculation in her eyes. "I think I should like to meet this disagreeable—"

"Insufferable," Violet corrected.

"*Insufferable* man who is immune to the beauty, wit, and

vibrancy of Violet Hawthorne."

"You may get your wish. We're drawing up to the house now." The carriage pulled to a stop and a few moments later, Evan, their footman, opened the door. He held an umbrella and offered his hand.

"My ladies."

Violet let him help her out of the carriage and waited under the umbrella for Patience. Evan held it over them while they rushed up the front steps to the cover of the arched doorway.

Their butler met them at the door. He took their shawls, gloves, and damp bonnets to hang to dry. "Lady Violet, Lady Cradock, the Countess is in the drawing room by the fire. Shall I prepare tea?"

"Yes, please," Violet said. "I need to warm up."

"It's dreadfully cold outside," Patience added.

They found Lily curled up under a blanket on a chaise in the library with a book balanced on her legs. She brightened when she saw them. "I wondered what you two got up to this morning. What could you have possibly needed on a blustery day like today?"

Violet stood in front of the fire, soaking up the heat. "Nothing as important as all that—"

"We went to the chemist for willow bark root," Patience said. "For your brother."

Violet glared at her. This wasn't meant as a grand gesture. She was helping an extended member of her family. Honestly, it wasn't as if she'd scaled a mountain looking for the root and battled a dragon for it.

"What is it?" Lily asked, sweeping a few loose strands of caramel hair off of her forehead.

"It relieves pain," Patience said. "My mother uses it regularly for the headaches she says I give her."

"Doesn't she also get them when you are not at home?" Violet asked.

Her friend nodded with a sparkle in her eye. "Is that not

curious? My spirit of annoyance must linger for days."

"If that were true, I doubt Noah would have married you," Lily added with a teasing grin. "Do you think it will help Archer? He doesn't want to admit it, but I see the pain on his face with every step he takes."

"Since Gabriel does not allow laudanum in the house, I thought this might help." Most people wouldn't understand her brother's adamant refusal of a drug used daily in some households. Doctors carried it to dispense for everything from pain to sleeping disorders.

Violet thought of her mother, languishing away at their small estate in Nottingham. People of the *Ton* were not willing to admit the devastating effect the medication could have but Gabriel and Violet knew it well. She hadn't seen her mother in years and tried not to think about their last visit, where the woman had fluctuated between extreme contentment and indifference to their presence.

"The white willow bark is best steeped into a tea," Patience said.

"Tea sounds lovely right now," Lily said and placed a hand on her lower belly. "I'm hungry."

She glowed with happiness. Violet could admit to herself that she wanted that same happiness. "Henry said he would... there he is now."

"Your pardon, my lady," he said as he entered with a silver tray laden with a teapot and china cups. Behind him, a footman carried another tray with sandwiches, biscuits, and pots of jam and cream.

Henry set the tray on the table between them and then arranged the plates of food. "Shall I serve?" he asked.

"No, thank you. However, Lady Violet has returned with willow bark for my brother."

Violet removed the small sack of bark from her reticule and placed it in the butler's waiting palm. "The chemist said to boil some in water for about ten minutes, then allow it to steep with an immersed cinnamon stick."

He nodded. "Will Mr. Bennett join you ladies for tea? Or shall I wait to have this prepared?"

Violet looked at Lily, unwilling to acknowledge the way her stomach suddenly dipped at the prospect of seeing Archer once more. *He told you to stay away, remember?*

"I would like to meet him," Patience said.

"Would you please have some prepared and ask my brother to join us? He may wish to avoid our social occasions, but he can at least join us for tea."

The butler nodded and departed with the footman.

"Patience, are you and Noah attending Lord and Lady Kensington's soiree tomorrow?" Lily asked.

Violet poured tea for the three of them and placed a few of the little sandwiches on a plate for Lily.

"Yes. I'm quite excited. I ordered two new gowns last month and I'm excited to wear one. Violet, do you remember that lovely carmine silk that we found? I had it trimmed in black ribbon."

She nodded even as her heart gave a hard thump in time with the sound of the cane landing on each step of the stairs. *Archer.* Would he avoid speaking to her again as he had last night? Would he appreciate her gift of the tea or be embarrassed? She bit her bottom lip and stared into her teacup. Her stomach fluttered uncomfortably.

Then he was there, and all the breath left her lungs in a rush. Violet set her plate and tea aside while she composed herself.

He wore a gold embroidered waistcoat and dark blue tailcoat that accentuated the delightful width of his shoulders and the muscles in his arms. He would be the most handsome man she'd ever seen, were it not for his grumpy demeanor that was a little too close to Gabriel's for her liking. With their matching dark hair and green eyes, they could be brothers. Fortunately, they were not. She shuddered, imagining growing up with two grumpy brothers instead of the one.

"Archer, there you are," Lily said. She made introductions to

Patience.

Archer nodded, and then his gaze drifted to Violet.

She inclined her head, not sure what to say. *Since when have you been stuck for words, Vi?* Gabriel would laugh were he here.

The look in Archer's eyes went from guarded to cool disinterest as she stared.

Violet ducked her head, fighting the sinking feeling of disappointment. Why must that singular look have such an impression upon her feelings? She sensed him taking a seat on the sofa opposite.

"Would you like some tea, Mr. Bennett?" Patience asked.

"No, thank you," he murmured.

Patience nodded and turned to Lily to chat about the upcoming outings planned.

Violet felt every second of the silence between Archer and her like a smothering blanket. She should say something to break the awkwardness, but what?

"It's... not normally this cold in May," she murmured and glanced at Archer from beneath her lashes.

He met her gaze and made a noise.

Was that a *hmm* in agreement, or a *hmpgh* of disagreement? Violet narrowed her eyes. He could at least make an attempt to be civil. He may want her to stay away from him, but they lived in the same home. What did he expect of her? That she would lock herself in the attic until he found a way to leave? She folded her arms across her chest.

A spark of humor flitted over his face until he looked away.

She clenched her teeth. The man was maddening. Why, she had half a mind to—

Henry arrived with another tray of tea. "White willow bark tea for Mr. Bennett." He removed the teapot and a cup from the tray, then a jar of honey, and departed.

Archer frowned at the cup.

When he didn't reach for the tea, Violet bristled. "It is to help with your pain," she growled. "Add the honey because the flavor is bitter." She snatched up her own teacup and swallowed a mouthful. The tea was tepid now.

He shot her a quizzical look and reached forward to pour the tea into the cup. He sniffed it. "It smells… woodsy."

"I imagine that it would since it is *bark*." Violet pasted on her sweetest smile.

"Literal bark? From a tree?"

"Is there another kind?"

"Violet," Patience said in admonishment. Then to Archer, "It is very good for pain. My mother uses it. Although, like Violet, I do advise the honey to make it palatable."

Archer stirred a bit of honey into his cup and took a sip.

"Violet thought you might benefit from it," Patience added. "We made a special trip to the chemist for it this morn."

Violet widened her eyes at Patience, trying to will her into silence.

Her friend blinked back innocently.

Archer looked out the bay windows at the dark clouds and falling rain. When he turned back to Violet, she couldn't read his expression. If possible, the man seemed more guarded than ever.

"Thank you," he murmured. His eyes moved over her face and rested on her lips. Then he looked away.

Violet flushed. "You're welcome."

Henry reappeared in the doorway with a small tray.

"What is it, Henry?" Lily asked.

"Lady Violet has a delivery," he said.

Violet set her tea aside again, feeling a trill of excitement. What could it be?

Henry held the tray for her. On it sat a delicate, light pink rose half-open in bloom. On its stem was a bow of matching pink ribbon, and alongside it lay a card.

Violet lifted the rose to her nose and drew in the sweet fragrance. She loved roses. Hawthorne Hall had a rose garden that her grandmother had planted long ago and in the summer, the fragrant blooms filled her bedchamber.

She opened the card and removed the paper within.

You are a beautiful pink rose amid the bramble. Too lovely for words.

Your faithful admirer.

The messy scrawl was the same as the note delivered with the peonies which now decorated her dresser. Her heart sped up and a flutter of intrigue danced in her belly. How exciting! If Archer wanted her to keep her distance, then she would. Instead, she would try to find this mysterious author. Maybe he was a dashing gentleman who was too shy to approach her yet. Or perhaps a man of lesser means, afraid to ask Gabriel for her hand.

Violet smiled, searching the faces of her memory to see if she could discern the man's identity, and closed her eyes to draw in the sweet scent once more.

When the note was plucked from her hand, it startled her, and she opened her eyes.

Archer stood over her, scowling at the note. He flipped the card around and scanned the contents, then gave her a black look. "Who is sending these?" he growled.

"An admirer," she said slowly as if speaking to a child. Honestly, the card was signed, *An admirer*. What was so difficult to understand?

"Admirer?" Patience sat forward. "What admirer?"

Oh dear. She'd been so caught up in purchasing the willow root bark for Archer that she'd forgotten to tell Patience of the other note she'd received. Her friend gave her a pointed look. "It's nothing," she said with a wave of her hand. "Someone sent flowers before."

"Who?"

Violet smiled at her. "It's a mystery. Isn't that delightful?"

Patience leaned forward. "How intriguing."

"Hardly," Archer said in a dark voice. "He saw you today. He's been following you."

"Don't be ridiculous." Violet snatched the note back.

Archer tucked his cane under his arm and pointed at the

script. "He called you a beautiful pink rose."

"I don't see how that signifies."

He waved at her dress. "You're wearing pink, Violet."

She looked down, startled to realize that her dress *was* a close match to the color of the flower. "That is a coincidence, surely. Even if he did see me today, it is not so unusual. Women of my station often shop on Bond Street. He may have simply spotted me and thought to send a lovely note."

Archer turned that glare back on her.

"I'm certain it is nothing," she said, ignoring him.

"I think it's exciting," Patience added.

Lily made a small noise. "It's probably nothing sinister, Archer." To Violet, she added, "However, you should be more careful on your outings."

"I always take a footman with me. At events, Aunt Josephine is my chaperone." If anything, that made Lily frown.

Archer looked no less pleased.

"Gabriel is the one who appointed Aunt Josephine as my chaperone," Violet pointed out.

"Because he knew that he would also be in attendance," Lily said. "He told me that once he realized that Aunt Josephine spent more time with her friends than observing you, that he insisted on going with you *both* to parties given by the Ton."

That was one of the things Violet appreciated most about her aunt. She waved away their concerns. "I shall be perfectly fine. This admirer is probably afraid of my gargoyle brother. In time, I'm sure he'll make his introduction."

"Any man afraid of your brother isn't much of a man," Archer muttered.

Violet scowled at him.

"At any rate, I'll ask Aunt Josephine to be more diligent. In the meantime, Gabriel and I will try to stay close by in case you need us, beginning with Lady Kensington's dinner."

"I'm not a child who needs a nursemaid," she sputtered. "I'm a woman of marriageable age. That is also where Gabriel intends to introduce me to Lord Mansfield."

Lily protested, "Vi, I'm just worried that Aunt Josephine won't be—"

"I'll go," Archer said.

They turned to him in unison.

"I'll be your chaperone," Archer said, his voice stern. "If someone means you harm, they'll have to go through *me*."

"No," Violet said.

At the same time, Lily exclaimed, "That's a great idea!"

She shot Lily a glare. Having Archer there, frightening potential suitors away with his disapproving stare, would be as bad as having Gabriel as a chaperone. She'd *never* get a marriage proposal. "*Lily.*"

"Violet, you'll have no better protector than Archer."

He tapped his cane on the floor. "Unless you think I'm not capable."

She saw the flash of vulnerability that he tried to hide in his eyes and understood the reason for his challenge. *Oh, blast.* Violet's shoulders sank. If she said *no* to his protection, would he think that she found him lacking because of his injury? Of course, she didn't. But a stubborn, proud man like Archer might see it otherwise.

He's just being overprotective, like Gabriel.

Did that mean that he *cared* about her?

She couldn't begin to decipher the mind of Archer Bennett, nor why she wanted to protect his feelings when he didn't give a whit about hers.

She crossed her arms over her chest. "If you insist. However, I shall remind you that you were the one who suggested that I stay away from you."

"Things change, Violet," he rumbled in that delicious voice that sent shivers of awareness through her. He leaned down to pin her in his gaze. "Now I plan to stay *very* close."

CHAPTER SIX

I F GABRIEL WAS a gargoyle, then Archer Bennett was a dragon. The man may as well be breathing fire at the poor souls who wandered a bit too close to her. It was a wonder that Lord Mansfield hadn't had his eyebrows singed in his attempts to speak with her.

After a sumptuous supper hosted by Lady Kensington for thirty guests, the ladies retired to the drawing room. Violet sat on a flowered chaise that reminded her of the garish flower patterns Aunt Josephine preferred in all decor, and tried to feign interest in what Lady Parling was saying about the proper etiquette to display when one encountered a tart on the street. Normally, such conversation enthralled her, and she'd be full of questions. Beginning with how Lady Parling knew the etiquette for such things, and how often she'd put such proprieties into practice. Instead, she could scarcely think of anything but that dratted Archer Bennett. He had nearly ruined her introduction to Percy Mansfield at dinner.

Shortly after their arrival, Gabriel had found Viscount Mansfield in the drawing room and introduced them. Percy conducted himself in a genteel fashion, especially when compared to Archer's gruffness. Where Archer was dark, Percy had light brown hair and blue eyes, and a clean-shaven jaw. She found him quite handsome and thought him to be a couple years older than

Gabriel. Perhaps thirty-four. He stood a couple of inches shorter than Archer. In looks and temperament, the two men could not be more different.

She had the seat between them at dinner, though if that were by design or happenstance, she didn't know. Lord Mansfield attempted to engage her in conversation several times. She learned that he owned a home an hour away from their country estate in Hopton, which meant she could visit Gabriel and Lily often should she and Percy suit. He'd just come into his title while serving his family at their Scotland estates and now looked for a wife so that he could carry on the family line. Yet the moment he asked her a question, Archer would lean forward to answer as if Percy asked the question of the entire table. After the fourth time, Lord Mansfield politely nodded at her and remained silent until the ladies withdrew for tea, sewing, and—in Aunt Josephine's case—gossiping while drinking liberal amounts of port.

Violet wished she could pour the tea over Archer's head and kick him soundly in the shins for his impertinence. Instead, she rose as gracefully as she could muster, smiled at Lord Mansfield, and left without a backward glance at the vexing Mr. Bennett.

The cushion dipped beside her as Lily lowered herself to the chaise. The peacock-blue satin gown she wore covered her stomach where she was beginning to show the child growing within. Lily smiled at her. "Enjoying your evening? I'm dying to know what you thought of Lord Mansfield."

Violet clenched her fingers together in her lap. "He is quite polite."

Lily eyed her. "Polite?"

"Polite," Violet huffed. "I couldn't learn more with your brother speaking over me to answer all of Lord Mansfield's questions. Perhaps the two of *them* should court."

Lily coughed to cover her laugh. "I don't think he's my brother's type."

"Type of what?"

"Type of lover."

Violet flushed scarlet and pressed her lips together. She hadn't thought *that* when making the jest. Could two men even do that? She looked at Lily from beneath her lashes, the question brimming on her lips.

Lily covered her lips with her fingers, which didn't hide her wide grin, but it apparently stopped her words. "We can discuss *that* later, in private," she whispered.

Violet held back a smile. Lily knew her well. They'd become friends not long after Lily had arrived in their time seven months past. "I only meant that Archer insisted on inserting himself into our conversation. I know he took it upon himself to chaperone me, but he is worse than Gabriel."

Lily chuckled and smoothed a caramel-colored curl away from her face. "I know that it doesn't seem like it now, but having a strong protector is a good thing. It means they care what happens to you. Archer has always been that way. He told me once that the reason he joined the military was because his best friend disappeared when he was thirteen. Archer hadn't protected her from the strange man who'd been talking with her. He decided right after that he would do whatever he must in order to look out for the people he cared for. He heard about the Navy SEALS and decided that was what he was going to be."

"What is a Navy SEAL?"

"The SEALs are a special unit in our military. They are specially trained to go anywhere in the world on secret missions for the government. They fight to keep people safe. Archer doesn't talk about it, but I know that they often went into dangerous situations that few people have the courage to endure." She smiled. "They're known as some of the toughest warriors in the world. The kind that can kill a man before he even thinks about drawing his weapon." Her eyes rounded. "Oh, sorry, Vi. That's probably not an appropriate thing to say. I don't mean to...well. He's not the average man."

She thought of how he'd rescued her from being trampled,

even before he knew who she was—or where he was. Not the average man, indeed. And *that* made him even more fascinating. *Except, you don't want to be fascinated, remember Violet?* The dratted man. Everything about him stirred her curiosity.

She smoothed the skirt of her gown. She hadn't felt that same curiosity about Percy. Surely that would come in time without a bothersome chaperone leaning over her shoulder?

As if manifested by her thoughts, Archer Bennett entered the drawing room, followed by Percy Mansfield. While she'd woolgathered, the men had finished their cigars and decided to join the women. The two of them cut striking figures standing beside one another, Archer with his dark hair, in the black silk suit emphasizing his wide shoulders, and Percy with his light brown hair and dark green tailcoat over tan trousers.

Her heart beat harder at the sight.

Lady Kensington stood and called for games of cards and dancing. Servants entered with more tea and trays laden with cakes and cleared a space for dancing. Gabriel appeared at Lily's side to coax her into a dance.

"Enjoying yourself, Violet?" he asked.

"Immensely, dear brother," she lied. She would have been enjoying herself far more without Archer's interference.

Gabriel narrowed his eyes.

How could he always see through her small falsehoods? Violet pasted an innocent smile on her face. "Don't keep your lovely wife waiting."

"Where is Aunt Josephine?" he asked.

"Somewhere watching my every movement for propriety, I'm certain." *Or gossiping like a magpie…*

"Hmm." Gabriel gave her a look that said that he didn't believe her earlier statement of her enjoyment of the dinner party, didn't think for a moment that Aunt Josephine was paying her the least bit of attention, and that he expected her to behave like a proper young lady. Somehow, he'd perfected the art of communicating all of that in a single glance.

She watched him lead his wife to the gathered dancers as a quartet of musicians took seats in the corner and prepared their instruments for the first dance. She wondered if she would have the opportunity to join them. Were there any young men in the room who would ask her to the dance floor? She did so enjoy dancing...

A clean, woodsy scent swirled around her moments before Archer stood beside her. That dark green gaze moved over her like a sensual caress. "Violet."

She suppressed a shiver at the sound of his husky voice. The man had no right to sound seductive when ruining her chance to learn more about a serious suitor. "Mr. Bennett."

He frowned, then sat next to her and rested his cane beside him. "It's Archer."

"It's improper," she said. "A woman may not call a man by his Christian name unless they are in the company of close friends. Such a woman should also not sit too close to a man that she is not courting." She resisted the urge to lean into him as she spoke or place a hand on his arm. Would she feel his muscles beneath his clothes?

You won't find out because it would be improper.

His lips twitched. "Have I told you that you look lovely tonight, *Violet?*"

The contrary man! A quick scan showed that none seemed to have heard his brazen disregard of common etiquette despite the hours they'd spent teaching him. "Thank you," she grumbled.

"I mean it. That burgundy dress is very lovely. It makes your skin glow."

I should tell him such compliments are inappropriate. Violet met his gaze again and words failed her as her breath caught. The deep-green depths of his eyes sparked with something that filled her with heat. Like a hundred flames licking along her skin and gathering at the junction of her thighs. Every breath she drew filled with the scent of the forest. Something wicked curled low in her belly and made her nipples harden and tingle.

She licked her lips, her mouth dry as sand.

His eyes hooded as he traced the movement, and he tilted his head. Did he lean closer?

She ducked her head, fighting with the desire to ask him for a kiss. It seemed terribly unfair that a man as undeniably attractive as Archer Bennett should be so unsuitable for her in every way.

He chuckled, and the sound seemed to have a dark edge. "You would tempt even the coldest of hearts, wouldn't you?" he murmured, the words spoken for her ears only.

Would she? The end of her second season drew near, and she hadn't so much as been courted by a man. Not in person, anyway. Only by flowers.

"Violet. I…" Archer shifted on the chaise and cleared his throat. He looked away from her and across the room at the dance floor.

The silence stretched between them. She clasped her hands in her lap and tried to look composed. Inside, her stomach flipped over, and her heart thudded in her ears as she picked at a nonexistent thread on her gown, so she didn't have to look at him.

Archer shifted beside her, moving his cane between his knees, and spread thighs. The man took up so much space! It was…disconcerting.

"I don't like Mansfield," he announced then. "Something seems… *off* with him."

"What?" She had to look at him after that. "Whatever do you mean?"

He continued gazing across the room and she realized his attention was pinned to Percy, currently dancing with Miss Merriweather. "You should stay away from him. I sense… *something.*" His jaw worked beneath his dark beard.

"You sense *something.* What could you possibly sense about a man that you only met this evening?" Violet crushed down the ridiculous spurt of disappointment that rose. She'd thought he might say something else, maybe more seductive, inappropriately sweet words that made her heart flutter.

"I spent years honing the skill to sense danger," he growled with a glower. "He's *dangerous*. To you or in general, I don't know. But you have to trust me and stay away from him."

Stay away from the only suitor that Gabriel would allow within twenty leagues of her? "I will *not* avoid him. He has acted as nothing but a gentleman. If he should do otherwise, then I will keep my distance. I can manage unwanted advances." She'd done so with that odious Lord Musgrave at Gabriel's house party several months earlier. "But you will not ruin my only chance at happiness, Archer Bennett."

"Fuck, you're stubborn," he muttered. "That man isn't your 'only chance at happiness.' Look at you, Violet. You're gorgeous, vivacious, and a hell of a catch. Men must be lining up to win your hand or whatever they call it."

She didn't know what "hell of a catch" meant but his delight-ful swearing made little difference. "*Men* won't approach me at all because of *men* like you and my brother," she argued. "And your language is scandalous. Gentlemen should not swear in front of a lady."

He muttered another curse in response.

Oh, this man! Violet bristled. "Mr. Bennett—"

"Lady Violet?" a male voice said.

She turned to see Percy, Lord Mansfield, approaching. She smiled and wondered if it looked as forced as it felt. "Lord Mansfield."

He stopped in front of her, much as Archer had, and swept his gaze over her. "Your beauty outshines everyone here."

She flushed. "How kind." She thought she heard Archer growl beside her but chose to ignore him.

Percy extended his hand. "Would you grant me the honor of a dance?"

Archer had not asked her to dance. He'd refused to even try to learn the dances of their time. If she wanted to dance, this would be her only opportunity.

Violet smiled wide and placed her hand in his. "I would be delighted."

He drew her to her feet, and without a glance back at Archer, followed Percy to the dance floor.

ARCHER CURSED HIS injured leg as he stalked across the drawing room to where Christian leaned against the mantle of the large marble fireplace. Bellamy sat at one of the tables nearby, concentrating on her hand of cards. Dinner had been a dozen courses served with gossip, sniping, and petty jealousy from people with more money than sense. He tugged at the knot in his cravat to loosen it. He'd done well enough to act the part of a man newly arrived from America, which helped cover any slips in etiquette, but the whole affair was damned uncomfortable.

And then there was Mansfield.

He glared at the small dance floor where Violet skipped lightly along in a complicated dance with her suitor. He knew when he'd approached her that she wanted to dance. It was in the longing look that she gave the gathering dancers and her hopeful sweep of the room, searching for anyone who might ask. Violet was the type of woman who enjoyed every moment of fun she could squeeze out of life. A long time ago, he'd been the same. Now, he couldn't ask her to dance even if he wanted to.

His injuries—and his pride—prevented it. He'd refused to learn the dances of this time period, not only because he meant to return home as soon as possible, but also because he didn't want his leg to give out on a dance floor full of people and embarrass Violet. He refused to put her in a position that would lead others to gossip about her, something she seemed particularly sensitive to.

"Bennett," Christian said in greeting. He held a small tool, his attention on something that he continued to tinker with, in his hand.

Archer nodded at the man, grateful for the distraction. "Huntington."

When he reached Christian's side, he realized that it was a piece of that cursed clock that brought them all here. The red enamel and gold filigree glinted in the candlelight. "Any luck figuring out how that worked?"

Christian shook his head. His blond hair seemed long for the current fashion and his cravat looked like he'd twisted it a few times in agitation. Not that Archer was an expert on such things. He tugged at his own to make it more comfortable.

"A number of the pieces have a gritty white powder coating them," Christian murmured. He angled the little red door toward the light so Archer could see it. "I am unable to determine if it was from the road or the clock."

"The clock," he replied. "I didn't see the white dust anywhere else on the road. If it had come from a carriage wheel or a horse hoof, it would have been in other spots nearby. There was nothing."

Christian looked up from his work and smiled at Archer. "You are as bright as your sisters. I admire that. Intellect is not always valued in this society." He stood to his full height, a frisson of energy visible as a small smile touched his mouth. "The thing I find quite perplexing is that nothing in my original design would produce any sort of white powder. If it did come from the clock, then I believe we have stumbled upon the key difference. I've assembled the remaining pieces, and save for a few small parts that are missing, I believe the egg was largely the same as it was originally. Meaning that this added element could very well be what caused the time anomaly."

Archer couldn't share the man's excitement. How would they possibly be able to tell what the white powder was? What kind of scientific labs did they have here?

Christian placed a hand on his shoulder. "This gives me a direction in which to look for answers. I believe this is a good sign."

Archer nodded. As the music drew to an end, his gaze sought out Violet. She dipped into a graceful curtsey to Mansfield. Her breasts heaved in that low-cut gown and her cheeks were flushed from the dance. She smiled brightly, happiness evident in every inch of her beautiful face.

Jesus, she was gorgeous. When he'd sat beside her on the chaise, she'd turned those big, amber eyes on him, her plump pink lips so close, and he'd almost kissed her. The desire to lower his head and take her mouth with his had been so strong, it had shocked him. His surprise was the only thing that kept him from acting on the impulse, which in retrospect was also shocking. He'd locked down his needs as he'd trained his body until both were completely under his command and yet—in a matter of days—Violet blasted right through his control as if it never existed.

On the dance floor, Mansfield bowed low over her hand, lingering a little too long for Archer's comfort. The back of his neck bristled. If he couldn't do anything to help Christian with the clock, then he'd spend his time figuring out why Mansfield lit up his every protective instinct when it came to Violet. He'd honed that instinct for danger for the purpose of protecting women just like her and he wanted her to keep that innocence as long as she could. That meant finding out what Mansfield was into.

"What do you know of Mansfield?" he asked Christian.

"Nothing. He's just back from Scotland, Gabriel tells me. He had family dealings there, I believe. Other than that, I only know that he has expressed interest in Violet." Christian eyed him. "You don't care for the man."

"No. Something's off with him."

Christian nodded and returned to the clock in his hands. "Is your interest in the matter solely for the protection of Violet? Or is there a personal consideration?"

Archer squeezed the handle of his cane until his knuckles turned white. He tracked Violet as Mansfield escorted her away from the dancers. The man led her toward the windows, where less people gathered. "It's her protection. What else could there be?" If Mansfield laid a hand on Violet, he'd lose the appendage before the night was over.

Christian murmured a non-committal noise that Archer ignored.

The musicians prepared another song, and more dancers took their places. Gabriel led Lily off the dance floor and escorted her toward him and Christian. She smiled as brightly as Violet, and her caramel curls bounced as she walked, highlighting the blue-green eyes she got from their mother.

"I do love these dances," she gushed. "I wish you would reconsider learning them, Archer."

He lifted his cane higher. "Don't think I'd be too graceful out there, Lils."

She made a face at him. "Or maybe it would be good for your healing. By the way, how is the tea working? Is it giving you any relief? You seem less like a rampaging bear."

He snorted at her description of him. The willow tea worked surprisingly well. It didn't eliminate his pain, but it took the edge off, and he didn't have the horrible brain fog from the prescription painkillers the docs gave him. "It's helping. Tastes like licking a tree though."

"Did you have to do much of that while in the military?"

She had no idea. Archer planned to keep it that way. He'd once had a gash in his leg sewn shut without painkillers. Damn, he missed his team.

"That's classified," he said.

Lily laughed. "Right. How are you enjoying the dinner party?"

"It's marginally better than licking a tree."

"I quite agree," Christian added.

Gabriel crossed his arms over his chest. "You could have remained home, Huntington."

Christian's eyebrows rose. "If I had, you would have stomped to my chamber door, thrown my tailcoat at me, and dragged me from the house to come to this blasted party."

The corner of Gabriel's lips tipped up. "It's what friends do."

Christian huffed. "I shall remind you of that the next time that you want to—"

Lily put her hand on Christian's arm to stop his retort. "Is that Violet's suitor, Lord Mansfield?" she asked.

"Indeed. He seems solid," Gabriel replied.

Archer couldn't hold back his rumble of disapproval.

Lily cocked her head, silently asking him why he disagreed.

He avoided her penetrating stare and kept an eye on Mansfield instead. Violet waved her hands as she talked, a smile playing about her lips, which the man seemed fascinated with.

Archer clenched his teeth and forced himself to remain where he was instead of marching over there to yank her away from him.

Lily made an annoyed sound, then turned her attention to Christian. "Is that a piece of the clock?"

"With Archer's help, I believe I've discovered something important," Christian replied. "See this white dust? He didn't see any of it in the dirt around the clock, so whatever caused it must have been inside. It may be the very thing that brought you here."

If anyone had told him a week ago that white dust had made him time travel, he'd have thought that they were in a drug-induced fog, probably caused by that very same powdery substance.

"Oh!" Lily fluttered her hands. "Oh, I remember something." She latched onto Christian's arm again. "When I first found the clock on my boss's desk, it was broken. I took it home to fix it, and when I opened it, there was a little crystal inside."

"A crystal?" Christian studied the small piece in his hand.

"It was an opaque white stone with a bit of a light blue hue. That's all I remember."

Christian closed his fist around the piece. "I need to return to my workshop and look through my notes. I think… no, I can't be sure. I must check." He strode across the drawing room to Bellamy's side.

When Archer looked back at Lily, she had twined her fingers together, shoulders slumped. "I wish I hadn't told him. I don't want you to go."

His heart dropped. He hated disappointing either of his sisters. He'd done enough of that for a lifetime and now, seeing them and their disappointment that he didn't want to stay—it was hard. But he couldn't remain. "Sorry, Lils. I don't belong here."

"Do you belong *there?*" she asked.

He didn't know how to answer that.

"Perhaps we should all retire for the evening," Gabriel said. "Aunt Josephine looks one glass of sherry away from sleeping in that chair, and I know you tire easily now, love."

Lily nodded. "Let's collect Violet."

His gut clenched as he followed her to where the couple stood by the window. Mansfield leaned a little too close to Violet for Archer's liking. "I'll ride with her and Aunt Josephine," he said.

Gabriel studied Archer. "Lily says you're concerned about the person sending the gifts to Violet."

Archer nodded. Was it Mansfield? Or someone else? "I have a bad feeling about it."

"Then I thank you for protecting Violet. She is strong willed but reasonable. As Lily helped me see, she is also a capable young woman. If she argues, tell her you go with my blessing."

Good. Although Archer had been prepared to ride with the ladies whether he had Gabriel's permission or not. "I don't trust Mansfield," he added.

"I sensed as much. I will have someone look into his dealings before signing any agreements for their union."

Their union. Archer grimaced but remained silent.

Gabriel placed a kiss on Lily's temple and left to collect his aunt.

She and Archer approached Violet and Mansfield.

"It's time to go, Lady Violet," Archer said. He took her elbow and urged her a few paces back from her suitor.

Violet narrowed her eyes at him and pulled her arm free. "Thank you, Mr. Bennett." She growled his name like a curse.

If the tension running through his body wasn't wound so tight, he might have laughed. "Your brother is collecting your aunt now. Let's go."

Her chin went up a stubborn notch and her amber eyes sparked with willfulness.

Something about that rebellious spirit fired his blood. Archer stepped closer, his cock growing hard as those plump lips beckoned him. One kiss was all it would take to prove that he wasn't her brother.

Lily's fake yawn interrupted him. "I'm quite tired tonight," she told Violet. "I hate to cut your evening short, but I'm afraid that I must go home." She placed a hand on her stomach to emphasize her silent point.

Violet's eyes softened when she looked at Lily. "Of course." She glared at Archer, then turned a friendly smile on Mansfield and extended her hand. "I do hope we may speak again."

"You may count upon it, my dear Lady Violet," the man said. He bent low to brush his lips across the back of her glove.

He's lingering. Archer reached for her elbow again.

Violet side-stepped out of reach and withdrew her hand from Mansfield's. She bade the viscount goodnight, then whirled around to loop her arm through Lily's. Together the women left the room.

The moment the ladies turned their backs, Mansfield's smile dropped. He met Archer's gaze with a coldness in his eyes that hinted at something darker, the veneer of civility gone.

Archer nodded once, then walked away. He'd seen what he needed to. Even if Mansfield wasn't the one sending Violet the odd notes and flowers, Archer didn't trust his intentions. He wasn't letting Violet spend another moment alone with him.

Once their party gathered cloaks and hats, they stepped outside. A lengthy line of carriages crowded the street as the guests began to depart. The ladies chatted about the party, their breath crystallizing into puffs of white in the cold evening air. Strains of music and laughter echoed from within the mansion and horses whinnied nearby.

Archer scanned the area, cataloging the people standing around them, the carriages, and the alleyway across the street. The habit kept him alive on peaceful nights, just like this one, when anything could happen. Memories of a high-pitched whistle followed by shouts and explosions crowded into his thoughts. His throat closed and he shuddered. Pain shot down his leg, as fresh as the shrapnel that caused it. Archer dragged in a breath, held it, and let it out slowly. With effort, he pushed the memories back down and tried to focus on the safety of the people around him.

He drew a second breath, this one laden with cinnamon.

Violet.

She inched closer to him, then with a quick glance at the others, raised her hand to run it down the back of his arm. The simple gesture soothed him and relaxed his tense muscles. She offered him comfort even when he knew she was irritated with him.

He tamped down the rioting emotions in his chest and nodded his thanks.

Her lips quirked and she put a respectable space between them.

The entire silent exchange lasted only a moment. In his heart, it lingered longer. The innocent touch to his body felt stronger than any lover's caress in the power it had over him. She posed a danger to him that he'd never faced before. She could wreck him in a way that even the terrorists he'd fought couldn't when they'd attacked his team. He swallowed hard.

Gabriel and Christian's carriages arrived, and Lily and Bellamy climbed into one, Violet and Aunt Josephine into the other.

With a final nod at Gabriel, Archer entered the coach behind

Violet and settled on the red velvet seat across from the women. The carriage was comfortable, with curtains covering the windows and candles behind glass sconces to light the interior.

"Where is that nephew of mine?" Josephine asked loudly. She stifled a yawn behind her lace fan.

"He's with Lily, Aunt Josephine," Violet replied.

"He decided to ride with Huntington and my sister," Archer added.

Josephine tutted and slapped her fan on his knee. "You will exercise good manners, young man. I'll not have you take advantage of us vulnerable young ladies. I know how you men are."

Violet's eyes widened. "Aunt Josephine!"

"Of course. I will be a perfect gentleman." That seemed to mollify the older woman.

She pawed her unnaturally bright red curls away from her face and blinked, eyelids growing heavy. "See that you do."

The carriage rocked as the footman climbed aboard and soon bounced along the rutted road. He shifted his position on the tufted seat. Violet sat directly across from him, staring out the window into the darkness.

Was she thinking about Percy Mansfield? He knew that Gabriel would investigate the viscount. Gabriel seemed to have a similar need to protect others as Archer, and he knew the earl would take special care with his sister. But in many ways, Violet was as rebellious as a young Bellamy. It would take substantial proof of a man's underhanded dealings, or worse, to sway her to stay away from Mansfield.

When preparing for an op, his team had spent days going through mission details, learning all they could about their target and the location they would infiltrate. But here, Archer didn't have the starting intel or even a team, and he didn't have much time. He'd talk to Gabriel tomorrow to learn all he could about Mansfield. Together, maybe they could—

The carriage jolted to a halt. Shouts rang out from outside

and the coach dipped, then rocked back as someone climbed down from the driver's seat. The door opened and the footman, Ethan, stuck his head inside. He opened his mouth to say something, but Violet held up her hand and then pointed at Josephine.

The elderly woman rested her head on the window, a bright red curl stuck to her open mouth as she slumbered.

Ethan lowered his voice. "There's a cart stuck up ahead, my lady. It lost a wheel and spilled goods on the road. No one can go 'round until it's cleared. Be a few minutes, I say."

"Thank you," Violet whispered.

The footman closed the door quietly after promising to get the carriage underway as quickly as they could. Archer didn't offer to assist. His priority was the safety of these women.

Silence settled between them. Violet looked back out the window.

"Violet," he breathed.

The glare she turned on him surprised him after the comfort she offered earlier. *She didn't want to see me in pain even though she was angry with me. She cares for me.* Perhaps even more surprising was the realization that he cared for her as well.

"You may have declared yourself to be my chaperone, Archer Bennett, but that does not give you the right to grip my arm like I'm a wayward child and embarrass me in front of a suitor. You may not see my circumstances as important, but they are to me. I do not want to be like Aunt Josephine," she grumbled. "Of an advanced age, in my cups, and sleeping in a chair in a stranger's drawing room at the end of a dinner party, waiting for my family to collect me because I have no husband or child of my own."

Josephine snorted in her sleep, then began to snore.

Violet blinked rapidly and crossed her arms.

Archer saw the moisture rimming her eyes and cursed. He hadn't meant to upset her. He wouldn't apologize for trying to keep her away from Mansfield, but maybe he could have handled the situation better. "I didn't mean to treat you like a child," he murmured. "As for the rest, there's no way you'll ever be a spinster, Violet, but you can't accept the first man that comes along out of fear for what might happen if you don't. Fear what might happen if you *do*. Most marriages of the upper class are arranged in this time, right? But don't most women want to marry for love?"

She nodded, not meeting his eyes.

"Do you?" he asked.

"Y-yes."

"Then why this urgency to marry right now? You're young."

"I'm of marriageable age," she insisted.

"Yes, but is it more important to make a suitable match or to find a man who will treasure you?"

She dropped her hands to her lap and clutched her fingers together. "How would I be able to tell if a man would treasure me? I am not permitted to be alone with one and most conversations are not private."

"You don't need privacy to tell, Violet. Sometimes you don't even need words."

She met his gaze and the vulnerability he saw there made his heart clench.

"How can I tell without words?" she asked.

"It's in the way that a man looks at you. The way he touches you in public. The way he treats you."

Her brow furrowed.

She was so innocent in these things, she probably didn't know what to look for. God, maybe the only way to get through to her was to show her.

Josephine slept soundly, her snores filling the carriage. His mind insisted that this was a mistake, but fuck it, he'd already decided. He would show her what he meant and then she could decide for herself if Mansfield—or anyone else—would treasure her as a man should. He leaned to the side and shut the curtains on one window, then the other.

"What—?" Violet began.

He leaned forward, gripped her waist, and pulled her into his lap.

Violet squeaked, then clamped her lips shut.

Neither moved, barely breathing as they watched Josephine for a reaction. The older woman mumbled, then resumed snoring.

Archer settled Violet's bottom on his thighs, her legs across his lap. She gripped his shoulders, eyes wide as she searched his face.

"It's the small touches," he whispered. Archer trailed his fingertips over the satiny skin of her cheek. He tucked some of her curls behind her ear and traced the shell.

Violet's lips parted but she didn't speak.

He lowered his other hand to the small of her back. "It's when his hand lands here to assist you into the carriage or through a door." He skimmed his fingers down and around to cup her neck, then feathered his thumb over the soft skin beneath her jaw. In the candlelight, her amber eyes glowed. Thick, dark lashes, slightly damp with unshed tears framed them, drawing his gaze. Her features were delicate, her lips inviting, yet there was stubbornness and determination there. The mix of beauty and spirit was sexy as hell. "It's in the way he looks at you," he whispered.

Violet leaned closer. One of her hands slid around behind his neck to spear into his hair. "What does it mean when he looks at me like that?" she asked.

"It means he thinks you're beautiful. That you are unlike anyone he's met, and he can't look away or you may disappear like a mirage in the desert."

"Men have looked at me with longing before. How can I know which look is the right look?"

Archer pulled her closer. The air felt thick between them. Every breath he took filled his senses with her cinnamon scent. She smelled delicious. "There will be appreciation as well as lust in that look. His small touches mean that he would see to your well-being, and sometimes, that he can't keep his hands to himself, even in a public setting."

"What if he does these things but is afraid to speak to Gabriel on my behalf?"

"Any man worthy of you would fight the devil himself to make you his wife."

"What if the man does all of those things, but he isn't suitable because of his station… or his background." She looked at him from beneath her lashes.

"Then you will have to determine what matters to you most, sweetheart. Your heart, or your address."

"I think I could live anywhere so long as I had love," she whispered. "Someone I could love and care for in return." She slipped her other hand beneath his coat to press over his heart. "Someone who will love me as passionately as Gabriel loves Lily."

Violet would be a passionate lover. He could tell by how she leaned into his touch, even if she didn't realize she did so. His last lovers had been quick tumbles to take the edge off. With a woman like Violet, he'd want to spend hours—maybe days—coaxing every ounce of pleasure from her body.

They stared at one another in the dim candlelight, Josephine's light snores were the only sound in the carriage.

Archer's heart beat faster. His gaze dropped to her plush lips. He nearly groaned when she licked them, leaving a trail of moisture on her bottom lip. Would she taste like cinnamon?

There were reasons that he shouldn't find out. Reasons he shouldn't touch her at all. Holding her in his lap, her warm breasts pressed against his chest, he couldn't remember a single one. Their breaths mingled as he slowly lowered his head, giving her time to pull away.

Violet leaned forward to meet him.

He pressed his lips to hers once. Twice. His hand tightened on the back of her neck, and he tugged her mouth closer.

Josephine snorted and shifted on the opposite bench. The

older woman could wake at any moment. He shouldn't…

Violet sighed against his lips, gripping the hair at the back of his neck.

That small yank snapped something inside him. All thoughts of slow, and light, and gentle, and Josephine evaporated in that moment. Archer crushed his mouth to hers, kissing her hard.

Violet gasped.

He had a moment of worry that he'd been too rough before she wrapped both arms around his neck and kissed him back.

Her kisses were strong, yet unsure. Archer tilted his head and coaxed her mouth to move with his. He opened her mouth and stroked her tongue with his own.

Violet sat back, eyes wide, and pressed her fingers to her lips. "Is that a normal kiss?"

Jesus, she was sweet. "It is. But if you don't want—"

She pressed her mouth back to his and licked his lower lip.

Archer held her close and opened his mouth. He couldn't deny her when he wanted this kiss just as much.

He stroked his tongue against hers again, teaching her how to kiss. Showing her without words that he admired her. Her breathy little moans of pleasure from his kiss made him hard, and the mad thump of his heart drowned out any thoughts of stopping this madness. He traced a hand up her spine to the curve of her neck and down the velvety skin above her breasts, wanting to touch all of her. He wanted to lay her out on his bed and strip the gown from her, kissing every inch of skin he revealed.

The kiss went on and on. Violet matched his movements, growing in confidence with each press of her lips and stroke of her tongue. It was intoxicating.

Archer kissed his way along her jaw and down her throat, breathing her in. Tasting her.

She shivered and let out a breathy laugh. "Your beard tickles."

He grinned against her skin and kissed lower, down to the low-cut neckline of her gown. He wanted to see those plump breasts. Suck them until her nipples were hard on his tongue and she squirmed in his lap, begging him for more. But another snort from Josephine made him reverse course, kissing up to the other side of her neck. Archer worked the little puffy sleeve of her gown off her shoulder to press kisses along her collarbone.

Violet rocked her hips against his hard cock.

He barely stifled a moan. He fastened his mouth on hers and kissed her again, savoring the rush of heat running through his body after months of celibacy.

A loud shout outside broke through the haze of lust in Archer's head. He gentled his kiss, pressing a few light kisses to her lips before raising his head.

The carriage dipped and voices drew closer outside.

"I think we're about to see the footman," he said.

Violet pressed her lips to his cheek, then nodded.

Archer was just helping her back to her side of the carriage when the door flung open, and the footman looked inside. His eyebrows rose when he saw Archer's hands about her waist, but he didn't comment.

Violet resumed her seat and straightened her skirt.

"My lady, the other cart is out of the way. We'll be off now." He looked anywhere but at them, as he spoke.

Archer glanced at Violet and realized that her breasts were nearly spilling from her dress and that one sleeve was off her shoulder. Her lips and parts of her neck were red from his beard. They'd been even more passionate in their kisses than he'd realized. He made a small gesture with his hand to her, and she quickly adjusted her gown.

"Thank you," he said to Evan, who bowed and shut the door with a loud click. The noise startled Josephine.

She blinked owl eyes at them. "Huh? What goes?"

"The carriage had to stop for an accident in the road, but we are about to resume the trip home," Archer said.

"How inconvenient," Josephine replied, her eyelids already drooping. Moments later, her snores began anew.

Violet's cheeks were flushed, and her head was down.

"Okay?" he asked softly.

She nodded and pressed the tips of her fingers to her lips, now puffy from his kisses.

"Will the footman say anything?" Not that the man saw anything Archer considered scandalous, but this time period was far more reserved, and he knew Violet would be concerned for her reputation.

"No," she said. "But that can't happen again."

As much as he knew she was right, that it shouldn't have happened in the first place, a part of Archer growled in frustration. The part that wanted Violet. He shut that part down. Violet would never be his. She belonged here. He didn't. It was as simple as that. Leaving this century was what he wanted.

CHAPTER SEVEN

ARCHER ASCENDED THE stairs of Gabriel's townhouse, heading for the study. So far, the mission to return home was a disaster. He had no way to help Christian figure out how the damn time travel clock worked, his sisters were pleading with him to stay, and he'd been distracted by amber eyes and hot kisses. And damn, those kisses had scorched him.

Violet, who'd seemed so innocent, responded to his touch the night before with a heady enthusiasm that heated his blood and scattered his thoughts. When she'd tugged his hair and breathed against his mouth... It was the sexiest thing Archer had ever experienced with a lover and his body turned almost painfully hard. He'd gone to bed with the lingering taste of her on his tongue and he hadn't been able to sleep until he took himself in hand. Even now, the memory threatened to send a shiver of pleasure through him.

Shouldn't have kissed her, asshole.

Yeah. Well... he couldn't exactly take that back, and if he were honest, he didn't want to. Kissing her wasn't going to happen again anyway. Violet had sense enough to know that too. Any caveman claims telling him that she was his would have to be ignored.

Hell, the only thing that had improved over the last week was his injury. Surprisingly, the tree bark concoction Violet bought him had reduced some inflammation in his leg and he was in less pain. He'd even gone for a walk this morning to learn the area better. The weather was mild and stretching his muscles felt good. Maybe the physical therapist had been right. If he used those muscles more, his strength might return. Perhaps Gabriel could recommend somewhere to exercise. Both he and Christian looked in good physical shape. Better than many of the gentlemen he'd seen at the Kensington party last night and neither man did hard labor, so they must use other means to maintain their physique.

Archer reached the second-floor study and found Lily's husband bent over a ledger of some sort, grumbling under his breath. He knocked on the door frame.

Gabriel looked up from his seat behind a large, carved desk and waved him in. He slapped the ledger closed with a thump and tossed a quill pen on the desk. "Come in, Archer. I can't look at these figures a moment longer."

"What are they?" He took the chair Gabriel indicated on the other side of the desk. The study was comfortable, with dark wainscoting, light yellow walls, and heavy, navy-blue curtains. Bookshelves lined one wall, packed with leatherbound books, which gave the room that scent of an old library. Lily must love it.

"Accounts for all the Rothden holdings. Tallies of sheep, stores, and income from tenants." Gabriel ran a hand through his hair and then rubbed his eyes. "I am responsible for a great many people's livelihoods. Every column of figures is important."

"Don't you have someone to do that for you?" Archer asked.

"Indeed. Malcolm, my steward, manages the accounts when he's not hovering outside my doorway eavesdropping like a dowager waiting for gossip. He remains at my country house when we come to Town and dispatches the books to me monthly for review." Gabriel sat forward. "I'm certain you didn't come here to hear about my accounts, although I admit that I am glad to see you. I hoped that we might come to know one another better. I imagine it is quite a shock to not only find yourself in the past but also that one of your sisters is married and expecting her first child, while the other is nearly engaged."

Archer set his cane against the edge of the desk, choosing his words. "Can't say I've ever had a week quite like this one." It was nothing compared to Hell Week training for the SEALS. In the longest five days of his life, he'd learned the limits of his body physically and mentally, and that he could handle twenty times more than he thought. That week had defined him as a man and taught him who he was. Or who he used to be before he lost his team. He shifted in his chair. "I see the way you take care of Lily. I haven't seen her this happy since before we lost our parents."

Gabriel smiled, a look of tenderness in his eyes. "I'm glad to know that. She is everything to me."

Archer nodded. "And Violet?"

"What do you mean?"

"I know you're considering a marriage between her and Mansfield."

Gabriel sat back in his chair. "My sister can be quite willful when it comes to the things she wants most. I want to see her happy, but I won't risk her safety. Mansfield seems to be a man of character and means, and he met her list of requirements."

Violet had a list of requirements for a husband? Why was he not surprised? "What do you know of him?"

"His family has held the Viscount Mansfield title for three generations. They have a moderate income and a decently sized holding in the country, as well as land and business in Scotland. I'm aware you have reservations about him, and I've sent some inquiries to associates to see if they are aware of any-thing…untoward." Gabriel eyed him. "But what I really want to know is—why the interest in whom Violet marries?"

"I've seen a lot of harm done to innocent women who fell for a charming façade." An image of sweet Amanda, his childhood best friend, flashed through his mind from the last time he'd seen her. Her skin had glowed in the late afternoon sun while they sat outside the ice cream parlor, talking about their math teacher. She'd laughed until she cried when he gestured with the ice cream cone in his hand and the top scoop of mint chocolate chip dropped right in his lap with a splat he could still hear in his mind. He loved that memory, and he also hated it. Maybe if he had begged her not to meet the mysterious guy sending her notes the next day, she would have listened. She might have lived.

"Is that the only reason?" Gabriel asked, pulling him out of his thoughts.

Archer blinked and buried Amanda back in his past, where she belonged. Keeping Violet safe mattered now. "Isn't keeping her from harm enough?" he replied. He sure as hell wasn't going to tell Gabriel that he'd kissed his sister in the carriage last night. "Once Christian figures out the time travel clock, I'm heading home. I may as well put my skills to use while I'm here. Maybe prevent your sister from marrying the wrong man."

"Violet and I have been at odds over her choosing a husband for two Seasons. I assure you that I have her best interests in mind, even if I must pick the man myself."

Archer didn't know much about Violet, but having her brother pick the man she was going to marry did not seem like something she would appreciate. He also didn't envy Gabriel meeting with all the "suitable men" who would want Violet for a wife. Just the thought of it raised Archer's protective instincts and made him want to shield her from the whole matter.

Shit, he was glad he wasn't responsible for finding husbands for Lily and Bellamy.

"Are you so ready to leave your sisters behind?" Gabriel asked.

No... Yes.

Archer rubbed the back of his neck as Lily's question from last night played back in his mind.

Do you belong there?

She'd made him question his decision to return to the future. "They've done well without me for a long time," Archer said, as much to himself as to answer Gabriel.

"That may be so. However, I suspect if they were given the opportunity, they would much prefer to have you near."

Would they want him to stay if they knew what happened in Afghanistan? No, and he'd never tell them. There was no sense in discussing it further. Archer rose and grabbed his cane. "Has Christian made any progress on the white substance on the clock?"

"I don't think he's left his workshop since we returned from the Kensington dinner last night."

"He seems to spend all his time there. How does he stay fit?" Archer asked.

"He fences as well as engaging in some pugilism. When we're in Town, we sometimes go to Gentleman Jackson's boxing saloon."

Boxing took good footwork. That might be exactly what he needed to regain muscle memory in his leg.

"If you're thinking of your injury, then I have a suggestion that might seem peculiar. You should allow the ladies to teach you to dance." Gabriel held up a hand to stave off his protest. "The country dances can get quite vigorous and require a certain amount of stamina. They could teach you the steps here, in the privacy of the townhouse where you can practice without public observation."

When put that way, the idea had merit. He still remembered the longing in Violet's eyes when the dancing began last night until Mansfield swooped in for the opportunity. If he learned to dance, then Violet would have no reason to dance with the man. She would dance with him. His stomach swooped at the idea of holding her in his arms again.

Archer cleared his throat. "I'll consider it."

Gabriel smiled. "You should know that I am with your sisters in this regard. I too hope you will stay."

Archer lifted his chin in acknowledgment and left the study. He found Christian in a cluttered room at the back of the basement, bent over a large worktable scattered with tools, gears, and what looked like a rose made with silver-hinged petals.

"Find anything?" Archer asked.

Christian lifted his head and blinked. He held what looked like a short telescope and a piece of the clock.

"What is that?" Archer asked.

"A monocular opera glass. Since I hate the opera, this seemed a better use for it. It successfully magnified the powder, verifying that Lily did indeed see a crystal inside the clock."

"What kind of crystal? Could you tell?"

"Not precisely. However, given the properties I've seen and the understanding that it somehow operated within a clock, I gather that it isn't your average gemstone, such as moonstone or quartz. In the right light, it has a light blue tint."

Archer had no idea how to recognize gemstones.

"It's like nothing I've seen before," Christian said with a grin.

If he hadn't seen it before, why was he so excited? "How does that help?"

Christian set the opera glass aside. "There is a man who I ran into several weeks ago. A collector of the unusual…" He touched a silver petal on the rose, tracing its shape. "If anyone might know of such a stone, it is he."

"Where can we find him?"

One side of Christian's mouth quirked. "That is part of the issue. I don't know."

Archer crossed his arms and leaned against the desk. "You need to find this collector, but you don't know where to find him." Finally, something he could help with. Finding those who wanted to remain hidden was one of his best skill sets. He'd already studied Gabriel's maps of London and the countryside, acquainting himself with the area. Knowing the layout of a city in advance had saved his ass numerous times. "I can help. Tell me what you know about him and what he looks like."

"His name is Carter. He's slim, a bit shorter than you, with dark hair, and favors the look of a dandy." At Archer's quirked brow, he added, "Colorful breeches, tailcoats, and waistcoats in satins and velvets at any hour of the day."

"Where did you run into him?"

"Vauxhall Pleasure Gardens."

Sounded like a strip club. Did they have those in this time period? It was a place to start anyway.

"Too bad Zeph isn't here," Christian murmured. "He found Carter the last time."

"Locating people is my specialty. I'll find him."

"When you do, I'd like to speak with him. We have unfinished business."

Something about the way Christian spoke told him that their previous meeting had not been over tea. "Tell me about Vauxhall," Archer said.

Christian averted his eyes. "It's a large garden area in the city where—" A knock on the door interrupted him and he gusted out a breath that sounded relieved.

The butler entered and gave a short bow. "Lord Huntington. Mr. Bennett. Lady Rothden wishes to inform you that Lord Lael has just arrived."

Christian chuckled. "Ask, and he appears." He stood and gestured for Archer to proceed him back to the stairs. "Seems we shall have help after all. Zeph has arrived, the moment we needed him."

Zeph. He'd heard the man mentioned several times over the last week, both with fondness and puzzlement. His gut clenched with a bit of trepidation. Archer frowned at the foreign sensation. He'd entered buildings with dozens of terrorists without a moment's hesitation. Meeting an enigma of a man shouldn't even rate on the nervousness scale. What the hell?

"VIOLET, YOU MUST tell me all about your night last night,"

Bellamy said. She leaned forward, eagerness shining in her sapphire blue eyes. "Christian said you danced with Lord Mansfield."

They sat in the drawing room with Lily after spending a torturous morning with Aunt Josephine paying calls to her dowager friends and listening to news of the same scandal at each house they visited. After the fourth call, Violet began to suspect that she knew more about Lord Warding's exploits with Lady Fairchild than they did themselves.

"Lord and Lady Kensington put on a lovely dinner party," she replied to Bellamy. Of all the topics that Violet would happily discuss, last night was not one of them. She blew a curl out of her eyes and set about filling a china plate with sweet cakes.

It may have been her suggestion that Archer not kiss her again, but the dratted man didn't have to *agree* so quickly. She picked up a fork and stabbed it into a strawberry pastry, then set it on her plate. Was her first kiss so poor that he was relieved to not have her begging for another?

No. He'd enjoyed the kiss. He must have. Throughout the kiss, he'd held her tight, and she felt the hardness pressed against her hip. The stubborn man confused her. Indeed, she'd lain awake half the night reliving that kiss in her memories. She'd never expected that kissing would make her stomach flutter and her heart race.

"Lily and I were there for the lovely dinner party," Bellamy said. She placed a sandwich and two small pastries on a plate. A moment later, she added a third. She'd begun to eat more in the last few weeks since she decided to stay with Christian, and her overly thin frame was beginning to fill out, making her even more beautiful. "I want to know what you thought about Lord Mansfield. He was pretty handsome, I thought."

"Yes. How was your dance with him? I know dancing doesn't allow for much conversation, but you must have learned something," Lily said as she rubbed a hand on her stomach.

"I learned that I shall not have to have my slippers lined with lead, should we dance again. He is quite graceful," Violet replied.

Lily arched an eyebrow and gave Violet a look that said she wasn't to be put off. "Violet Hawthorne, almost from the moment we arrived in London, you have regaled me with every tiny detail you could learn about a potential suitor. Now you expect me to believe that all you discovered about Lord Mansfield during the ball was that he could dance well enough not to maim you?"

Violet stirred her tea and avoided her gaze. She hadn't learned all that much about Lord Mansfield, which frustrated her. Not because the gentleman hadn't been willing to share details, but because she hadn't asked him anything. He was handsome, titled, and presumably well enough off to care for her and any children they might have. He seemed to be a perfect match in every way. If he wasn't, she should be inquiring about him enough to determine that. Instead, she'd been distracted by Archer, who was unsuitable in *every* way.

"Vi?" Bellamy called softly. "Is something wrong?"

She stirred her tea in the other direction. "Do you suppose that attraction always happens when you first meet a person? Or can it come later once you become more acquainted?"

"It can come later," Bellamy said. "I've known people who were friends for years before they suddenly realized that they were attracted to each other."

"Is that what is bothering you, Vi? You're not feeling instant attraction to Lord Mansfield?" Lily asked.

She nodded. "I feel as if I should. Do you suppose something is wrong with me that I'm not?"

"No, Vi. Nothing is wrong with you." Bellamy reached out and squeezed Violet's hand. "Maybe you just don't know Mansfield well enough to decide. Or maybe he isn't your type."

"My type of what?"

"Your type of man," Lily said, smiling. "Some people have specific types of suitors they are attracted to. Some are only attracted to men with dark hair, others to men with money. Or accents. Or arrogant types. For others, it's nothing so specific." She shrugged.

"Some are only attracted to men like their fathers," Bellamy added.

Lily waggled her eyebrows at Violet. "Or their *brothers*."

Violet's mouth dropped open. "Grumpy, overbearing, dark-haired men are most certainly *not* my type of suitor."

"Not even a man like Archer?" Bellamy asked. Her eyes gleamed with a look Violet refused to acknowledge.

"Love *Archer*? Don't be ridiculous. Falling in love with your brother is a bit too much like falling in love with *my* brother."

Lily shared a look with Bellamy and then said, "Who said anything about love, Vi? We were talking attraction to potential suitors."

"Aren't I supposed to love a potential suitor?" She took a sip of her tea and realized it was growing tepid.

"You're supposed to love the suitor you plan to marry. But you're right. I suppose strong, honorable men who've seen far too many terrible things in life would be too grumpy... too injured... for love," Lily said.

Bellamy nodded. "Yes, I fear Archer will be alone for the rest of his life. He'll run off any woman even remotely interested in him with his overbearing attitude and the dark parts of his soul that are scarred from the things he's seen and done. And I know he feels as if people already look poorly upon him for his limp. Who knows what terrible scars are under his clothing? He probably wouldn't want to show them to a lover. She might be disgusted."

"Poor Archer. Can you imagine going the rest of your life without kissing? Or even the simple touch of a person who truly desires you?" Lily asked as she reached for another pastry.

"Anyone who cares for Archer wouldn't be disgusted by his scars," Violet argued. She set her teacup on the table a bit more forcefully than intended. "He just needs someone to show him that he is desirable and to bring some light back into his life. If he could stop being overbearing for a moment, he might find someone like that. Someone who would adore those hungry, passionate kisses. And anyone who thinks he is too injured to love or even to acknowledge isn't worth his interest." Violet swallowed, suddenly realizing she'd said a lot more than intended.

"Hmm. Well, perhaps after he's returned to his time, he'll find someone like that. I fear the women of this day are not strong enough to address any insecurities Archer might have, as well as willing to appear with a man who limps and walks with a cane," Bellamy said. She glanced at her sister. "Too bad we shall never get to see him happy."

Lily nodded. "I wish somehow that we could."

The thought of Archer not being happy for the rest of his life twisted Violet's emotions in a way she couldn't identify. The very notion seemed… too awful to conceive. Maybe he would find a woman in his time who would love and care for him. Someone to make him laugh. Her heart clenched, and it wasn't in happiness.

A knock at the drawing-room door drew her attention away from the troubling thought.

Henry entered and gave a slight bow. "Lord Lael, to see you, my lady."

Lily grinned and rose. "Show him in! And please let Rothden and Huntington know."

Henry bowed once more and held the door open. Zeph swept into the room with a wide grin.

"It must be a good day indeed to find myself in the company of the three most beautiful ladies in London," he declared.

Lily hugged him. "Where have you been for the last week? We've missed you."

He guided her back to her chair and then took the open seat by Violet. He winked at her, making her grin.

With his unusual almost silver-white hair and his pale silver eyes, he was striking. Violet often thought that his hair color should make him look in his dotage, but Zeph was young and fit like Gabriel, and the sparkle of mischief in his eyes could never be mistaken for someone elderly. He wore perfectly starched cravats and cutaway tailcoats tailored to perfection that showed his fine form. He was exceedingly handsome, a man of good fortune, and even if he wasn't declared an unsuitable suitor by Gabriel because they were friends, Violet didn't feel an ounce of attraction toward him. Maybe there *was* something wrong with her, despite Lily and Bellamy's insistence otherwise.

"I visited someone dear to me," Zeph replied, bringing her back to the conversation.

That piqued Violet's interest. She'd seen Zeph dance with many ladies, but he never courted one. She sat forward. "Is it a lady? Do you have someone special? Is she your mistress? Because you've never brought anyone to an event during the Season."

Zeph chuckled and accepted a cup of tea from Lily. "I'm sorry to disappoint you, Violet. She is more like family to me."

That interested her even more. "I wasn't aware you had family nearby. You never speak of them. Is it your sister? You should bring her to dinner one evening. We'd love to meet her."

"I'd admonish Violet for being too forward, Zeph, but I'm terribly curious myself, so you'll just have to accept the invitation and bring your family," Lily replied.

He laughed. "I'm afraid that is not possible, though I thank you for the invitation. The travel would be... difficult for her."

Before Violet could pry more information out of him about this mysterious family of his, the door opened, and Christian arrived with Archer. The moment she spotted him, she forgot all her questions for Zeph.

She dropped her gaze to her hands and twisted her fingers together in her lap. She didn't know how to act around him now that they'd kissed and then decided that it shouldn't happen again. Should she act as if nothing happened? *Could* she act that way?

She felt like a different person today. Like the world had opened and spilled a secret that only some people knew—how passionate a kiss could be with someone you cared for.

Bellamy went straight into Christian's arms and kissed him. A flush appeared on his cheeks, and he wrapped his arms around her, pulling her close.

Violet's chest pinched as she watched their greeting. It was as if they'd been apart for months, not hours. Violet wanted a man to look at her the way Christian looked at Bellamy, or Gabriel at Lily. Someone who would eagerly draw her close for kisses and be with her for every adventure. It was a fanciful, and altogether impractical wish. Women of her station rarely married for love. Perhaps that's why she wanted it so badly.

Zeph rose and joined the men.

Bellamy took her seat as Christian shook Zeph's hand and said, "It's good to have you back, my friend. This is Archer Bennett, brother to Bellamy and Lily. Archer, this is Zeph Lael. I believe he can help with that other matter."

Archer gave a single nod to Zeph, who responded in kind.

"Another Bennett," Zeph said to Lily. "Are there any others we should know about that might pop in unexpectedly?"

She laughed. "No. This is the last of us." As she spoke, her smile faded. "It's just been the three of us for a long time." Bellamy reached over and squeezed her hand.

Were they thinking of their parents who died years ago? The event had changed their lives forever. She snuck a glance at Archer and saw him frown. Warmth spread through her, making her want to go to his side and offer comfort. But he didn't want that, especially from her.

Archer met her gaze, then chose a seat nearest to the door. As far from her as he could get without sitting in the dining room next door.

Violet clenched her hands in her lap. Was he so honorable that he not only agreed that they shouldn't kiss again but also planned to avoid her? That would be challenging since they lived in the same house. And if it wasn't difficult enough, then Violet would make it so that he couldn't avoid her. *Ha!* He may not wish to court her, but he'd kissed her. A man who kisses a woman should never avoid her after. It was inconsiderate and somewhat hurtful.

"Was your visit with Raina?" Christian asked Zeph. "She's the only family you've ever mentioned."

Zeph nodded and returned to the seat next to Violet. She smiled at him, grateful that *someone* wanted to sit by her since Archer clearly did not.

"Yes, I've known Raina since she was a little girl. I still spend as much time as I can with her." Zeph's chuckle had an edge of mischief. "Though sometimes I think she would prefer otherwise after I've rearranged her workshop."

"That's the most you've ever told us about your family," Violet said.

"Is it?" Zeph asked with feigned surprise.

She lightly elbowed him. "It is. Do you annoy her as often as you do me?"

"I fervently hope so."

Violet laughed. Archer watched their exchange from across the room and his frown deepened. Maybe he was not as unaffected as he wished to show.

"Gabriel is reviewing accounts in his study, but I know he'll want to see you. Maybe you could join us for dinner?" Lily asked.

"I'd be delighted."

"Excellent. That will allow Archer and I time to speak with you on another matter," Christian said.

"And inquire about Lord Mansfield. Do you know him, Zeph?" Lily asked.

"Only in passing."

"Lord Mansfield has expressed an interest in Violet," Lily explained. "We were just encouraging her to spend a bit more time with him to decide if he is someone she wishes to court."

"Oh, I have an idea," Bellamy said. "Let's go for a stroll at Hyde Park tomorrow. It's a Sunday so much of the ton will be out. We may see Lord Mansfield."

"Violet could get to know him in a public setting where it's perfectly respectable to walk or ride with a gentleman." Lily nodded. "An excellent idea, Bells."

"That sounds… lovely." She tried to smile. It didn't sound lovely at all. A large part of her didn't want to know more about Lord Mansfield. *You're almost on the shelf, Violet. Can you truly afford to be picky at this moment?* No, she couldn't. Perhaps attraction would come as she learned more about him.

"No," Archer said. "That's a bad plan."

"Why?" Lily asked before Violet could.

"It's not safe. We don't know who is sending Violet those notes or what their intentions are. I can't protect her in a large, open public setting like that. There will be too many variables. Sorry, Violet. You have to sit this one out."

The presumption of this man! "Those notes are perfectly harmless and meant only as flattery. Furthermore, if I wish to go for a stroll at Hyde Park with Lily, then I shall do so. I do not need your permission, *Mr. Bennett*." Violet crossed her arms over her chest as she spoke and glared at him.

He glared back. "I'm trying to keep you safe," he argued.

She huffed. "There's no threat, so there is no need."

Lily raised her hands up to stop the argument bubbling up between them. "It is just a stroll, Archer. There are long paths through the park, and we shall all remain together."

His jaw worked. Finally, he nodded. "And Carter?" he asked Christian.

"I had hoped to spend time looking for him tomorrow."

Zeph chuckled. "If you wish to find Carter, you have no need to look further than Hyde Park on a lovely spring day. When I sought him out for you a few weeks back, that was one of several places he was known to frequent."

Christian looked at Archer. "It would allow us to find Carter and give you an opportunity to watch over Violet." He lowered his voice and said something more.

She thought she heard him say "horse." It would make sense. Archer could ride alongside them so he didn't have to limp his way around the park, which would no doubt tire his leg out, but also make him somewhat of a spectacle. Something she suspected that he wouldn't care for.

"It's settled. We'll go to the park tomorrow," Lily declared. She grinned at Violet. "Maybe we can find you a handsome gentleman who isn't overbearing and too much like your brother."

Violet thought she heard a muffled curse from Archer but chose to ignore it. She needed to find a husband soon. She couldn't continue to live with Gabriel and Lily into her dotage, turning into Aunt Josephine more with every passing year.

That thought decided it then. Violet felt her excitement rise at the prospects ahead. She grinned at Lily. "I think it will be a grand adventure. Perhaps we'll see Lord Mansfield, or finally meet the gentleman sending the anonymous notes."

Archer spun and stomped from the drawing room.

CHAPTER EIGHT

"CAN YOU SHOOT?" Violet asked Archer as they strolled along one of the crowded pathways in Hyde Park.

The weather had warmed, and the skies were a perfect, clear blue. The smell of fresh grass, horses, and many bodies mingled together in the air, making Archer's nose twitch. If he concentrated, he could detect Violet's cinnamon scent underneath it all. She walked beside him, wearing a pretty blue gown with gold embroidery, her head just reaching his chin. Her bonnet had matching blue ribbons that tied under her chin and kept her dark hair covered. He'd never paid much attention to fashion, but the nobility of this time seemed to relish it. He pulled at the knot in his cravat.

Violet shifted closer to him, her arm brushing his through his coat sleeve. The sun shone down on her fair skin and highlighted the gold in her amber eyes whenever she looked at him.

Damn, she was pretty. The way she'd molded her body against his in the carriage after the Kensingtons' party made his heart beat faster every time he thought about it. She'd learned to kiss quickly and had a natural passion that made him want to explore more. Tug that dress off and see how her silky skin tasted as he…

Head out of the gutter, Bennett. She's eighteen. Old enough to make her own decisions and accept the consequences, but he couldn't pursue her. Their life experiences were too different. Seeing the bleakest part of humanity put shadows in his heart while Violet radiated innocent excitement about everything in life. They didn't fit, and yet, he wanted her.

"Well?" she prompted, pulling Archer back to her earlier question.

He cocked an eyebrow, unsure he'd heard correctly. "You're asking me if I can shoot?"

"Yes. Do you shoot when you go hunting?"

He cleared his throat. He'd been the best marksman on his team. "A bit."

"Can you teach me to shoot?"

Archer stopped on the path, earning a few grumbles from the people packed in around them. "Why do you want to learn to shoot? Did you receive another note?"

Violet rolled her eyes. "No. Why shouldn't I like to learn? Or do you believe that a woman shouldn't learn such manly pursuits?"

The way she said it made him think she'd heard that quite a bit. What other manly pursuits did Violet want to learn besides shooting? Could be anything, knowing her. "It's not that. I've known several women who were excellent shots. But—"

"You *have?*" Violet's eyes lit up. "Did they enjoy it? I think I would enjoy it. I'm quite a good rider, and I should like to join one of Gabriel's hunts one day."

Her eyes took on a faraway look as she no doubt pictured herself on a hunt. Violet with a gun? God help him and anyone around her. He pinched the bridge of his nose. "I'm not certain that Gabriel would want you to learn to shoot."

She glowered at him and stomped down the path, calling over her shoulder, "When I marry, my brother will not have a say. Only my husband, and I won't marry anyone who won't teach me to shoot."

He hurried to catch up to her, leaning a bit on his cane. The strain from the long walk was catching up to him and his leg was beginning to ache. Stretching the muscles was good for him though, so he pushed through the pain. *The only easy day was yesterday, Bennett. Suck it up.*

He caught her elbow to slow her down. Ahead, Lily walked with Zeph, and in front of them, Bellamy held Christian's arm as they meandered on the path. Lily glanced back and winked at Violet, then returned her attention to Zeph.

"Dammit, I didn't say I wouldn't teach you," he growled. An older woman gasped as she passed, shooting him an alarmed look, and whispered to her companion about his language. *Blend in, remember Bennett?* He composed himself and focused on Violet. "You're not married yet, so your brother will have a say if I teach you to shoot."

She stared straight ahead.

Archer could practically see the steam pouring from her ears. "Why not ask Gabriel?" He'd noted how protective the earl was of Violet. The only reason that he wasn't with them now was because he was with Josephine in the open-air carriage, where, as she'd put it, "She would show those women who had the better hat." Gabriel had looked irritated as he had the carriage brought around, and Archer imagined the man would look the same if Violet approached him about learning to shoot.

"I have. He refused. Either he doesn't think a woman should shoot or he doesn't think that *I* should shoot. If you won't teach me, then I'll just have to wait until I marry."

He scowled. "I don't understand your rush. You have a long life ahead of you. Maybe you should travel a bit, get to know yourself before getting married."

She looked at him like he was crazy. "I'm nearly on the shelf. If I wait too much longer, *no one* will marry me. They will assume that there is something untoward about me because no one has offered for my hand, and it won't matter in the slightest that my brother is an earl. Or he'll be forced to accept a suit from someone in his dotage. Zinnea Parling found herself in a scandal with Lord Twisden last year and was forced to marry a man nearing sixty years old." She shuddered.

Jesus. Talk about robbing the cradle. The reminder that societal expectations about marriage in this time was an unwelcome one. As a SEAL, in non-Western countries and cultures, he'd seen girls married off to men four and five times their age all throughout the world. He was positive that Violet wouldn't be forced into a marriage like that. Lily would never allow it.

The topic set off memories he'd buried, of screams and seeing things best forgotten. Darkness descended on his spirit as images of clearing apartment buildings that should have been condemned but were instead packed with large families in spaces far too small for comfort, of his team's voices in his earpiece, and rapid gunfire. His heart clenched and pain speared him.

He breathed deep and held it, forcing his body to regain calm.

"Archer?" Violet called softly. She pressed a gloved hand to his bicep.

He looked down into her concerned eyes and tried to pull himself out of the darkness. It was an effort. Every day, it was an effort. "Yeah. I'm good," he murmured. The lie slipped out easily. He wasn't, and he didn't think he ever would be. The nightmares proved that if nothing else did. He was too damaged to be around people. Especially innocent young women too beautiful and spirited for their own good. Or sisters who'd found love and happiness in life. No way in hell would he drag them down with his inner demons. After everything that had happened with their parents, and then after, Lily and Bells deserved to be happy. He wouldn't ruin that.

A soft smile touched Violet's lips as she stared up into his face. Chocolate-brown curls brushed her cheek in the light breeze, highlighting her creamy skin and that pretty mouth that beckoned him to take another kiss.

He dragged his gaze away from her tempting lips and scanned the people around him. Carter, the man he and Zeph were looking for, could have strolled right past him during those few moments that he'd been caught in his memories and then Violet's gaze, and Archer never would have known it. He rubbed a hand over his jaw.

"You trimmed your beard," Violet said. "I think it looks quite handsome."

He huffed. "I borrowed the scissors from Lily's sewing kit." The handles were almost too small to get his fingers through, but they'd done the job. He'd trimmed it close to his jaw, remembering Violet's comments. Clean-shaven faces were the style, but as he'd stared at his reflection that morning, he realized that he wasn't ready to expose his scars. Lily and Bellamy didn't know the extent of them. Violet would probably be horrified.

She laughed. "We shall have to get your own along with a proper razor."

He shook his head. "Won't be here long enough."

Violet's shoulders sagged a bit. She didn't respond and the silence grew between them.

They continued walking along the gravel path that led toward Kensington Gardens. In the midst of hundreds of noisy people in the park, the silence between him and Violet felt pronounced.

"Do you think I will become like Aunt Josephine?" Violet suddenly asked.

He didn't follow her thought process from shaving to Aunt Josephine. "Does she also shave her chin?"

She laughed, and the sound washed over him in soothing notes. Her laugh was light, yet genuine, and her amber eyes sparkled with humor.

Archer wanted her to laugh again, just to see her beauty in its fullness.

"Perhaps, though she'd probably never tell." Violet twined her fingers together. "I don't want to be the unmarried aunt who is barely tolerated by her family."

He heard the worry in her voice. The fear that seemed to drive her desire to marry. "You want a family of your own."

"And love. Although in my position, I should be happy to

have friendship and companionship with my husband. I shall probably not be one of the lucky few to love the man they marry."

How could any man spend time with Violet and not come to care for her? He cared and he'd known her less than two weeks. "I wouldn't say that." The words slipped out before he could stop them.

"Have you ever loved?" A light pink blush colored her cheeks.

"I loved my parents and my sisters." *I loved my brothers on my team, until I failed them.* "But I've never been *in* love."

"How does one know when one is in love?"

"I'm not sure. But if you're willing to give your life for that person, you love them." The void in his heart reopened and pain stabbed at him. He clutched his cane handle harder and leaned more of his weight on it.

Violet nodded, intelligence shining in her eyes as she worked through what he said. "Do you intend to marry, Mr. Bennett?"

The handle of the cane bit into his palm, and it was only then that he realized that he was squeezing it. "Once. Not after..." He swallowed past the lump that had formed in his throat. "Not anymore."

Violet searched his face. Her gaze dropped to the scars that ran from his ear to his jaw and down, where the high starched collar of his shirt hid them from view. When she met his gaze again, he couldn't read her expression.

Whoever married Violet Bennett would... He froze the moment the thought began. *Hawthorne*, not Bennett. Whoever married Violet Hawthorne would be a lucky man. *Shit.* He had to distance himself before caring for her, caring about her, turned into something...more.

Archer ushered her forward with a hand on her lower back. "Let's not get separated from the others. There are too many people here." He scanned the surrounding crowd, looking for a man Zeph had described as a dandy, wearing brightly colored clothing made of velvets and satins.

Unfortunately, there were quite a few men who dressed that way. From what Christian and Zeph told him of their earlier encounter with the mysterious Carter, he'd always been surrounded by muscular men. What sort of man kept his own security detail in this time? Someone famous? Or infamous?

He wanted to ask Zeph more about the man, but he and Lily were up ahead. Observant and caring as usual, Violet had slowed her steps to match his halting, pained ones. Her concern vexed him and pleased him by turns. He offered her his arm, but only to keep her close he told himself. *Not for any other reason.*

"Have you found the man you are looking for?" Violet asked, taking his arm.

"Not yet." They approached an area on the path where even more people lingered, and the clop-clop of horse hooves grew louder. A flash of yellow caught his eye through a gap in the crowd. He leaned on his cane, hoping for a better angle, and spotted a dark-haired man wearing bright yellow trousers with a light green tailcoat. Two wide men stood behind him as the man spoke with an older woman.

Zeph and Lily appeared to realize they were behind and had stopped to wait for them; Zeph, too, was watching the man in yellow trousers.

"Is that Carter?" Archer asked Zeph as he and Violet drew closer and nodded toward the colorful man.

Zeph's nearly white hair blew in the light breeze as he followed Archer's nod. "Yes. If anyone may know something about the crystal you seek for Christian's clock, it is he."

Lily's eyebrows rose. "Do you know about the clock, Zeph? That it is…special?"

Zeph raised her gloved hand to his lips. "Everything Christian creates is special, my dearest Lily." To Archer, he said, "Christian can look after the ladies while we speak to Carter."

"I should like to meet him," Violet said.

"This gentleman is known to collect beautiful things, Violet," Zeph said. "You must stay here, so he doesn't collect you." He winked at her, but the comment made the hair on the back of Archer's neck rise. He'd seen too many things, including men who had a propensity for collecting beautiful women. The thought chilled him to his core.

"Stay here," he repeated to Violet, who stood on tiptoe to get a better look. "*Don't* follow us."

Violet made a disgruntled face and waved him off. "Go to your clandestine meeting then. I shall find something else to keep myself entertained."

Lily groaned and linked her arm with Violet's. "Come on, Vi. Let's go see the carriages in the Ring."

Archer waited until they were with Christian and Bellamy before he followed Zeph toward Carter. They weaved between groups of finely dressed people, all vying for attention from those around them.

He turned to avoid someone and bumped into another. "Excuse me," he said.

A large man in an ill-fitting coat looked down at him. His lips turned down as he studied Archer, then nodded and pushed past.

"One can never account for the pleasantries of others," Zeph said. He swung a black cane with a gold ball handle in a casual circle at his side, narrowly missing a group of ladies walking by him. They murmured in alarm. He tipped his top hat at them and chuckled.

Archer side-eyed the man as they walked. Zeph seemed more amused than apologetic about the whole event, making him wonder if the man hadn't swung the cane dangerously close to the women on purpose, just to elicit a reaction. "How do you know Carter?" he asked.

"He introduced himself to Christian and me at gunpoint on the Dark Walk at Vauxhall Gardens several weeks back." Zeph spoke as if they'd met in the cereal aisle of the grocery store. "He was there to purchase one of Christian's inventions from the thief who'd stolen it. Fortunately, Bellamy arrived at an opportune moment."

"What the hell was my sister doing there?" Archer growled. The pain from this walk was almost unbearable. A bead of sweat rolled down his spine.

"Bellamy was enjoying an evening at Vauxhall, I suspect, until the moment Wainsright separated her from Gabriel and Lily and made her join our little party."

Archer swore under his breath.

Zeph's eyebrows rose. "We're all well, as you can see for yourself. Christian rescued her from Wainsright, and Carter and his men disappeared into the darkness. I assure you, if Christian hadn't assisted her, I would have."

Archer glared at him. "She shouldn't have been in danger to begin with. She shouldn't have been there."

Zeph shrugged. "Ordinarily, the Gardens are an amusement, and quite safe." He glanced at Archer. Though his tone was light, his eyes were serious, and in their unusual, silvery depths, Archer recognized something of himself. "I'd suggest you take the matter up with Wainsright, but I'm afraid he's at the bottom of the Thames. Unless, of course, they pulled his body out after I shot him. Look, Carter's done holding court. Let's go talk to him before he starts speaking to someone else." He stepped around a couple with a little boy and hurried toward the man.

Archer could not get a read on Zeph. He'd honed his senses until he could size up almost anyone instantly, allowing him to make fast judgments on whom he could trust, at least on the surface. Zeph seemed to dance a line between good and bad. Could he trust the man? If Carter pulled a weapon on them, would Zeph help? He'd just admitted to shooting a man possibly to protect Bellamy. What sort of man protected and killed easily?

A man like me. Like my brothers on Team Three.

That brought Archer up short. He paused on the gravel walk, earning a mutter from a gentleman behind him.

If the question were reversed, he knew some might find him difficult and dangerous to trust. But he was a man of honor. He began to suspect Zeph might be the same. A man who didn't quite fit into the ideal of good versus evil. Sometimes you had to do shitty things to accomplish a mission for the good of all.

Moments later, they caught up to the collector. He walked along the edge of the path, with two bulky men just behind him.

"Carter," Zeph called.

Carter turned at the sound of his name. "Lael." He glanced at Archer, standing at Zeph's side. His gaze swept over Archer's frame, focused on his cane for less than a second, then turned back to Zeph as if Archer was of no consequence.

Appearing weak was often an advantage. Archer hadn't considered that when it came to his cane until this moment. If the situation turned, Carter would probably underestimate him, and he'd have an edge.

"To what do I owe the pleasure of your company, Lael?"

Up close, Archer could see that Carter had dark brown hair and eyes. He was a bit wiry, but his tailored clothes hinted at muscle beneath. He was also quite colorful. Besides his light green tailcoat, he wore a patterned blue cravat, a waistcoat embroidered in purple flowers, and bright, yellow trousers. Christian had described him as a dandy, an almost flamboyantly dressed, upper-class man. But one look in Carter's shrewd eyes said that there was far more beneath the surface.

Archer's muscles tensed as the hair on the back of his neck stood on end. He scanned the path and surrounding people, cataloging their numbers and the fastest route back to his sisters and Violet, should they need to leave quickly. He spotted Bellamy leaning into Christian's side, with Lily beside her.

Violet stood smiling brightly beside an open carriage pulled by a matching pair of chestnut horses.

He started to turn back to Zeph and Carter when the man descending from the carriage caught his attention. He offered his hand to Violet, which she accepted and climbed into the carriage. It looked as if the rig would only seat the two of them.

What was she doing? Wouldn't it be unacceptable for an unmarried woman to…

Archer's heart skipped a beat, then began to pound when the man turned, and he recognized him. Violet had just accepted a carriage ride with Percy Mansfield.

⫸⫷

"THANK YOU FOR joining me on this fine day, Lady Violet. I admit it was a surprise to find you in this crush, but I find the day all the brighter in your presence." Lord Mansfield smiled at Violet, his handsome face bright with happiness, then returned his attention to the pair of horses as he guided the curricle around the Ring where dozens of other carriages rumbled around them. He cut a fine profile with his clean-shaven jaw and light brown hair that curled under his beaver hat. "I realize that we do not know one another well, but I feel we will suit marvelously."

"You do?" Violet clutched her reticule in her gloved hands and offered a polite smile. Lily's plan to find Lord Mansfield in the park today had worked marvelously. *You're delighted, remember?*

"Indeed. You are a handsome woman who possesses a good and kind spirit. A gentleman should count himself lucky to find such a woman."

"Thank you." Violet knew he meant the words as a compliment, but since Lily and Bellamy came into their lives, she'd only heard "handsome" applied to men. She much preferred it when Archer—*or anyone*—called her "beautiful."

Lord Mansfield guided the horses out of the Ring and onto the road toward Kensington Gardens, where he slowed the curricle to a sedate pace. "There, now we can talk more."

"You are an excellent driver." She winced internally. After attending dozens of dreadful teas with Aunt Josephine, surely she could make better conversation.

He chuckled. "Thank you. I'm not certain I've received a compliment on it before. Do not feel nervous, my dear Lady Violet." He patted her gloved hand. "Is this your first time on a ride with a suitor? On my honor, I will be a perfect gentleman."

Violet refused to acknowledge the part of her who didn't want a perfect gentleman for a suitor. That path led to the ruin of her reputation. She mustered up another smile. "I confess that it is. My brother is quite protective of me."

"As he should be. A more unscrupulous man might take advantage of having a charming miss all to himself. Might try to take what he has no right to."

Violet saw his light blue eyes turn frosty as he spoke, and a line deepened between his eyebrows as he stared ahead. Who was he thinking of? Whomever it was, he appeared to dislike them immensely. "Then I count myself lucky to be with you," she said. It wasn't a complete lie. Lord Mansfield had shown nothing but interest in her as a true suitor would and was quite polite. He was almost Archer Bennett's opposite. Not that she should compare the two of them, of course, since Archer Bennett wasn't a suitor.

"I'm delighted to hear you say as much. I realize that you haven't given your permission, but I hoped that you might allow me to call you by your Christian name? You may, of course, call me Percy, in private. It is my hope that we may begin courting."

His eyes shone as he spoke, and he truly did look hopeful of their suit. *Archer plans to return to his own time. He has no intention of pursuing you, and even if he did, he is not a man of title or means.* Percy would be here long after Archer was gone. Archer might not think that Lord Mansfield was her last hope for a good match, but Violet knew full well that as each day passed, her prospects grew more limited. She *needed* this match. They would suit... and, they would... grow... to love each other. The smile she offered this time felt more genuine. "I should like that, Percy."

His breath caught and he looked at her as if she'd granted him his heart's desire. After a moment, he reached for her hand and tucked it in his.

Violet felt... *absolutely nothing*. Not attraction or revulsion, and certainly not the quickening heartbeat that she had when

Archer kissed her. None of that mattered, however. Bellamy said that a man and woman could start as friends, and it could become more. That is what she would do with Lord Mansfield.

"I will give you everything you want," he murmured. "Silks, jewels, a fine house here and in the country. My estate is not so far from Hawthorne's. We can visit whenever you like." Percy slid his gaze down her body and back up. "I shall give you children, of course. As many as you desire, and as often as you desire."

"You're very generous." The way he looked at her... She saw the desire in his eyes, the appreciation for her beauty and her form, but instead of making her feel desired, a shiver of something she couldn't name went down her spine. She slipped her hand from his and looked around at the people they passed. Where were Lily, Bellamy, and Christian?

Where was Archer?

"You'll find that I'm willing to give you everything, darling, once you're mine. I shall speak to your brother at once."

Her heart skipped a beat. "So soon?"

He gave her a sharp look.

"I only mean, what if we come to know one another as we court and find we do not suit? Breaking our contract would look poorly."

"You misunderstand my dedication, darling." His voice lowered to an intimate tone. "Since the moment we met, I have wanted you and no other."

She gasped in surprise. "How can you be certain after so short a time?"

"I know what I want, and I do not allow anyone to stop me from taking it."

What was wrong with her that words he no doubt meant as a promise and encouragement sounded more like threats? Had she read too many gothic romances in the dark of night?

"Do you want love, Lord Mansfield?"

"Of course. What man wouldn't want the love of a fine

woman?"

He didn't offer to love in return, she noted. Did he mean to imply that he would love the woman even though he didn't say so? She clenched her hands together in her lap to avoid rubbing at her temple in confusion. Why weren't men easier to understand? Why couldn't they say exactly what they meant as women did?

"I'm certain that we will grow to love, darling. Have no fear in that regard. I shall take care of you."

She nodded, unsure what to say. He seemed to be expecting a response, however, as he kept glancing at her. Finally, she said, "I shall consider your suit, Percy."

He nodded, seeming pleased. "Not too long, darling. I'm not a patient man."

They lapsed into silence for several moments, allowing her to ponder their conversation as she gazed at the pretty park setting. She felt unsettled, but surely that was only nerves about finding a suitable gentleman willing to court her. One who seemed intent on marrying her and who promised they would grow to love one another. It was everything she wanted. Wasn't it?

As if her thoughts conjured him, a feeling of warmth filled her chest, and she spotted Archer several yards away. "Oh, there's Archer and Zeph," she said, pointing to the men talking to three other men near the Serpentine canal.

"Violet, I must insist that you not keep a casual acquaintance with Lord Lael and… Mr. Bennett is it? It would not be appropriate." He slowed the curricle as they neared.

Violet looked at him askance. Formality with Archer? Or for that matter, with Zeph? Zeph would laugh heartily over the idea. She hadn't called him Lord Lael since she first met him over a decade ago. Did that mean Percy also wanted her to be less formal with Christian, who was nearly a brother to her? *Pish.* In an informal setting, they would always be Christian, Zeph— and—while he remained—Archer.

Instead of replying to his ridiculous remark, she studied the man with Archer and Zeph. He was not handsome, but neither was he plain. If not for his dandy dress, he wouldn't stand out in a crowd of people. The two large gentlemen with him stood back a few paces, surveying their surroundings. They reminded her a bit of the Regent's guards protecting their future king.

Percy stopped the curricle several yards away and watched the men with a keen interest that seemed out of place for their conversation. What about them made him watch with such concern? "Are you acquainted with Lord Lael?" she asked, doubting Archer had been there long enough to earn such a reaction from him. *Although Archer's grumpy nature could put anyone off.*

Lord Mansfield didn't reply. He was too focused on the men and appeared as if he wasn't listening to her at all.

Violet turned back toward them just as the dandy's head lifted. His gaze roamed briefly over her, then met Percy's stare with one of his own. She could see the man's lip curl, even at this distance. Heavens, his expression was the same as Gabriel's when she did something to displease him.

She turned back to Percy to ask him if he knew that gentleman, but the words died in her throat. His eyes had frosted over, and his eyebrows slanted low. Then he offered a slow, chilly smile to the man.

It sent a shiver down her spine.

Percy flicked the reins and turned the horses onto a side path angling away from the group. Once they began moving, he looked toward the copse of trees near where the men stood beside the canal.

Violet followed his gaze but saw nothing of interest. What was he looking for?

"Are you enjoying our ride, darling?" he said almost absently and reached for her hand again.

"Who were those men?" She gently pulled her hand from his and made a show of straightening her skirt.

"Hmm?"

"The man to whom Lord Lael and Mr. Bennett were speaking. It seemed as if you knew him."

"No one of consequence." She must have looked unconvinced because he added, "Nothing to concern yourself with, darling. Enjoy this fine weather and watch for your friends. Wouldn't you like them to see you riding in my carriage?"

No. She turned in her seat. At first, she thought Zeph and Archer had gone, but a flash of movement near the ground caught her eye. She watched in horror as Archer raised up on his knees over a man in a brown coat, lifted his cane, and cracked it over the man's head.

She gasped.

Beside him, Zeph and the dandy fought two more strangers. She saw the dandy's guards slumped on the ground.

Her heart raced and she pressed a palm over it. "Stop! We must go back. There are men attacking Zeph and Archer!"

Percy ignored her and flicked the reins, urging the pair of horses to travel faster.

She leaned as far over the side of the curricle as she dared, to see the fight. "Stop, Percy!" Archer's leg already pained him. Could he fight his attacker off? Violet caught her breath, heart in her throat, as an enormous man with a club of some sort began swinging it at his head.

She couldn't tear her gaze away. How could she help? Was there someone she could call to aid them? Should she jump out of the carriage? Before she could beg Percy to stop or find a way to find help, Archer rushed the man with the club, turned his body into the attack, and flipped the man over his shoulder. The attacker landed on his back and struggled to move. The last thing she saw before the curricle turned a corner on the path was Archer's wide grin, and it took her breath away.

CHAPTER NINE

Several minutes earlier…

"THERE ARE A great many types of crystal in this world, and most are hardly worth my notice," Carter said, picking at an imaginary piece of lint on the cuff of his light green tailcoat. Two wide-shouldered, burly men stood behind him, watching the exchange.

"Indeed, but this one is quite rare: white but with a bit of a tint. Bennett, what color did Christian say the crystal was?" Zeph asked.

"A bluish tint," he replied, resisting the urge to search for Mansfield's carriage. Violet had climbed into it so easily in spite of his feelings about the man. With effort, Archer compartmentalized his irritation that the stubborn woman had ignored his warnings about Mansfield and concentrated on the conversation.

Zeph quirked an eyebrow at him, glanced back at where Lily and Bellamy stood and then smirked. It was as if Lael had read his mind.

Carter looked up from studying his sleeve. "A white crystal with a bluish tint. What do you want it for?"

Archer tensed. The man no longer sounded bored. Instead, his tone seemed carefully neutral. As if he hid a sudden interest. The man could have been a dealer at any of the markets in a third-world country, selling his wares and appearing innocent while trading on the black market in the shadows at the same time. Archer didn't like him. Could they even trust any information he gave them? "You know of one?"

Carter's shoulders lifted in a shrug. "I may have seen something."

Zeph chuckled under his breath. "One never knows what one might come across in one's travels."

The collector met Archer's gaze, studying him a second time. "Why the interest?"

Archer weighed his responses. From what Zeph had told him earlier, Carter collected the unusual and wasn't known to give anything for free. His own impression of the man told him that the clothes and the air of indifference were a foppish disguise, hiding the true nature of the man beneath. Carter's direct gaze showed shrewdness, and an air of darkness lingered, like an invisible cloak, about him. Would skirting the truth help or hurt them? Because they damn sure couldn't say—

"Bennett intends to use it inside one of Huntington's inventions," Zeph replied. He cocked his head, silver eyes considering. "If you had seen such a crystal, might it have been—"

Carter suddenly shifted, looking past Zeph. His shoulders tensed and a muscle ticked in his jaw as his pupils contracted.

Archer followed his gaze and spotted Mansfield—and Violet—several yards away. Mansfield and Carter glared at one another, and the air thickened with tension. He could see Violet talking, but at this distance, with the canal nearby, he couldn't make out her words. To his relief, she seemed unharmed, but that could change in an instant. Archer gripped his cane tighter as the hair on the back of his neck bristled. Zeph shifted to the side, watching the interaction.

Mansfield's lips shifted into a smile that promised pain as he continued to stare at Carter.

Beside Archer, the collector never took his gaze off Mansfield. His eyes burned cold.

Then Mansfield flicked the reins and guided his pair of horses into a trot, and they continued down the path.

Violet's eyes widened, and she looked at Mansfield, then back at them.

Archer fought the urge to go after them and get her away from Mansfield. He wanted her at his side, not alone with a man who made Archer's sense of danger go haywire. As he watched the carriage drive away, he saw Mansfield look toward the trees nearby with interest. Nerves tingling, he turned just as five men sprung from the tree line and rushed them. All were armed. Two had clubs, one a large metal pipe, another a pistol, and the fifth—a large, familiar form in an ill-fitting brown coat that he'd run into by mistake earlier—had a length of thick chain wrapped around his fist.

One of Carter's men shouted just as a shot rang out. He'd thrust himself in front of the collector and a second later, sagged to his knees as a bright bloom of blood spread across his chest.

The assailant with the pipe swung at Archer's head. He ducked, landed a punch to the man's ribs, then tackled him to the ground. They rolled and Archer came up on top. He ripped the pipe from the man's hands and tossed it away, then followed with two hard punches, knocking him out. Archer was on his feet in an instant, spinning toward the next attacker. A man with a club rushed him. Adrenaline surged in his limbs, and he relished the energy. He ran to meet the attack and at the last moment, turned into his opponent, reached for the man's raised arm, and used momentum to flip the man over his shoulder. The attacker landed on his back hard and wheezed for air.

He grinned, feeling better than he had in months. More himself.

Archer grabbed the man with the chain by his coat and spun him, so they faced one another. The man whipped the chain at him in a snap of metal. Archer ducked and grabbed the chain before it could fall, then landed a punch to his abdomen. He followed with another to his jaw, snapping the man's head back.

Archer saw the whites of the man's eyes and watched as he crumpled.

Nearby, Zeph was trading blows with the attacker who'd had the gun. Pipe Man had roused himself off the ground and snuck up behind them with his weapon raised, ready to strike. Archer swept up the cane he'd dropped and ran for them. He brought the wooden cane down hard across the assailant's back. With a loud crack, it snapped in half, and the wood, along with the man, fell to the ground.

Zeph landed a punch that sent his opponent reeling. The man stumbled back, tripped on a root, and splashed into the Serpentine Canal. Zeph threw back his head and laughed. The pale skin across his knuckles was turning purple with a bruise and another darkened his jaw, but his eyes gleamed with excitement as he turned to Archer to breathlessly exclaim, "Any others?"

Of the five men who attacked, four were laid out in the grass. The last staggered to his feet in the shallow water, glared at them, and shuffled his way to the other side. He hauled himself out of the Serpentine and fled.

"This one's dead," Zeph said as he knelt at the side of the man who'd been shot. One of Carter's men. Carter and his other guard were gone.

"Did any of them say what they were after?" Archer asked, taking stock of his own pains. His leg had ached like hell from the walk, but now it throbbed. One of the men landed a couple punches on his ribs which hurt, but as he gently prodded them, nothing felt broken.

Zeph shook his head. "Judging by the state of this gentleman, I believe they meant to have a conversation with Carter. It is unfortunate for them that we found him first." He rose and collected his hat from the ground, dusting it off. "Sport like this on a fine day is almost a gift from the gods."

Archer chuckled and agreed. In that moment, he felt a bit of kinship with Zeph not unlike the brotherhood he'd felt with his team. "Not many men would consider getting jumped in the park by five thugs to be a gift of any sort."

"Then I count myself fortunate to be in good company." Zeph squinted down the road following the direction Mansfield's carriage had traveled. "I fear if Violet saw any of this fight she is even now contemplating leaping from the carriage to rush back."

He snorted at the image Zeph painted. It wouldn't surprise him. "She shouldn't have gone with Mansfield in the first place." He spotted the other half of his cane on the ground. Damn, there was no fixing that.

"Leave it. The groundskeepers will take care of it."

Archer dropped the other half beside the first, already dreading the walk back. He flexed his hand, feeling his knuckles start to swell. He was injured, but he'd just proven to himself that he could still fight, could still protect. He wasn't totally fucking broken, as he'd feared.

He retrieved his own hat, brushed it off, and put it back on. Then he took a few steps toward the path, noting with surprise that his gait felt a little smoother, even without the cane.

"What is it?" Zeph asked as he fell into step beside him.

"I expected to have more pain in my leg. It's throbbing, but I can walk." He took a few more test steps. He limped pretty badly without the cane, but he could walk on his own. That in itself was an accomplishment.

Zeph clapped a hand on his shoulder. "Good."

Maybe he *should* try learning to dance to improve his balance and stamina. What if he could finally leave the cane behind, this time forever? The thought buoyed his flagging energy. After all, he was stuck here for a while longer. They'd have to find Carter again, and Archer found himself eager to do so. But first, he needed to check on Violet and make sure that Mansfield hadn't touched her.

"Let's make certain the ladies are well and that Mansfield has returned Violet to them. If he has not, we may have more of a fight ahead," he said.

"Did you notice that Mansfield looked toward the trees just

before the attack?" Zeph asked.

"I did." He paused. "He knew the men were there."

"Judging by the intense glare between Mansfield and Carter, I'm certain of it."

Archer frowned. Any man who sent thugs after a target while cheerfully driving Violet around to show off his good fortune was not someone he wanted to associate with. Despite his pronounced limp, he walked faster. He needed to see with his own eyes that she was safe.

PERHAPS I SHOULD join the theater.

Violet stared at the gold embroidered canopy above her bed while the fire burned down to coals and the shadows grew thick in her bedroom. The curtains were drawn over the window, but a sliver of moonlight dared peek through a small gap in a vain attempt to add more light. It was long past midnight, but she hadn't been able to sleep with the events from Hyde Park earlier in the day spinning in her head like a country reel.

If I do not find a suitor, wouldn't the theater be better than spending the rest of my life on the shelf?

The thought hadn't occurred to her until after Percy had returned her to Lily, Bellamy, and Christian, and she'd given an inspired performance to them about her *delightful* ride with Lord Mansfield. Not even Lily suspected the truth.

After they'd left Archer and Zeph to fight off those large men, Percy had ignored her pleas to turn back and help them until she'd attempted to grab the reins. They'd ended up in a tussle that nearly spooked the horses. He'd finally forced her back onto her side of the carriage and said he was taking her away from the fight because a young lady shouldn't see such things, and that a man who could not hold his own in a fight was not worthy of their help. Violet had been incensed until she realized that—in his own way—he was trying to protect her.

That softened her towards Percy, but only a little. He didn't know Zeph or Archer, but he knew that she was well acquainted with them, and he made no effort to help them or soothe her fears until he'd stopped the curricle. Percy had taken her hand in both of his and pressed a kiss to her glove. He said he wanted only her safety, but as he spoke, all she could think about was the difference between his touch, and Archer's.

Lord Mansfield's grip was lighter, for one. He held her hand as if it were a delicate flower he was afraid to crush. Even in the warm sunshine, the heat of his skin didn't penetrate her gloves, and she'd suppressed a shiver as a chill slid down her back even though his eyes were earnest as he asked for her understanding and pressed another kiss to her hand.

"I will always protect you, darling."

As Percy spoke, she realized that she wanted to hear those words in a husky tone that warmed her insides and sent frissons of delicious heat through her body in a shocking and yet exciting way. The way Percy said them didn't do anything of the sort, but if Archer had spoken them, she would have burst into flames right there in Hyde Park.

Violet rolled onto her side and stared into the dying glow of the fire.

It's in the small touches, Archer had said the night he kissed her. *The way he looks at you.* That was how to know whether a man would treasure her.

Percy kept his touch proper at all times. When he'd helped her into the carriage or reached for her hand trying to explain his actions, he hadn't rubbed his thumb over the back of her hand or swiped a curl off her cheek. He pressed a kiss to the back of her hand, but Lord Kensington had done so at the dinner party several nights past, and it had felt exactly the same. And when Percy looked at her, she wondered if he saw her, or just the wife he wanted. True, they didn't know one another well, but he hadn't asked after any of her pursuits or hobbies. Did he even want to know about her?

She was coming to realize that she didn't *want* to know him. Not when her thoughts were constantly filled with Archer.

She'd been so relieved when she spotted Archer and Zeph pushing through the crowd. Both men were dirty and disheveled, and a little blood had crusted the corner of Archer's mouth, but to her, he'd never looked better. Until he started yelling at her for accepting a carriage ride with Percy, who thankfully had left by that time.

Violet sat up in bed and tossed her pillow aside. Archer Bennett was the most frustrating man she'd ever met, which said a great deal when she had a brother like Gabriel. Every conversation they had left her either wanting to kiss him or yell at him and today had been an odd mix of both. She'd been so afraid for him and Zeph when she'd seen those men attack in the park, then awed by his fighting skills because she'd never seen anything of the sort. When they'd returned largely unharmed, she'd wanted to kiss him in relief, but when he'd yelled at her about Percy, she'd lost her temper and yelled back.

She covered her face with her hands and groaned. She'd *yelled* at him in Hyde Park on a Sunday, in the midst of a very crowded footpath where every elite member of society was sure to hear. Even now, the gossip mongers would be talking about the event. A lady of good breeding did not raise one's voice, especially not in public, and they most certainly didn't shout at a gentleman and call him a dunderhead.

He made her forget herself. Whether he was kissing her or yelling at her, she lost all sense of propriety around him.

She lowered her hands to her lap and twined her fingers together. Finding a suitor with him here would be next to impossible. No one would marry a lady prone to shouting matches in the park.

What was she to do now?

A small noise, like a moan, came from somewhere nearby. She held her breath and listened. Was that Archer in the room next door, or the house settling and letting out a low creak?

Violet slipped out of bed and pulled a light wrapper over her nightrail. She lifted the candlestick with its sputtering candle from her side table and left the room. The hall beyond her door was heavily shadowed, with only the light of the moon filtering in through the windows, washing the furnishings in silver. She tiptoed down the hall, thankful for the carpet to muffle her steps, and stopped at Archer's door, listening. She didn't hear any movement inside.

Violet pressed her lips together, debating with herself over what she'd planned. Ladies did not enter a single gentleman's room. If they were discovered, they would be ruined, even if nothing happened. But this was her house, and everyone was asleep. Unless she and Archer began to argue again—which was unfortunately a possibility that she had to consider—no one would know she'd been there. Dare she risk it?

She smiled to herself. Gabriel would forgive her, she was sure. She reached for the handle and turned it, relieved to find it unlocked, and pushed the door open. The dark orange glow of the burning coals barely illuminated the furnishings. She could just make out Archer's big body in the bed.

He gave a low moan and flipped onto his side, punching the pillow nearest his head.

Was he having a nightmare? Violet closed the door and then crossed to the bed. Archer lurched, tangled in the sheets, and flopped over onto his back with a deep groan.

The primal noise sent a shiver down her back and made her nipples bead beneath her silk nightdress. She crossed her arms over her chest, willing the reaction to subside.

He's having a nightmare, Vi. Now is not an appropriate time to feel attraction.

He moaned again and heat speared between her thighs. She bit back a groan and reached for Archer. The least she could do was wake him from the nightmare.

Archer rolled toward her. His face was drawn in an intense frown, the lines at the corners of his eyes deeply shadowed in the dying firelight.

She willed her fingers to stop trembling and touched his shoulder. He wasn't wearing a shirt and his skin was very warm. There were strange markings on his chest which she couldn't make out.

Then the world spun as she was yanked off her feet and rolled beneath him.

Violet yelped, then winced at how loud it sounded in the quietness of the house, but she didn't have time to consider it further as Archer rose above her, scowling with a ferocity she'd never seen. Then his hand wrapped around her throat and stole her breath.

"Archer," she said, pulling at his hand. He held her in place but didn't squeeze as she expected. "Archer, wake up."

He didn't move.

Violet slid one hand up his brawny arm and cupped his cheek. "Wake up, Archer," she said more forcefully.

He blinked once, twice. His brow furrowed and his thumb stroked over the hollow in her throat. "Violet?"

"Yes. It's all right now. You were dreaming."

"I'm still dreaming," he murmured, then lowered his head and kissed her.

Violet shivered in pleasure as he took her mouth again in a heated kiss. She remembered their kiss from the carriage and mimicked his movements. Heavens, she shouldn't be here in Archer's bed, but nothing short of Gabriel *and* Aunt Josephine dragging her out would make her leave. She arched against him, her body moving by instinct, and speared both hands in his hair to hold him closer.

Archer moaned and shifted his hips, settling between her thighs.

Violet gasped when the hard contact of his member pressed against her womanly parts. This was what Lily and Bellamy whispered about when they didn't think she could hear. This was what women wanted in their marriage beds, she was sure. As sure as she was that she couldn't have this kind of passion with Percy. Her body wanted Archer, and she was beginning to think her heart did too.

Archer trailed kisses along the line of her jaw to her ear. He nibbled her earlobe and sucked it into his mouth, then continued kissing lower. He rocked his hips, pressing his cock against her core. The friction felt so delicious that she arched against him for more. Her nipples had hardened and dragged against his chest when he moved, the silk shifting against the sensitive peaks, heightening the intense feelings.

She felt his hand slide up the outside of her thigh, dragging her nightrail and wrapper with it, until he shoved the material aside and put his warm palm on her bare skin.

"Archer," she whispered, body on fire with his touch. She didn't know what she meant to tell him, whether she wanted him to stop or continue until he could no longer deny what was between them.

He murmured something low and moved his hand until his fingers dipped between her thighs and slid through an embarrassing amount of wetness.

She caught his hand, suddenly unsure. "Archer, wait."

He drew still and blinked, then shook his head a little.

"I'm not... not sure..." Heat crept up her neck to her cheeks. She wasn't sure what she was doing. What she wanted. What she was even trying to say.

He sat back and alarm crossed his face. "Violet?" He scrambled off her so quickly that he nearly fell out of bed.

She grabbed his arm before he could flee. "Don't go." She might be unsure of herself in these matters, but she did *not* want him to leave. "Please."

"Shit, Violet. What the *hell* are you doing in my bed?" His wide chest was carved with muscles, narrowing down to a trim waist. Thin cotton drawers molded to his strong thighs and dark hair covered his calves.

Heavens, he was handsome. "You were having a nightmare. I

tried to wake you, but you pulled me down and then you kissed me."

He scrubbed a hand over his face, and she thought he paled, though it was hard to tell in the near darkness of the chamber.

"I… I touched you?" He struggled away from her.

Violet launched herself at him, holding him close. "No! No. You thought you were dreaming I think and… I liked the kiss. I didn't want it to stop."

He tried to pry her off him. "But you didn't consent to it."

She clung tighter and shook her head. "Would you have heard me if I'd shouted it? You were sleeping."

"Goddammit, Violet, that doesn't make it right. I—"

She pressed her mouth over his, cutting off his words. Before he could move, she pulled back. "There, now you did not give leave for my kiss. We are even."

He stared at her. Then he chuckled. "I never know what to expect from you." He traced a finger over her cheek and shifted her hold on him.

Violet realized that he had one leg off the bed, the other tucked under them, and that she was completely wrapped around him.

He lifted her and set her back against the pillows before he stretched out beside her. "Never try to wake me again. I could have hurt you," he said.

"You didn't try to harm me even when you had the chance. I think you are a protector at heart, Archer. Even when you aren't aware of your actions, you won't hurt me."

He blew out a breath. "I wish I had your confidence." He flopped onto his back and flung an arm over his eyes.

Violet sat up and looked down at his beautiful body. The markings she'd glimpsed earlier were drawings, she realized, one on each side of his chest. His stomach muscles were defined in a way she hadn't known they could be, and a slim line of dark hair arrowed down towards parts she very much wanted to see.

"Violet," he groaned.

She lifted her gaze and realized he'd been watching her as she examined him. "Will you tell me what your nightmare was about?"

"*No.*"

She narrowed her eyes, vowing to herself that she would get him to talk about the nightmare eventually. "What are these?" She traced a finger over the drawing of a frog.

He hissed and caught her finger.

"Did I hurt you?" She attempted to pull her hand back.

He tightened his hold enough to stop her struggle. "No, it doesn't hurt. Your touch is… stimulating."

Oh.

"Those are my tattoos. People have had them for thousands of years, so I'm sure some do in this time. This one is my bone frog."

He angled his body toward the dying firelight, and she could just make out a skeletal frog holding a trident. *Odd.*

"It is in honor of the brothers I lost in battle." He spoke the words softly.

Violet heard the rasp of pain in his voice and wanted to comfort him. She snuggled down beside him and traced a finger over the frog. "Lily and Bellamy said something terrible happened when you were injured. This symbolizes that?"

Archer nodded and turned his left arm to show her his "As does this."

She squinted, trying to read what appeared to be a list of seven… "Names?" A chill stole through her, along with the certainty of what those names meant. She wanted to ask who they were. Who they'd been to him. But his face had closed off.

Archer nodded and wrapped his arm around her, tugging her against his side. He drew a deep breath, then said, "The other is the SEAL trident."

She traced what looked like a bird with a three-pronged fork. "What does it say below?" It was too dark to make out the words, but she felt raised ridges at the edge. His scars?

"Death before dishonor."

Violet smiled at that. Three words that seemed to describe him perfectly. "I think you are one of the most honorable men I know."

"Do you include Mansfield in that?"

"No," she huffed. "I don't know him that well."

"Well enough to get in his carriage."

"At the behest of your sisters so that I could come to know him better. But I don't wish to talk about that."

"I warned you to stay away the fuck from him, and we *are* going to talk about that."

"I believe you said everything you needed to say when you yelled at me in Hyde Park." She thrilled a little that he didn't censor his language around her. "The gossips will talk about it for weeks. You've now made it even harder for me to find a suitable match."

"Good! You shouldn't be forced into a marriage you don't want. Especially to Mansfield."

Violet huffed in irritation, sensing he was about to take up their earlier argument.

"Something about that man isn't right. Maybe he's the one sending you these creepy notes—"

"They're not creepy. They're sweet gifts, and you don't know who they're from any more than I do." Would he never cease this talk of bad men out to get her? She was a grown woman, and she'd taken care of herself before. She would do so again.

"That is why you should be concerned! There are too many men all too happy to take advantage of innocent women. And Violet, you are *very* innocent. Mansfield could have—"

Violet growled, frustrated to her core with the man, and did the only thing she could think to stop his words. She cupped his face and kissed him.

CHAPTER TEN

ARCHER MOANED AS Violet moved her mouth over his, licking his lower lip and tangling their tongues together. Whatever argument he'd had vanished the moment she kissed him. He loved the way she tasted, like tea, and cinnamon. Her slim curves pressed against his side, and he could feel the warmth of her skin beneath the thin silk of her nightgown. His blood heated as he imagined taking the weight of her breasts in his hands and thumbing her nipples until they hardened. In seconds, his cock filled to an aching fullness he hadn't experienced in a very long time. Since before the attack on his team, but he didn't want to think about them now. Not when he had Violet in his bed.

She sucked his lower lip, then kissed his chin and gave him an impish grin. "Do be quiet, Mr. Bennett. I have no wish to argue."

It took him a moment to figure out what she was talking about. One kiss from Violet and he'd forgotten about Mansfield and the odd notes. Archer dropped his head back on the pillow and groaned. "You're maddening."

"It's my finest quality," she said with a clear note of pride in her voice.

Archer chuckled. "I bet your brother disagrees."

"Perhaps, but that is why I don't listen to his opinion on the matter."

"Of course you don't." He fingered a strand of her silky dark hair and tucked it behind her ear. It was the first time he'd seen it down instead of pinned up in curls. Her hair reached her waist and gave him dirty thoughts of wrapping it around his fist while he pumped into her from behind. "You shouldn't be here with me, Violet," he said, voice deep with lust.

"Should I have let you continue to thrash in your nightmare?"

"Yes."

"*Pish*. Don't be ridiculous." She waved away his answer as if irrelevant. "In any event, I had not intended to find myself in your bed, however now that I am here, I find it quite exhilarating." She traced his lower lip with her thumb. "Might I kiss you again?"

There were dozens of reasons why he shouldn't, not the least of which was that he would be leaving this time as soon as he was able, but his body had other ideas because he'd already pulled her down to lay on his chest, her lips a breath away.

She's far too young for you.

She's looking for a husband, not a lover.

She's innocent, for fuck's sake.

None of that mattered when he closed the scant distance between them and kissed her. Violet melted into his embrace, kissing him back with growing confidence in her skills. Archer lost himself in the pleasure he felt just from her lips and the slight weight of her body against his. Kissing hadn't felt this good since he'd been a teen figuring out what went where. He tangled his hands in her hair and deepened the kiss, stroking her tongue with his.

Violet pressed closer and gasped when her leg brushed against his hard cock. She broke the kiss, gaze darting down to the sheets at his waist. She nibbled her lip, glanced up at him, and then back down to the one-man tent he'd pitched under the linen.

The desire in her amber eyes, lit by the dim firelight, was killing him and overriding all his rational protests until the need to show her pleasure was all that remained. He captured her hand where it lay over his frog tattoo and slowly moved it down his body.

Her lips parted on a breath as she watched their hands move lower, over his stomach, to the edge of his drawers. Archer stopped there but he continued to let his hand rest lightly atop hers. Their gazes met and an emotion he couldn't name moved through him. It clenched his chest tight and made it hard to draw a breath.

Her eyes softened and she leaned into the hand cupping her head, her lips curving the tiniest bit.

Nothing had ever felt like this moment, like magic filled the air and time had stopped only for them. As if he moved too fast the spell would break, and his beautiful Violet would disappear, nothing more than a dream he couldn't grasp.

God, he wanted this. He wanted her kiss, her touch... just *her*. As much as he'd fought his feelings for her, they only increased with every interaction, and every one of her smiles that sent light straight to his battered heart.

Before he went further though, he had to know she was with him. "Do you want to touch me, Violet?"

"Yes," she whispered without hesitation, though her hand trembled beneath his.

Archer slid their hands lower until he felt the velvet heat of her skin on his shaft. A bolt of pleasure shot through him, and he shivered at the contact. He guided her fingers to wrap around his cock and showed her how to caress him.

A dark flush painted her cheeks pink and made her lips appear darker and fuller.

Archer kissed her while she explored his body. Her innocent touch excited him, making his body tremble and his heart pound with her every stroke. She was going to make him come and she'd only just started stroking him. He removed her hand from his cock and dragged in a deep breath.

"I don't want to stop," she whispered.

He was afraid that if he didn't, he would draw her into something she wasn't ready for. At the same time, it was hard to hold back his desire to show her pleasure.

"Please, Archer."

Damn. The "please" broke him. If he was going to do this, it had to be about her. He pressed his lips to her silky throat and breathed in her scent. He didn't want to fuck this up.

She sighed as his lips skimmed over her pulse, and he felt her tremble.

Archer guided her onto her back in the big bed and let himself linger on her beauty. Even clothed, she was one of the prettiest women he'd seen in a long time. He couldn't sleep with her, but he could give her this. He could show her how her body responded to pleasure and watching her come apart in his arms would be enough. It was all he could have and was far more than he deserved.

He reached down to stroke his hand up her calf, reveling in her warm, satiny skin, and then trailed his fingers beneath her nightgown to her thigh. She shifted closer and pressed a kiss to his lips.

They kissed, long and slow, while he explored her hip and the curve of her backside. The more he touched her, the more she opened for him, unconsciously trying to guide his hand where she needed it.

He felt her hands drop to her waist and fumble with something. Breaking the kiss, he saw that she was tugging at the tie of her robe.

"Want that off?" he asked against her lips.

She nodded and he slipped it off her shoulders, revealing creamy skin and a white silk nightgown that barely covered her breasts. Violet crossed her arms over her breasts for a moment, then slowly lowered them and moved her hands to his chest.

Archer skimmed his fingers over her cheek and down her neck to trace the neckline of her nightgown, then followed them with his mouth. She moaned when he flicked his tongue in the hollow of her throat and arched her back, pushing her breasts closer to his hand. He cupped one breast and rubbed the silk of her gown against her hardening nipple with his thumb.

Violet gasped and pressed her breast closer.

Taking the invitation, he dipped his head and scraped his teeth gently over the silk-covered peak, and sucked it into his mouth. He teased her nipple, then switched to the other, wishing he had his mouth on her skin. But he knew that the moment he removed her nightgown, whatever sanity he had left would be gone. It had been too long since he'd had sex and he wanted her too badly. One word of encouragement from a naked Violet and his good intentions would vanish.

Death before dishonor. Archer considered himself a man of honor but tempted by a siren, he wasn't sure he would have the strength to walk away. He kissed his way back to her lips, savoring the feeling, and caressed her thighs, pushing the material higher until it reached her hips. Shadows clung to the area between her legs, hiding her from his view. He stroked his thumb low on her belly. "More?"

"Yes," she whispered, her eyes shining bright.

Archer dipped his fingers between her thighs, tracing the soft slit, wet with her excitement.

Violet's eyes flared wide in surprise, and before he could remove his hand or ask if she was all right, she arched her back and rubbed herself against his hand, breathing out an undeniable sigh of pleasure.

Archer stroked her folds, watching every expression that crossed her face, making certain that she wanted his touch. She writhed and gasped, then grabbed his hand and pushed it closer.

"M-more," she said raggedly.

He smiled a little and paused his movements.

Violet whimpered and rocked against his hand.

"Let me kiss you, Violet." She looked adorably confused until he stroked between her folds. "Here."

Her eyes widened. "There?"

He chuckled. "Right there. I promise, it will feel good."

She nodded.

"Yes?" he prompted.

"Yes. Kiss me everywhere, Archer. Don't stop."

He kissed her lips, then her cheek, and the spot beneath her ear, then moved lower, settling between her thighs. Her scent was thicker here, headier. He dipped his head and placed a kiss at the top of her mound, then another lower.

Violet put her hands in his hair and gripped the strands.

He waited to see if she meant to push him away. When she didn't, he flicked his tongue over her folds and barely held back his moan of desire. His aching cock rubbed against the sheet, adding a friction that had him on edge while her flavor overwhelmed his senses.

She arched against him, asking without words for more.

Even so, he checked to make certain she was with him. In answer, she tugged his head closer to her body.

Archer dragged his tongue slowly through her folds to flick at her nub. He sucked the bud into his mouth until she panted, reading her every move. He kissed and licked her, sucking until she bucked against his mouth for more.

"I don't... what... I feel..." Violet's breath hitched.

"Let go, sweetheart. Feel that coiling in your body and let it release," he said. "You will feel amazing, I promise."

She nodded, though he wasn't sure she knew she did so, and clenched her thighs around him.

"That's right. Let go." He sucked her nub into his mouth and felt her body go taut.

Violet gasped as she found her release, eyes going wide. A tiny cry of pleasure escaped her lips, and she slapped her hand over her mouth.

Archer laughed softly. His breath fanned over her wet heat, making her arch against him. He placed another kiss on her bud, then licked her folds. Her body clenched on a second orgasm, and he moaned at her taste.

She pushed weakly against his head.

Archer looked up to find her eyes closed, her lips puffy from where she'd bitten them to hold back her moans. He kissed her hip, then her thigh, as he rose to his knees and leaned forward to cup her cheek. "Are you okay?"

She nodded, a soft smile touching her mouth when she met his gaze.

The look she gave him pierced the armor around his heart, and he felt it like a gunshot—hot, intense, and surprising. Before he could recover, she kissed him, and cemented her place in his heart.

At that moment, Archer knew that no matter what the future held, Violet would always have a special place in his memories. She'd made him feel when he thought he never would again, and that both thrilled and terrified him.

He lay beside her and pulled her into his arms, draping her over his chest. He'd only meant to give her pleasure, he hadn't expected that in doing so, he'd be changed irrevocably.

Shit. He was in trouble.

VIOLET DABBED A little more rice powder over the red mark beneath her ear where Archer's whiskers had abraded her skin most deliciously last night. She reveled in the mark, because it meant that the events of last night had been real, and she'd studied it in the mirror, right up until she received the summons from Gabriel to meet him in his study. Now she was desperately trying to lighten it and hoped her very observant brother didn't notice.

Archer made her body feel things she hadn't known were possible. The rush of pleasure she'd felt with his mouth between her legs made heat curl in her stomach every time she thought about it. She wanted to find him and make him do it again just so she could re-experience those wonderful feelings. No wonder Lily and Bellamy sometimes looked dreamy in the morning. How could she hide that from Gabriel when she felt as if she floated above the floor?

She checked the mark in the mirror and gave up on the rice powder. If her brother noticed, she would simply say that she scratched herself there during the night. Still, she tugged a curl down a little more, hoping it would help hide the mark, and left to find her brother.

Gabriel sat behind the large mahogany desk in his study, illuminated by a strong shaft of sunlight coming in through the mullioned windows. He looked happier than she'd seen him in a long time, with fine lines beginning to show at the corner of his eyes from laughing, and in a relaxed pose instead of one where his shoulders nearly bunched around his ears. She had Lily to thank for his good humor. Lily's appearance in their lives had changed everything, but most especially her brother. Even Violet's shouting matches with him were much improved.

"How fine you look this morn, brother," she said as she entered. He always looked impeccable in his tailcoat, even when at home, but the deep green he wore today matched the color of his eyes.

"Flattery before breakfast?" he asked, not looking up from his ledger. "What have you done now?"

"Can I not compliment you without rousing your suspicions?"

He snorted and set his pen aside, then motioned for her to sit. "You may try, but since your penchant for trouble is only exceeded by Zeph's, you must admit that my suspicion is warranted." They grinned at each other.

She loved her brother dearly, and a great part of that love was due to their banter. The rest was because he'd raised her after their father died and their mother decided to grieve with only her laudanum bottles for company. Violet sat in one of the chairs opposite him. "You sent for me?"

Gabriel pushed the ledger aside and leaned his arms on the desk. "Lily tells me that your carriage ride with Lord Mansfield went well. Are you finding him to your liking?"

She'd forgotten all about the ride with Percy after spending a few forbidden hours with Archer last night. How could she think of any other man after kisses like that? But Gabriel expected a response, so she said, "Lord Mansfield is a fine gentleman."

Gabriel quirked an eyebrow at her. She huffed. How did he always know when she attempted to lie or evade an answer? "The carriage ride was lovely until we came upon Zeph and Archer and saw those terrible men attack them. Then Lord Mansfield urged his horses on like he was racing on Rotten Row and refused to turn back to offer them help."

"I see."

"And before that, he said I was too familiar in calling them by their first names, and that I should stop doing so immediately."

Gabriel chuckled. "Am I to assume that he is now acquainted with your more spirited side?"

She smoothed out a fold in the skirt of her morning dress and looked for any others. "I may have attempted to turn the carriage back myself by fighting him for the reins."

He sighed heavily. "Violet."

"I couldn't allow them to be attacked and not try to get help for them."

"*Violet.*"

Honestly, did Gabriel expect her to be decorative and mostly useless? She raised her chin a notch. "Did you honestly raise me to turn away from people in need, especially when they are our friends? You didn't, so I don't see what is so terrible about—"

"Violet!" Gabriel growled.

She pressed her lips together. When he growled at her, she'd usually gone a step too far in her explanations.

"Zeph and Archer can take care of themselves, as you clearly saw when neither man was injured."

She leaned forward in her chair, thrilling at the memory. "You should have seen the way Archer fought! Do you know he took on several men by himself?"

"Be that as it may, they did not need the sister of an earl pushing her would-be suitor out of the carriage and rushing to their rescue."

"I did no such thing!"

"But you considered it when you fought Mansfield for the reins."

How in heavens did he know that? "Have you developed an ability to read minds? Do you know what I'm thinking now?" She pictured adding salt to his coffee as she'd done once as a child.

"No, and I'm afraid to ask. Despite your rather eventful carriage ride, and your argument with Archer after, Mansfield has sent word that he wishes to meet with me in regard to your future. I think he wishes to offer for you."

Violet sat back in her chair, stunned. "He still wishes to court me?"

"I believe he does. Perhaps he finds your spirit as charming as I do," Gabriel said.

Was that possible? Even though he refused to turn the carriage around, he'd promised to protect her and care for her. Did he truly enjoy her company, or did he simply want an earl's sister for a wife?

"He meets all of the qualifications on your list," he reminded her.

"Yes, he does." He should have been a perfect match, but Violet didn't feel anything for him even close to what she felt for Archer.

What was she to do? Archer hadn't said he was staying. Even when he'd kissed her so sweetly goodnight, there'd been no promise for more.

He still plans to leave.

"You don't want Mansfield," Gabriel said.

"I should," she whispered. "He's handsome, he can provide for me and any children we might have, and he lives near our house in the countryside so I could visit often." She twined her fingers together in her lap. "He still wants to court me after yesterday and he might be the last man of quality to show an interest once the gossips relate my actions in the park."

Her brother rose and rounded the desk to take her hands in his. "Violet, the one thing you've said often is that you want a marriage of love, like I have with Lily. Do you think you could come to love him?"

No. The answer was in her heart before she even asked it the question. She shook her head. "No, I—" *think I love someone else.* Not that she could voice that.

"Then we shall keep looking. I want you to be happy, Vi. If that takes a month or years, it will always be true."

"Will you love me when I've turned into Aunt Josephine?"

Gabriel released her hands and leaned back against his desk. He looked uncertain. "Ah, well… I love Aunt Josephine. However, I do not think I can love *two* of them. If it is your intention to turn into a woman like her, then you will have to fight her for the position in my heart. I do hope you understand."

Violet gasped and swatted him on the arm. "Gabriel Jacob Hawthorne, you are a rotten brother!"

He laughed and pulled her into a hug. "And you, Vi, are a wonderful sister. You will find the love you desire. As everyone who knows you is aware, it is impossible not to love you."

Her eyes misted and her throat turned thick. "I hope you're right."

"Of course I'm right. I'm your older brother. But if you should have a doubt, then all you must do is look in the mirror. The Violet I know and love will always go after what she wants." He put his hands on her shoulders and set her back a step, holding her gaze. "And *who* she wants."

She swallowed. Did he know she wanted Archer? Without thinking, she touched the mark on her neck.

Gabriel's eyes followed the movement and his eyebrows lowered.

Violet gave him a kiss on the cheek and fled before he could ask about it. She blew him a kiss when she reached the door. "Thank you, Gabriel. I just remembered that I promised to talk to

Bellamy about the ball at Almack's."

He stared at the ceiling as if praying for patience. "I didn't want to know anyway," he muttered.

Biting back a smile, she slipped from the room and went downstairs. The hall was empty, but she could hear Bellamy and Lily in the drawing room. Violet turned toward their voices, but a flash of red caught her eye. On the table was another single rose and beside it, a small, wrapped package bearing her name. Violet slowed and looked for Henry or a servant, wondering if anyone saw who sent it. No one seemed to be about.

She took the card from the package, noting that it was blank save for her name, and set it beside the rose. Then she untied the twine and unwrapped a book of poems. A blue velvet bookmark was placed inside, and when she opened to the page, she found a poem about a man comparing his love to the finest rose.

A shiver went down her spine as she looked back at the blood-red rose lying on the table. Who'd sent these gifts, and why? Though she'd never thought them sinister, something about the poem made her uncomfortable.

Don't be a ninny, Vi. Archer's warnings are getting to you. What harm can come from a book? People read them all the time.

She would put it with the other books of poetry in the drawing room. Taking it to her bedroom seemed too intimate. A silly notion, considering it was just a book, but one she couldn't dismiss.

Violet paused in the doorway to the drawing room and spotted Lily and Bellamy sitting near the window sharing a pot of tea. Lily smiled at her sister as they spoke, warming Violet's heart. The two had spent a great deal of time together since Bellamy had arrived several weeks prior, and their relationship improved daily. For the first time, Violet knew what it was like to have sisters instead of only a brother who delighted in ordering her about, and the difference was wonderful. Thank heavens for Christian's genius with his automatons. If it weren't for him, none of the siblings would have come to their time.

Her thoughts returned to Archer, as they so often did, and she wondered what he was doing at this moment. Heat curled in her belly when she remembered their kisses last night and the way he'd touched her body. She'd never expected to end up beneath him in bed, but with his heavy weight pressing her into the mattress, their bodies lined up so that she could feel his thick member between her thighs… she hadn't felt crushed but surrounded by him. As if he used his body to block out the rest of the world and only the two of them remained, secreted away together. However did Lily and Gabriel leave their room if that was how it felt to be abed with a lover?

"Eavesdropping, sweetheart?" a husky voice whispered in her ear, sending delicious shivers down her spine. *Archer*. She felt the warmth of his chest against her back, and her nipples beaded beneath her stays and thin muslin gown.

Violet nearly moaned when his lips grazed the sensitive skin at the back of her neck and his warm palm slid down her spine in a gentle caress. She swayed back against him, *needing* to feel him against her, even as she looked to see if Bellamy and Lily had spotted them in the doorway. Fortunately, whatever they discussed was riveting enough to keep their attention.

She leaned back against his shoulder and tilted her head towards his.

One corner of his mouth rose in a half smile, tugging at the edge of a scar.

Violet spun to face him. "You shaved!"

Archer ran his hand over his cheek and jaw, not meeting her gaze. "Yeah."

She sensed that he was embarrassed, and as his hand swept over his skin, she had a better view of the scars there. They angled from the corner of his jaw to his ear, more prominent without his short beard. Violet drew his hand away, then cupped his cheek. She swept her thumb over the damaged skin, then leaned up to kiss the spot. If possible, she found him even more handsome. The scars testified to his strength.

"Why?" she whispered. Why had he shaved if he was uncomfortable?

Archer ran the tip of his fingers down her neck, tracing the mark he'd left there. "I noticed last night that my beard scratched this soft, delicate skin. I hate the thought of marring such beauty. Plus, I don't want your brother to kick my ass."

She leaned into his touch, stirred by his words. Gabriel was strong and often went to the boxing saloon, which meant that most men of their acquaintance had no desire to cross him. After seeing Archer fight in Hyde Park, she knew he was far more formidable than her brother, so he truly had nothing to fear in that regard, which meant he was more concerned about her. He'd rather people see the scars he'd tried so hard to hide than mark her skin. Her heart melted at the realization.

"I borrowed Aunt Josephine's rice powder to try to cover it," she said, fighting to speak over the lump in her throat.

His eyebrows rose. "Did she know what you needed it for?"

"I may have waited until she left to do some shopping. But don't fret; she has plenty. Aunt Josephine would rather spend a week in debtor's prison than be seen without her rice powder."

Archer chuckled. He trailed his fingers over her shoulder and down her arm, watching his progress.

She realized that she still held the book of poems the moment he spotted it and her stomach flipped, knowing their sweet moment was over. She tried to hide it behind her back, but it was too late.

He plucked the book out of her grasp. "What is this?"

Violet grabbed it back. "It's a book of poetry that I'm putting in the drawing room."

Archer took the book back and flipped it to the marked page before she could wrestle it away. He scanned the poem, but Violet tugged it out of his hands again.

He scowled. "Did this come with the rose?" He pointed to the side table several feet away in the hall. "I saw the card with your name and the paper and twine from a parcel."

Violet glared back at him. Any moment, he would lecture her about the dangers of receiving unknown gifts. He was just like Gabriel—insufferable. She hugged the book to her chest, spun, and stomped into the drawing room. She heard his heavy footsteps behind her. "It is not your concern, *Mr. Bennett.*"

He wrapped his hand around her arm and tugged her to a stop. "Dammit, Violet. No man of honor hides from the woman he wants. If he wants her, he goes after her."

"Don't they?" she argued, pointedly looking him over. He'd done nothing but hide his feelings from her since the moment they met, yet he was one of the most honorable men she knew.

Archer put his hands on his hips and growled in frustration. "I have my reasons."

"Maybe whoever sends these gifts does as well."

"Or maybe he wants to gain your trust, and then he'll harm you."

"Don't be ridiculous. No one is lying in wait in the bushes waiting to leap out at me after sending me flowers and poetry!" Oh, this wretched man. One moment she wanted nothing more than to kiss him and in the next, she wanted to bash the book over his head.

He stepped closer, leaning in until she could smell the shaving soap on his skin. "If you won't heed my warnings, then I'm not leaving your side. The moment you leave this house until the minute you return, you're mine."

A flood of warmth rushed through her and settled between her thighs at his murmured words. *You're mine.* She wanted to be his in every way. Would he ever feel the same?

His protectiveness was both annoying and endearing, and as with everything else about this man, it tangled her emotions in her chest. Violet lifted her chin and gave him a teasing smile. "Then I shall be certain to go shopping for all manner of stockings, and stays, and... and chemises the next time I leave." No man wanted to spend hours with a lady shopping for underclothes.

Archer's green eyes glittered and his gaze dropped to her lips. "Is that supposed to scare me off?" he asked in a soft, seductive voice.

Her heart began to pound, and her stomach clenched. She did not want to kiss the overbearing man. Not when he leaned so close and smelled so good. And especially not when his lips looked as inviting as they did. Or even when the husky tone of his voice reminded her of his *other* kisses last night.

Violet grasped for the only other argument she could think of. "Then you best learn to dance because I intend to go to the ball at Almack's on Wednesday, and I will dance with anyone who asks."

"Then I better ask now," he said and tugged her forward until she hit his chest. Before she could protest, he leaned down and kissed her.

The moment their lips met, all thoughts left Violet's mind. There was only the firm press of his mouth and the hot sweep of his tongue against hers. She was dimly aware of him taking the book of poetry from her and the thud of it hitting the floor, before he wrapped his arms around her and held her closer.

She felt enveloped by his strength, protected, and even cherished when he cupped her neck and held her to him while they kissed.

A light cough sounded nearby, and then Lily said in a wry tone, "Should we step out and give you both some privacy? This argument looks as if it might last quite a while."

Heat flooded Violet's cheeks and she broke the kiss. *Oh heavens.* She'd forgotten all about Lily and Bellamy, and the two had just watched her and Archer passionately kiss. Perhaps Archer had been right to worry about her brother after all. Gabriel would surely hear of this.

CHAPTER ELEVEN

V IOLET STRUGGLED OUT of his arms and flushed scarlet in embarrassment, though Archer wasn't ready to let her go. He wasn't embarrassed about kissing her, but he was concerned about her reputation, since that mattered in this time.

"I… he was…" Violet sputtered and clapped a hand over the mark on her neck, drawing attention to it rather than hiding it. But her verbal search for a plausible explanation about why he'd just kissed the hell out of her was dismissed when Bellamy gave a soft gasp.

"Oh, Archer," she whispered and wrapped him in a fierce hug.

Lily covered her mouth, staring at his left cheek where the scars were now quite visible. "You shaved."

Bellamy released him and swiped away the tears from her cheeks. She sniffed and cleared her throat. "We knew you'd been hurt, but the military didn't tell us how badly. What happened to you?"

He flinched when she tried to touch the scars and her face fell. Dammit, he hadn't meant to hurt her feelings, but he didn't want to talk about his scars or the injuries. He didn't want to tell them about lying in a hospital bed for weeks, wishing he'd been the one to die on the road that day.

What did you expect when you shaved this morning, Bennett? Now everyone can see your ugly mug. Of course, they were going to make an issue out of it.

He gently set Bellamy away and stepped back, needing a little distance between them. "I can't tell you. It's classified."

She sputtered, then threw her hands up. "Dammit, Archer. We're in 1814. Who the hell are we going to tell?"

"It's not about who you tell. It's about who *I* tell. I gave my word and I'm not going to break it just because it's safe to do so here." Maybe that was a cop-out to avoid telling her, but right now he didn't give a fuck. He wasn't going to examine it too closely.

Bellamy narrowed her eyes.

Archer could practically hear her teeth clench. He crossed his arms over his chest, waiting for the storm that was Bellamy's temper.

Lily stepped up beside Bellamy and touched her shoulder. "We just want you to be okay, Archer," she said, her voice soft. "Maybe asking you to tell us isn't wise. I don't want you to relive painful memories to satisfy our curiosity."

Bellamy crossed her arms and looked away. It wasn't lost on him that she mimicked his pose.

"We worried," she ground out.

"I know. I'm sorry." There was nothing he could say that would help. If he told them what they wanted to know, they'd worry more, not less. They'd look at him differently. Bells and Lily were the only family he had left. He couldn't bear to see condemnation, disgust, or worse, *pity* when they looked at him. It was time to change the subject. "Violet intends to show me how to dance."

Bellamy sighed. "Fine. But we will talk about this again, Archer. I'll go get Christian and see if Gabriel is available for dance lessons." She marched out of the room, fists clenched.

"I should grow the beard back," he muttered, staring after Bellamy. What the hell had he been thinking? He shouldn't be kissing Violet, and then he wouldn't need to worry about beard burn or people asking uncomfortable questions about his scars.

"No, Archer. You're still as handsome as ever," Lily said. "It was just a shock. I suppose we weren't really ready to see your scars, especially since we don't know what you went through."

He rubbed a hand over his jaw. Apparently, the beard had done a better job at disguising it than he thought.

Lily exchanged a look with Violet, who'd been silent throughout the exchange. When she met his eyes again, he saw determination mixed with concern. "Will you tell us what—"

"No." Even if the mission wasn't classified, he couldn't talk about it. Not with them. Hell, he'd barely talked to the Navy therapist about any of it.

"Archer," Lily implored. "We want to help you. We want to share your burdens."

He shook his head. "Not this time. Besides, I'm the older brother. I'm supposed to take care of you and Bells. Not the other way around."

She wrinkled her nose at him.

Archer flicked her nose with his fingertip.

Lily smiled then and wrapped her arms around him. "I've missed you so much, Arch."

"Missed you too, Lils."

"Losing mom and dad doesn't mean that we will lose everyone else," she whispered in his ear. "Neither does time travel, apparently."

Archer heard the smile in her voice, and it softened the edge of anger and frustration he felt. "Not the way you do it."

She chuckled and then sobered. "We deserve every happiness. Mom and Dad would want us to be happy, no matter where—or when—we are."

Maybe they would. He couldn't think about them. Like his team and Amanda, the guilt he carried over their passing weighed too heavily, pressing down on his chest until he couldn't breathe. He cleared his throat and released his sister. From the corner of his eye, he saw Violet putting that damn book of poetry on the bookshelf to give them a moment to themselves.

"I'll go find Gabriel and pull him away from his estate books. That should give you two a few minutes to finish your uh... argument."

He snorted and nodded his thanks. Once she'd left, he turned to Violet. "Hiding it with the rest of the books?"

"No. I'm putting a book where it belongs. On the bookshelf. Surely you don't expect me to carry it around everywhere?"

"Depends on how enamored you are with this admirer."

She gave him a withering look. "How can I be enamored of someone that I've never met?"

He wandered closer. "You probably *have* met him. Otherwise, how would he know you?"

"It may come as a surprise to you that I *am* known in Society. As the sister of an earl, I've come to know a great deal of influential people and their families. I'm not a wallflower."

"Violet, no one who's met you would confuse you with a wallflower. A tempest perhaps, but not a wallflower."

"A tempest," she sputtered, shoving the book on the shelf and turning on her heel to face him. She clamped her hands on her hips and glared at him. "What do you mean by that?"

God, he loved riling her. She was beautiful anytime but fired up, she was stunning. Her amber eyes sparked a deeper gold and her plump lips pursed, begging for a kiss. "A tempest because you whirl into a room and leave nothing and no one untouched before you leave."

Her dark brows drew together. "Is that a dreadful attempt at a compliment?"

He laughed. "Maybe. Would you rather a more straightforward attempt?"

"Anything other than comparing me to a destructive whirlwind." Violet closed the distance as she spoke. Her breath came faster, and she licked her lips. "I am quite graceful and good-natured."

"As well as modest." The sheen of moisture on those plump

lips called to him. Arousal thrummed inside of him, rushing blood to his groin. He remembered the feel of her under him last night, the scent of her skin, and the way she tasted.

"And it is quite fortunate for you that I am all of those things, or I might be inclined to—"

Archer cupped her face and covered her lips with his. He angled his head and deepened the kiss, stroking his tongue with hers. God, he'd never enjoyed kissing a woman as much as he did Violet. She softened in his arms, wrapping her arms around his neck, and pulling him closer. They kissed until he heard the thump of boots on the stairs in the hall.

He reluctantly broke the kiss and pressed his forehead to hers, panting against her lips. "I could travel through centuries and never find another like you, Violet Hawthorne. You have the spirit of a warrior and the beauty of a goddess. How can a man not be enchanted by you?"

Her lips parted and pink tinged her cheeks.

He stroked his thumb over her lower lip and then stepped back to a respectable distance. But he couldn't look away.

Violet smiled and something passed between them. It was more than affection or longing, because it burned bright in the pit of his stomach and rose until it threatened to compress his chest. Leaving her to go back to his time was going to be hard.

As his sisters returned with their men, Archer shut the feelings down. He couldn't stay here and even if he did, he wasn't the man for Violet. But he could keep her safe. He'd learn how to dance so he could stick close to her while at the ball, and he'd talk to Gabriel and Christian about locating Carter once more. No matter the warm feelings Violet brought out in him, they couldn't be together. There were a dozen good reasons. But at that moment, he struggled to remember any of them.

"He didn't speak to me at all after supper last evening, Patience. When the gentlemen joined us in the drawing room later, Gabriel said he'd retired for the evening." Violet blinked against the sun's glare as she and her friend stepped out of the chemist's shop. Though the sun was high in the sky, and it was already June, the air still held the chill of early spring. She drew her shawl tighter around her and tucked the liniment bottle into her reticule.

Patience adjusted her shawl over her rose sarsenet gown and tutted at her. "Did you not just finish telling me that you spent the afternoon teaching him to dance?"

"Indeed. Why?"

Patience linked her arm through Violet's as they made their way past a haberdasher with a window display of the newest fashion in trimmings. "Dancing can be quite vigorous. I imagine that his injury pained him. Isn't that why we went to the chemist this morning for the liniment?"

Was that why he avoided her? Because he was in pain? She felt foolish for not considering that, for being more concerned with whether he spoke to her instead of the discomfort he might feel from their dance lessons. After his kisses yesterday, and the smoldering way he'd touched her the night prior, his absence after dinner had left her unsure of herself and how he might feel about her. Feelings that were not at all comfortable and left her unsettled. She'd slept fitfully, wondering if he had decided against seeing her more.

"When Noah and I were courting, he injured his ankle in a fall from a horse. It was nothing serious, but he refused to see me for three days because he was afraid of appearing... weak, I suppose. Although the word doesn't seem quite right."

"He didn't want you to see him as anything other than strong and capable?" Violet asked.

Patience nodded. "If your Archer is anything like Noah, then I imagine that he would have wanted to retire to his bedchamber for rest instead of having you see him in such a state."

Archer was like a warrior from centuries past. He valued

strength and skill with weapons, and she knew that his injury pained him more than he wanted to let on. Although he'd improved considerably in the fortnight that he'd been there, he still limped, and his scowl was fierce when his leg hurt.

"I've been a ninny," she said.

"Oh, indeed," Patience agreed, a little too eagerly for Violet's liking. "Though I expect little else when you talk about Archer."

She gasped and elbowed her friend in the ribs. "Wretch!"

Patience laughed and bumped her shoulder against Violet's. "If you are truly concerned, then take your liniment to him and offer to apply it to the ache in his leg."

Her cheeks flamed at the very suggestion. "That would be most improper."

"Violet Hawthorne, worried about being improper?" Patience stopped and peered closer at her. "Are you ill? Should I send for the doctor?" She pressed the back of her hand to Violet's forehead.

Violet swatted her off. "I'm not ill. Do you… do you think I dare?" The thought of Archer removing his trousers, displaying the thick, muscular legs she'd admired in the close-fitting confinements of his clothes, made her heart thump hard in her breast. Would she finally be able to see his handsome form and the tattoos in better detail, revealed to her in the light of day? She pictured smoothing the oil over his naked skin and clenched her thighs against the sudden thrum of desire.

"In all the time that I've known you, you've never once questioned an action you wanted to take, no matter how improper or wild. Why are you concerned now?" Her friend passed no judgment, instead looking at her curiously as they continued to walk past the busy shops.

Why did she hesitate? Patience was right; she wouldn't normally. But this was Archer. What if she did something he considered outlandish and thought she was mad—or worse, childish? She didn't have the same sweet, gracious nature that Lily did, and she wasn't elegant and refined like Bellamy. What if he wanted a woman more like them? "I'm afraid that if I act as I normally do, that he will leave. I've often been accused of being unrestrained. What if he doesn't like that in a woman?"

"Then he is not the right suitor for you. Vi, if you are to marry, wouldn't you rather marry a man who loves you for the woman that you are instead of the woman he thinks you should be? Consider how unhappy you would be playing the perfect, meek wife that society expects. You're far too impetuous, and that is one of many of your wonderful qualities."

Patience was right. She couldn't hold herself back for long. If she refused to do it when Gabriel wanted her to impress a suitor, why should she try to do it for Archer? "Whatever would I do without you?"

"Shop alone, I imagine." Patience grinned. "And have many boring conversations with Aunt Josephine who would no doubt be your chaperone on any outings."

She groaned at the thought.

"Besides, from what you've said, I think Archer fancies you. Any man might want to kiss a woman or protect her. A man who wishes to do both is one who carries affection for her."

"I do hope you're right. I'll take the liniment to him when I get home and make the offer." Her stomach fluttered in anticipation.

"You must tell me what happens! I want to know every detail. Especially if he kisses you again, the way you said he did in front of his sisters." Patience hummed. "I think I should return home and see if Noah is available for some kisses."

Violet smiled, finally understanding why Patience was so eager to see her husband. If Violet were married to Archer, she would be eager to return home for kisses too.

They walked past another few shops, admiring the goods in the windows, until Patience stopped and looked across the street. Lines of carriages and carts bumped along the dirt road, while men on horseback wove in between them. Just beyond, several carriages were parked in front of the shops.

"Isn't that Lord Musgrave's carriage? I recognize the crest."

Was it? Violet swallowed, remembering the last time she'd seen him at Gabriel's house party last autumn. He'd been perfectly charming up until the night of the masquerade ball. In truth, she regretted overreacting when he'd tried to kiss her. She should have excused herself and slipped away, not slapped him, elbowed him, *and* stomped on his foot. The thought mortified her. The poor man had left abused and scandalized. Just one more time when her impulsive nature led to an unwise decision. She really must try to think before acting. "Is it his carriage?" she asked, grimacing at the thready note in her voice. Could she duck into the nearest shop as if she were suddenly in need of new slippers?

Patience gave her an odd look. "Yes. Have you seen him at any of the parties this Season?"

She shook her head. "I think he is avoiding me and Gabriel. No doubt he's upset about having his nose broken by my brother and being turned out in the middle of the night."

"Hm."

Normally, when Patience said *"Hm,"* it was because she wanted to say something but hadn't quite decided how to broach the subject. Violet would then badger her until she said whatever it was. Right now, she didn't want to know. She started walking again. Ahead, a gentleman exited a shop. He swung his walking stick up onto his shoulder without care, nearly whacking the poor fellow behind him. It reminded her that Archer had lost his cane in the melee at Hyde Park. "Let's make one last stop before returning home. I have an idea for a gift for Archer."

Patience nodded and followed, a speculative gleam in her eyes.

An hour later, they returned to Gabriel's townhouse in Mayfair, where she said goodbye to Patience with a promise to see her the following evening at Almack's. Henry met her at the door to take her hat and shawl.

"Is Mr. Bennett back from his outing?" She'd heard Gabriel

say at breakfast that Archer and Zeph were going to search for the gentleman they'd met in Hyde Park who might know something about the mysterious crystal that had been in the time travel clock. A part of her hoped they wouldn't find him so that Archer could stay.

"He has just returned, my lady. I believe he retired to his room. Shall I...?" He reached for the gift she'd purchased for Archer.

"No, thank you. Are my brother and Lily in?"

"The Earl and Countess have gone calling, and Miss Bennett is with Lord Huntington." Henry's face colored, and Violet bit back a smile. No doubt Bellamy would distract Christian for a few hours. If she were going to approach Archer with the liniment, now was probably the best time.

Gathering her courage, she climbed the stairs and stopped before Archer's door. The air in the corridor felt cool to her heated cheeks and she shifted from foot to foot. What if he didn't want to see her? What if she tried to apply the liniment but he found her clumsy and inexperienced, and dismissed her? With how often he'd put distance between them, she wasn't sure of his reaction to any advances she might make.

Violet looked down at her gift and his words from yesterday came back to her.

How can a man not be enchanted by you?

His words had made her feel beautiful and he'd kissed her as passionately as Gabriel kissed Lily. That had to mean he felt affection for her as she did for him, and she wanted to care for him in any way she could. The last bit of hesitation fell away as she knocked on his chamber door.

A moment later, his husky voice called for her to enter.

Violet found him sitting in a chair before the fire, with his left leg propped up on a stool. She closed the door and set her gift aside, then crossed to him.

"Violet?"

Heavens, he was so handsome with a lock of dark hair on his

forehead and eyes as green as a forest looking at her in surprise. A bit of hair had grown back on his jaw, but not enough to hide the scars, or the fine form of his features. He'd removed his coat, waistcoat, and cravat, leaving him in just his linen shirt that gaped open to reveal the hard planes of his chest. She spotted a few dark hairs there, and wondered how they would feel. She hadn't been able to see or explore his body as she wanted to when he'd awakened from his nightmare. He'd been intent on her pleasure while denying her the opportunity to give in kind. Today she would. Starting with his leg.

She opened her reticule and removed the small bottle of liniment she'd purchased at the chemist. "I came to see how you were. I thought perhaps you were in pain from the dance lessons."

He grunted and looked at the fire. "The willow tea helps, but when I exercise the muscles, the pain is more intense. I can handle it though."

"I brought something else to try. It's a mugwort liniment that the chemist said is particularly good for pain in the legs."

One of his dark eyebrows lifted. "Mug wart? That sounds… unappetizing."

Violet stifled a laugh. "You don't drink it. It's an oil that's applied to the area that hurts." She handed him the brown glass bottle.

He frowned at it, then removed the stopper and took a sniff. His face scrunched and he quickly sealed it and handed it back. "That smells like a moldy orange."

"All the more reason not to drink it."

He chuckled, then his eyes softened. "Thank you, Violet. From the moment I arrived, you've tried to help with my injury when even my sisters want to avoid it."

She moved closer and set her reticule on the small table beside his chair. "I hate the thought of you in pain," she said.

His eyes darkened as he studied her. "Why?"

"I don't like when the people I care for are hurting." She

reached out and brushed the lock of hair off his forehead, letting her fingers linger at his temple.

Archer took her hand and brought it to his mouth, kissing it softly.

She couldn't look away. In less than a fortnight, everything she thought she wanted had fallen away until the only thing left, all that she needed, was him. "Archer," she whispered.

He turned her hand over and placed a kiss on her palm, lips brushing the tender skin. "Thank you, sweetheart."

"Will… will you allow me to apply it?" She wanted to touch him, to soothe his pain, and then bring him pleasure.

Archer went utterly still, lips pressed to her palm. A moment passed, and then another.

The fire crackled in the hearth behind her, warming her back until a trickle of perspiration slid down her spine. She held her breath, praying that he didn't push her away.

Then his lips skimmed over her palm to the inside of her wrist. He flicked his eyes up and the burning heat in them made her quiver with desire. She dragged in another breath, captivated by that smoldering, glittering green gaze. Desire burned through her, making her breasts feel full and her nipples tighten and settled in her core with a rush of damp heat.

"It is not my neck that hurts, sweetheart," he said softly, brushing his mouth up the inside of her arm to the tender skin of her elbow. The stubble on his jaw whispered over her skin after each kiss, sending sparks of pleasure through her.

She wanted to see him and feel his skin beneath her hand. Violet sank down to her knees between his thighs and reached for the liniment bottle.

His throat bobbed. Then he reached for the left hem of his trousers, sliding it up his calf.

Violet smiled at that. He may hurt there, but she knew his thigh pained him more. Setting the bottle down, she brushed his hand aside and started unbuttoning the fall of his trousers.

Archer sucked in a surprised breath. "Violet."

She slipped each button through its hole until the material fell forward and revealed his drawers. She reached for the string holding them up.

He covered her hands with his. "You're about to get an eyeful. You know that, right?"

An eyeful. She chuckled at the term. "I need to apply the liniment to your thigh, so you must remove your clothes."

He cleared his throat. "I could apply it myself. I don't want you to be uncomfortable." He smoothed a hand over his thigh and muttered, "Or horrified."

Violet slid her hand up his chest to cup his cheek. "I could never be horrified by you."

"My leg looks rough. Not like most men's."

"I haven't seen a man's bare leg, so you need not worry."

He ran a hand over his face. "I'm not sure that makes me feel better. Besides, if I take my clothes off, your brother will kill me."

She grinned. "Then I suggest not removing them in front of him."

Archer choked on a groan, but he didn't reach for his clothes. He looked away from where her hands rested on his legs and shifted in his chair. His forehead creased, and he seemed nervous. "The bomb did a lot of damage, Violet. Only the doctors have seen it."

A bomb? Violet had read about such things when news of Napoleon's campaigns was posted in the newspaper, but for Archer to have experienced a violent explosion… She swallowed and smoothed her hand over his thigh. She didn't know how to ease his mind. "Would it help to pretend that I'm your doctor?"

His lips twitched.

Emboldened, she reached for the tie of his drawers and tugged the string loose. Violet squared her shoulders and spoke in an authoritative tone. "As my patient, I must ask you to disrobe so that I can apply the medicine to the affected areas."

He snorted and the tension in his shoulders eased. "All right, Doctor." He touched her chin with his fingertip and met her gaze again. "But if you feel uncomfortable, I'll understand."

She smiled at that.

Archer reached for the hem of his linen shirt. He gave her one last, lingering look, then drew it over his head and dropped it to the floor.

His chest was broad with firm ridges on his stomach. She hadn't known the male body had so many muscles there, or that the sparse, dark hair in the middle of his chest trailed down to disappear into his drawers. As much as she wanted to explore where that intriguing line of hair went, she forced herself to take her first look at the scars on his chest and ribs. She'd felt them when she lay beneath him in his bed in the dark, but the shadows hid them from view. In the afternoon light, with the firelight flickering behind her, she could see each pink ridge. It looked as if a dozen sharp blades had carved into his left side, and her heart ached for him. If his side looked this way, how much worse was his leg?

Archer held still, focused on her face as if he waited for her to shriek in fear or shrink away. Or for her to show pity, a reaction she imagined he would disdain as much as her fear, especially after her conversation with Patience about how men didn't want to appear weak in front of women. She steeled herself not to react even though every bit of her wanted to cry over the pain he must have endured.

"I can't imagine how much you've suffered," she whispered.

His throat bobbed as he swallowed.

"Can I touch you, Archer? Can I help take the pain away?"

He relaxed into the chair and nodded.

Violet uncorked the liniment and poured a small amount into her hands. She warmed the oil between her palms, watching him carefully, and then smoothed it over his scars. With soft strokes, she rubbed the oil in, tracing every jagged pink line.

He made a noise in the back of his throat and settled deeper in the chair.

She worked the liniment up the side of his neck to the spot

beneath his ear and smoothed a little on his jaw.

"More?" she asked and waved toward his thigh.

"Is that what the doctor thinks is best?" His voice sounded rough and deep, the way it had when she lay under him in his bed.

Violet shifted, feeling her body responding to that husky sound. "Yes. You must remove the last of your clothes." She sounded breathless to her own ears, excited to finally see all of him. "As… as your doctor, I insist."

One corner of his mouth curled up in a half smile. "I suppose I must if I want to feel better." He reached for his trousers and drawers. Lifting his hips, he slowly inched the fabric down, revealing more dark hair.

Violet couldn't breathe and couldn't tear her eyes away as inch by inch was revealed.

"Jesus, sweetheart. You're making this difficult."

Before she could ask how, he slid his hand into his trousers and adjusted his cock until the head came into view. It was dark pink with a rounded top, and as she watched, it lengthened in his hand.

Archer pushed his trousers and drawers down and off his feet, kicking them aside, and sat marvelously naked before her.

She swallowed, taking in the sight of him for the first time. The scars along his left side didn't detract from his beautiful body. His muscles were strong, and she knew how they felt beneath her hands. The scars on his thigh were thicker and darker red, only fading where they traveled to his calf, and disappeared into the dark hair covering his skin.

Archer watched her closely.

Waiting for her to recoil, no doubt. But Violet wasn't disgusted. She wanted to touch him even more than before. To feel the difference in the texture of his skin beneath her fingers and beneath her lips. She laid her hand on his damaged thigh, then leaned forward and pressed her mouth to his. Archer's body trembled beneath her hand. He kissed her back tenderly and sighed against her lips.

When they parted, Violet held his gaze and poured a little more oil into her palms to warm it.

"Where does it hurt?" she asked, nearly breathless.

He reached for her once more, cupping her cheek and feathering his thumb over her skin. "Everywhere."

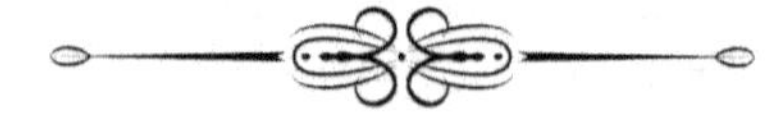

CHAPTER TWELVE

HIS LEG HURT like a bitch from hours of learning how to dance, but if it meant beautiful Violet would kneel between his thighs and put her hands on him, he'd do it every day for the rest of his life. Sitting naked in the chair, bare to her gaze, he marveled that she'd barely blinked at the scarred mess of his leg. Instead, her eyes heated and her pretty pink lips parted as she had her first look at a male body. At his body.

Violet licked her lips and rubbed the liniment oil in her palms as she looked him over. Her gaze settled on his hard cock.

Blood rushed to his dick, making him almost painfully hard from just her eyes on him. Jesus, what would it be like to have those slicked-up hands wrap around his length and pump him slowly? He shifted and gripped the arms of the chair to keep from reaching for her. Violet was innocent in every way. He couldn't move her hands where he wanted them. Couldn't wind his fingers in her hair and tug her mouth down until he sank inside it. Oh shit, just the fantasy of that made him tremble with need. If she so much as gusted out a warm breath on his cock, he would come.

"Violet," he whispered, voice ragged with want.

She blinked and licked her lips, finally, *finally* looking somewhere else.

God, that plump, wet mouth was killing him.

"Your body is like that of the marble statues at the museum," she said. Her warm palms settled on his thigh and smoothed the liniment over it. She rubbed the oil into his skin, fingers gliding through the hair on his legs as she traced each scar. "Although you are much warmer, and I find I quite like the way you feel under my hands."

He couldn't hold back the rumble of pleasure that came deep from his chest. "Feels good." Better than the doctors or the physical therapist. They didn't touch him with such an intimate exploration and thank God for that because his Navy doctor was pushing sixty and his physical therapist could have been a SEAL instructor for Hell Week. He didn't want either of them touching him the way Violet was. "It's okay to press harder."

Wide eyes met his. "Are you certain I won't hurt you more?"

Archer touched his fingers to her cheek, tracing the delicate bone beneath. "I'm sure. Push your thumbs harder against the muscle as you rub."

She dug her thumbs in on the next pass over his thigh.

After a few minutes, he felt the tightness in his bunched muscles ease. The liniment made his skin tingle. and the pain began to fade. Not a lot, but enough for him to draw a full breath as the tightness in his chest relaxed. Though that might have been more to do with Violet's hands on his body. Her touch sure didn't relax his cock.

Her fingers moved down the outside of his leg to his knee, over the top to the other side, and started a path up the inside of his thigh.

He sucked in a breath, gut-clenching when the tips of her fingers brushed his sac.

Violet went still, her hand inches from where he wanted it. "Did I do something wrong?"

Archer shook his head, not sure he could find coherent words.

"Do you want me to keep touching you?" she asked.

Her words were spoken in innocence but damn if they didn't

make him think dirty thoughts.

"Archer?" Her fingers flexed on the top of his thigh.

He slouched further in the chair, his body determined to maneuver until her hand was exactly where he wanted it, whether he consciously thought it or not. "Yes," he ground out.

"You want me to continue?" She stroked her hand back to the inside of his thigh, her eyes still on his.

His hips bucked. *Jesus.* "Yes." He wanted her badly.

"Where should I go next?"

"Anywhere."

She leaned closer. "Anywhere?" Her gaze dropped to his crotch and the pink staining her cheeks darkened to red. When she met his eyes again, there was a sheen of excitement in them.

Archer wrapped a hand around the back of her neck and tugged her forward until their lips were a breath apart. "Anywhere," he breathed against her mouth. "Everywhere. I want you to touch me everywhere, sweetheart." Then he sealed his mouth over hers and kissed her hungrily.

She met his kiss with matching passion, sweeping her tongue against his and leaning into his touch.

He held her in place while he plundered her mouth. The sound of something lightly landing on the floor brought him up for air. Several long strands of chocolate brown curls hung around Violet's shoulders, the pins holding them in place now on the floor. He'd ruined her hairstyle when kissing her and tunneling his fingers into the hair at the nape of her neck. Her cheeks were flushed, her lips plumped with a sheen of moisture, and her eyes were lowered to a lustful haze. She looked moments from being wrecked, and God help him, he wanted her that way. Archer speared his fingers in her hair and released the locks, pins pinging as they hit the floor all around them.

Violet's amber eyes twinkled in the firelight, and she helped remove a few he hadn't found. Then her hair fell in wavy ringlets across her shoulders, down her back, and over her breasts. Had a woman ever looked so beautiful? He couldn't remember any woman that had come before, and he didn't want to. Violet outshined them all.

She smoothed her hands over his shoulders and down his chest, as if trying to memorize him. "You're so handsome, Archer. Your hair here is softer than the hair on your legs," she said as she trailed her fingertips between his pecs and down his stomach to pet his happy trail.

"Not as soft as yours," he murmured, running several silken strands through his fingers. "I want to see this spread out on my pillow, surrounding you while you writhe from my tongue." Was that too coarse for her sensibilities? Many modern women liked a bit of dirty talk during sex, but Violet was not a modern woman. Thank God she also wasn't a proper young miss who only wanted a chaste kiss.

"Like when you kissed me... there?"

"*Mhmm.*" She tasted so damn good. He wanted that again tonight and every night. This thing between them had grown, despite his efforts to keep her at arm's length. It was more than sexual too. He liked her. He cared for her, and earlier when he'd sat before the fire in pain, he'd wondered what it would be like if he had a future with Violet. The thought should terrify him, but for some reason, it didn't.

Violet toyed with the ribbon on her gown as she eyed him. The next minute, she'd tugged the bow loose and stood to pull the gown off. Next followed her shoes and a slip, leaving her in just a thin, silk shift, stockings, and something a bit like a corset.

Archer swallowed. Even though she was still fully clothed, she was enchanting, with her hair falling around her shoulders and that sweet blush spreading down her neck to the tops of her breasts. He reached for her, pulling her between his thighs and running his hands over her hips. The silk beneath his fingers was so fine, he could almost make out the patch of curls beneath. He pressed a kiss to her stomach, wishing she was naked so he could explore her body more.

Violet held her arms over her breasts and shifted from foot to foot.

He stroked the outside of her legs and around her bottom, then back to her hips and pressed another kiss there. "You don't have to do anything you aren't comfortable with," he said.

Slowly, she relaxed, and her hands settled on his shoulders. "I… I want to touch you." She kissed him, and when she pulled back, he saw the determination he'd become quite familiar with in the short time he'd known her.

Violet sank to her knees between his thighs and wrapped her hand around his cock.

Archer sucked in a breath and tipped his head back, squeezing his eyes shut until he could get his body under control. He hadn't expected that. Although she'd warned him, hadn't she?

She moved her fist up his length. "You have moisture here," she said with a note of surprise. Before he could respond, she'd touched her finger to his pre-cum and swirled it around his tip. "I didn't notice that before."

He raised his head and looked at her hand wrapped around his cock. "It happens when a man is excited. Just as a woman can feel moisture when a man touches her."

She looked at him from beneath her lashes. "I feel that between my thighs right now."

Archer growled and reached for her, intending to stand her up, lift her shift, and sample that sweet heat.

Violet giggled and batted his hands away. "This time I want to touch you more. Can I… well, does a woman put her mouth on a man too?" She stared at where she worked her hand up and down and licked her lower lip.

He gasped for breath, harder than he'd ever been in his life. Violet's pretty pink lips wrapped around his shaft? He would be in heaven, right before he went to Hell after her brother killed him. He should send her away, now, before this went any further. But dammit, he couldn't.

"Yes," he said in a guttural voice. "Some women don't like it, and if you don't, just do whatever you are comfortable with."

Violet explored him with her hands, then pressed a kiss to the tip of his cock. She licked her lips, tasting the bead of moisture that she found there. Her eyes scrunched—deciding if she liked the flavor?—then she dipped her head and gave him a slow lick.

Archer shivered in pleasure, feeling that warm touch all the way to his toes. He threaded his fingers into her hair and guided her mouth where he wanted it.

Every silken touch enflamed him. He'd had his share of women, but not even the most experienced of them made him burn the way Violet did.

He moved her hand back to his shaft and wrapped her fingers around the base, showing her how to stroke him to bring added pleasure. It felt too damn good. The hot depths of her mouth sliding over his cock and the gentle way she sucked... he was going to come.

He cupped the back of her head and gently lifted her mouth off him. "I'm going to come," he rasped.

"Oh." Her eyebrows pinched in confusion.

She was so damn innocent that she didn't even know what he meant. "A release that gives me pleasure," he added. "Like you experienced."

She nodded.

Archer put his hand over hers and guided it up and down his shaft. Together, they jacked him, winding his body tight. Tingles erupted at the base of his spine a split second before he came, splashing on his stomach and their hands. It took every ounce of willpower to muffle his cries. God, the last thing he needed was Gabriel to charge in and find his sister between Archer's thighs with her hand on his cock and a smile on her lips.

When he could breathe again, he looked at Violet to make sure she didn't regret what had just happened. The dark gold around her pupils deepened, making the amber color seem to glow. A small smile teased the edges of her lips and a rosy flush still spread down her throat, beckoning him. On her knees before him, with the glow of the fire highlighting her skin and hair, she looked like a priestess worshipping at a temple. She could worship him anytime. *Holy shit.* He'd never come so hard and told her so.

Violet grinned like a satisfied cat. She stood and went to the side table.

He heard a splash of water, and then she was back with a damp cloth. He reached for it, but she shook her head and cleaned his chest and their hands. After she rinsed the cloth out, she returned to his side.

Archer took her hand in his and gently tugged her down into his lap. He kissed her, telling her the only way he could how much she affected him.

Violet placed one last kiss on his lips and then lay her head on his shoulder. "The day is almost gone. I suppose I should sneak out and change for supper. Do you feel well enough to join us?"

He hated that she had to sneak out. Violet shouldn't be a dirty little secret. She was too good for that. But what could he do since he was leaving? At least he hadn't taken her virginity. He ran a hand down his face and ground his teeth together.

"Archer?"

What had she asked? *Dinner.* "Yes, I am well enough. The liniment helped a bit."

She beamed at him. "Shall I apply a little more before I go?"

"I will never deny myself your touch, sweetheart." He would take every memory that he could between now and when he left, to linger over when he was once more alone.

Violet moved off his lap slipped back into her dress and retied the bow. Picking up the little brown bottle, she warmed more oil in her hands and reached once more for his leg.

It felt wonderful to have her massage his muscles, and while the oil had that pungent medicinal smell, the pain in his leg was definitely easing.

"I wish I could dance with you at the ball," he said softly.

She looked up from her ministrations. "Then I shall expect you to find me for the first quadrille. It is the slower of the dances and should not pain you." Then, "Too bad we can't dance a waltz," she muttered under her breath.

"Why not a waltz?" Not that he knew the steps to dance a waltz with her.

"It is too scandalous a dance for Almack's. And even if they did play it, Gabriel would never allow me to dance it unless I was spoken for. I've practiced the steps on my own in secret, but that's all."

Were they talking about the same waltz that his grandma and grandpa had danced to? People would have to dance it naked before it would be scandalous.

His confusion must have shown, because she added, "Lily says the dance is a little different in your time, but not much, and that people think the dance is outdated rather than appalling."

"Then I shall look forward to our quadrille." That seemed to please her, as she went back to applying the oil. Her touch soothed him, and he let himself relax once more.

Violet brushed her fingers over one of the thicker scars that ran from his hip almost to his knee. She looked at him from under her lashes. "Will you tell me what happened?"

He stiffened, as the relaxation vanished, like she'd thrown cold water over him.

She sat back on her heels. "I... I'm sorry. I shouldn't have asked. I know you can't speak of it, even to your sisters."

Archer squeezed his eyes shut and willed his body to loosen up. When he tensed, the pain flared in his thigh. A minute ticked by. Another. Finally, his tension eased, and the ache began to recede. He opened his eyes and instantly felt like an ass. She looked so dejected, sitting between his thighs. It was all he could do not to pull her up onto his lap. But he was still naked, and the next time he had Violet in his lap, he wanted her as bare as he.

"It's okay," he said. Damn that rasp in his throat. He reached for her hand and put it back on his thigh, searching for the words that would smooth the awkwardness that filled the air between them. "Soldiers fight in wars to keep the people at home safe. Not just to protect them from threats, but also from the knowledge of how terrible mankind can be to one another. We fight so the people we care for don't have to experience the dark, ugly parts. The parts that haunt a man even in his dreams and can never be unseen." Truth was, even if he wasn't bound by his oath, he didn't want to tell anyone. He'd failed his team. He'd failed Amanda. And in his present condition, he hoped to God that no one he cared about found themselves in a dangerous situation because he'd fail them too. It was a dark part of his heart he didn't want to share with those he loved.

When he'd been medically discharged, part of him had been furious. The Navy was his life. What the hell was he going to do if he couldn't defend his country? But another part of him had been relieved. If he wasn't responsible for people's lives, he couldn't let them down when they needed him most. That's why he needed Violet to be smart about her mysterious gift-giver. She couldn't count on Archer, and if she were harmed and he wasn't there to rescue her... His gut twisted.

"Gabriel once told me, after he met Lily, that having someone to share those dark moments with, made them easier to carry in his heart." She traced a circle on his thigh with a fingertip, not meeting his gaze. "When you meet a woman and fall in love, will you share those memories with her?"

Would he? *Could* he make himself that vulnerable? Share the deepest secrets of his soul and then wait to see if she fled? "I don't know."

"I would want to know. If I were the woman you loved, I'd want to know every detail."

His heart jumped at her words, and he had to clear his throat. "If you were the woman I loved, I wouldn't have a single secret. You'd twist the screws until I spilled my soul."

She grinned. "If that means that I would pull every secret from you, then you're right. Ask poor Patience."

Archer chuckled, his spirits lifting. The pain in his leg had diminished enough that he could probably walk, and Violet's unflinching spirit made it hard to dwell on those dark thoughts for long.

"I would want you to feel as Gabriel does. That sharing your dark moments with me would make them easier to carry."

"Even if you were to learn that I'm not the man you think I am? I've killed a lot of people, Violet, and more have died because of me. I don't think your brother can say the same. If he did, don't you think Lily would have returned to her time as quickly as she could?"

Violet held his gaze and rose to her knees. She reached for his hand and twined their fingers together. "You killed to keep people safe, Archer. You're a protector. And no, Lily wouldn't have. She loves Gabriel. Even the stubborn parts that drive everyone crazy. She loves the dark parts of him too because they are part of him. Part of the man she loves. Nothing he says will change that, but it will help her understand him. She'll know him as no one else does, and she will love him more for it."

Archer swallowed. Were they still talking about Lily and Gabriel? It felt like Violet was speaking to his soul, shining the bright light of her spirit in his dark corners. "You would do that for the man you loved?"

She nodded. "And I would share mine. Every time I disobeyed Gabriel to search for the fairy king in the garden or rearranged his desk when he wouldn't let me do something."

He bit back a smile. "Dark indeed."

She squeezed his hand. "Or I'd tell him about my mum, who prefers her bottle of drugs to her children."

Archer sat up. "What?"

Violet traced the fingers of her free hand over the stubble on his jaw. "When my father died, my mother was devastated. Though whether that was because she loved him or because she was suddenly a widow in charge of an earldom and two children, I don't know. Gabriel said she had several fits of hysterics. The doctor gave her laudanum to help her sleep.

"When my brother came home to help with the estate, he

spent all his time with my father's books. Apparently, our father had run through quite a bit of the family fortune and Gabriel had to work to build it back up so we wouldn't be destitute. I was young, so I don't remember much, but I didn't have a governess for some reason. Perhaps my father didn't want to hire one because of the expense. Mother spent most of her time in bed, so I was able to indulge in all my childhood fantasies.

"I believe that I was climbing a mountain shaped quite a bit like a tree to fight off trolls, when I slipped and fell. I was scraped up, but Mother was too 'tired' to help me, so I went to Gabriel. He was furious to realize that while he'd been trying to save our estate, Mother had let me run wild. You see… she liked the way the laudanum made her feel, and she took more and more. She started getting her own from the chemist, so Gabriel didn't know how much she had."

"She became addicted," Archer said. "Laudanum. Doesn't that come from opium?"

Violet nodded. "There are opium dens in Town, and I've heard that the people who go to them haven't a care after. Much like my mother."

"What happened to her?" Archer rubbed his thumb over the back of her hand.

"Gabriel sent her away to one of our other estates. At first, I was angry because I didn't understand. But several years ago, I visited her. She looked terrible, thin, and pale. But she didn't seem to care that I was there. I cut my visit short and came home."

He raised their joined hands to his lips and pressed a kiss to her skin. He appreciated that she realized when she was wrong and made changes. She'd been angry with her brother for sending their mother away, but when she realized that he'd been right, she'd come back home, where she belonged.

They sat in comfortable silence for a time. The fire cracked and popped, and somewhere in the house, a door closed and muffled voices drifted up. The sky outside his window was deepening to twilight, making the room darker. In the hall, he heard the clock chime the hour.

"Supper will be served shortly," she said. "I must go."

Their stolen time was at an end. Archer felt a pang in his chest that tasted like disappointment. He helped her to her feet, then stood and pulled his trousers back on.

Violet gathered her scattered pins and her reticule.

He steadied his balance, cursing his leg, then guided her toward the door.

"Oh! I almost forgot. I brought you a gift." She picked up an item leaning against the door jam and handed it to him. "I know that Gabriel lent you a walking stick after yours broke in Hyde Park, but I thought you might like your own. I hope you like it."

She'd gifted him an incredible walking cane made of ebony, with a brass knob and end cap, inlaid with ivory. He was both touched by her thoughtfulness and yet, hurt. When Archer was with her, he didn't feel like an invalid. He felt like the man he once was. With this gift, was she implying that she saw him as a man who couldn't get by without it?

"You don't like it?" She looked crestfallen by his lack of response. "Or is the height wrong when you lean on it? If so, we can find another."

Because he would have to lean on it, wouldn't he? He ground his teeth and leaned the cane against the chair. "It's beautiful. Thank you."

"You're upset. Why?"

He stalked to the other side of the chamber near the bed. He hated that he needed the damn thing. That he looked weak in her eyes. He spent years in Special Forces proving to himself that he wasn't weak, only to end up that way anyhow. Clenching his fists, he said, "It's fine. Thank you. Just leave it and go."

"Archer?"

"Just leave," he growled. "Take the liniment with you. I'm not an invalid and I don't need to be coddled." Not by his sisters, the doctors, his therapist, and certainly not this beautiful young woman who was too fucking young for him anyway. She didn't need to be stuck with an older man who couldn't walk without assistance. She was too vibrant for that. As if he needed more of a reminder of why it wasn't a good idea to kiss her.

"Coddled?"

He heard her march across the chamber after him.

"You think that's why I'm here? To *coddle* you because you're injured?"

His teeth clenched as she wound up for an argument that he didn't want to have. He didn't want to talk about his injury, and he couldn't face the pity that would be in her eyes. "Leave me alone, Violet."

"I will not." She rounded in front of him and thrust the liniment against his chest.

He put his hand over hers, holding the bottle to him, and glared down at her.

She glared back, clutching the cane in her other hand. "I don't think you're weak."

He blanched and looked away. "Don't you? You came here with more ointment and a cane for the man who can barely walk on his own and can't dance without being in pain?"

"I came here to help relieve your pain so that you can dance with me at Almack's tomorrow. And as for the cane, I wanted to replace the one you broke with something more suitable to a man who's fought to protect others." She yanked her hand out from under his, leaving him grappling to keep the bottle from hitting the floor.

While he fumbled, she lifted the cane. He heard a soft *snick* and the wood slid free from the hilt, revealing a thin blade.

"It has a knife in the handle?" He'd seen cheap knockoffs of sword canes before, but this looked as if it was quality-made.

"Every warrior needs a weapon," Violet said. "When I saw this one, I thought of you."

He dropped the liniment on the bed behind him and reached for the cane. The knife edge was sharp against his finger and the weight was balanced between the blade and the brass knob. He studied the carved ivory and craftsmanship of the cane, then slowly slid the weapon back into its hiding spot. A tiny lever just under the knob released the catch and allowed the knife to slide free with ease.

All his anger dissolved, quickly replaced by warmth for this woman. She said she saw him as a warrior, and this gift proved that she wasn't just saying that to make him feel better. A small smile touched his lips.

Violet waved at the cane. "You will cut such a striking figure at Almack's tomorrow, I fear you will need that to fend off the debutantes and their mothers."

Archer snorted. He rested the cane against the wall and turned to her.

She twined her fingers in front of her stomach, somehow managing to look both hopeful and nervous about his reaction.

He wound an arm around her waist and pulled her flush to his body, slanting his mouth over hers.

She melted against him.

Archer kissed her for a long moment, then pressed his forehead to hers. "Tonight, once everyone is asleep…" What was he doing? He couldn't ask her for this.

"Yes," she whispered against his lips. "I'll come to you."

"Violet…" He wanted to retract the request immediately. He had no right…

She covered his mouth with her fingertips. "I'll see you downstairs." Then she slipped from the room and was gone.

ARCHER PACED IN front of his bedroom window, overlooking the small garden below. Light from the moon spilled in through the glass pane, illuminating a square spot on the floor that he walked through every few steps. When he'd returned to his room from dinner earlier, he'd watched the moon crest the buildings as it climbed in the sky, silver-white and in that strange place between full and half full.

He'd yanked off his jacket, waistcoat, and cravat and tossed them over the chair by the fire, unsettled by the sight. He loved the moon. Always had, and he'd spent hundreds of nights under the stars with his team, staring up at the moon as it shifted through its phases. The sight had always brought him peace. Tonight, that partial phase where it wasn't quite one thing or another, echoed back the confusion he felt about his own state.

Everything felt different, heightened at dinner. He'd been intensely aware of Violet's every move. Her light laugh, the way she hummed when she enjoyed a dish, the creamy skin above the low neckline of her deep red gown where he had pressed his lips just hours ago. Though he tried to keep from staring at her, a pointed look from Gabriel told him that he'd failed.

After the ladies had retired to the drawing room, he'd sat with Gabriel and Christian in the dining room drinking brandy and trying to pay attention to their talk of Bellamy and Christian's impending marriage, and Christian's desire to avoid the ball at Almack's. Gabriel had insisted that Christian go, and it seemed that this was a common argument among them that they enjoyed.

He'd had that relationship with Church, his platoon leader. An ache bloomed deep in his heart for his lost friend and all the others he'd failed. He focused on his breathing to blank his mind and paced to the window again.

What the hell had he been thinking, inviting Violet to his bedroom? His cock perked up, answering the question. Maybe she wouldn't come tonight. Maybe she'd get nervous, or shy, and stay tucked in her bed where it was warm and safe from him.

Archer snorted. *Nervous* and *shy* were two words no one would associate with Violet Hawthorne. Which meant she would come to him. Would he have the strength to push her away? In the SEALS, he'd mastered control over his body until he could fight through anything. Pain, fear, lust... nothing could break through his will.

Violet waltzed through his control as if his walls didn't exist. One alluring look and whatever good intentions he'd managed to muster evaporated as if they'd never been. Somehow, if she did come to him, he'd have to restrain himself.

Or she could restrain him.

Visions of Violet riding him while his wrists were bound to the bedposts filled his head, making him even harder than he'd been moments ago. *Shit.* How the hell would he keep himself from taking her? And he couldn't take her. She was meant to go to her marriage as a virgin. Bellamy had mentioned that fact during one of their etiquette lessons, along with her belief that it didn't happen as often as people seemed to think. Give a young couple some time alone and passions ignited.

They couldn't happen with Violet though. What kind of man would he be if he took her virginity and then ghosted her to return to the future?

A discreet knock on his door pulled him out of his panicked thoughts and sent his stomach plummeting to his toes.

Archer crossed to the door, reached for the handle, and hesitated. If it was Violet, and he knew in his heart that it was, he'd treat her with the respect she deserved. He was only a man, but he could do that for her at least.

The knock came again, just as soft as the first.

Archer turned the handle and swung the door open to the sight of Violet in her silken robe, with her hair down in soft waves around her beautiful face, amber eyes wide as they skimmed down his body.

"May I come in?" she whispered.

He stepped aside and waved her in, then closed the door and turned the key in the lock, sealing his fate.

Violet wandered closer to the fire, the flickering light highlighting her curves.

Archer moved toward her, unable to keep his distance. She'd

come to him. She wanted to be here with him and damn if she didn't see through his scars to the man beneath. He settled his hands on her shoulders and pulled her flush against his chest. Her hair smelled like cinnamon, and as he trailed the tip of his nose along her temple, he realized that her skin smelled that way too. He'd never thought of cinnamon as a seductive scent, but the warm, sweet scent settled him in a way that he couldn't describe. Like coming home to the one you loved after being away too long.

He brushed a kiss over her temple, her cheek, and the corner of her jaw.

She settled back against him and tilted her head, granting him access to more of that delicious skin.

He curled his arms around her waist, anchoring her to him as his mouth trailed down her neck. "I should make you go," he said against her soft skin.

Violet gripped his arms, holding him in place. "No, you shouldn't."

"You're supposed to go to your wedding a virgin. Untouched by a man."

She chuckled. "I suppose it is too late then, Archer Bennett. You touched me before dinner. What's more, you touched me in a place no other man has. My heart."

Archer closed his eyes, lips resting at the place where her neck met her shoulder.

You touched me too.

"I can't offer you what you need."

"Do you know what I need? Or, like my brother, are you merely presuming to know?"

"I know you need a husband who can take care of you. I know you don't want to turn into your aunt, living on the charity of your brother for the rest of your life." He opened his eyes to stare into the fire, a truth he hadn't wanted to admit to himself on the tip of his tongue. "I know that I'm not capable of taking care of you, Violet. Even if I stayed here, I can't... I have no income, no home."

"None of that matters," she protested.

"Yes. It does, and you know it. But, Violet, even if I had those things, I still couldn't be with you."

She spun around and put her arms around his neck, giving him a look of mulish determination he'd become quite acquainted with. "Tell me why." She didn't ask. She demanded.

Archer cursed under his breath but couldn't find it in him to release her and put distance between them. Before he'd consciously had the thought, he pulled her closer until her breasts pressed into his chest and her warmth stole into his being trying to revive a soul that had long since gone cold.

"I can't. If you knew…"

"If I knew, I'd be able to argue against it until you gave in." She gave him a cheeky grin.

He snorted a laugh and spanked her ass. Even in the midst of his fears, she made him smile. "You probably would, little minx."

Violet rose on her toes and pressed a lingering kiss to his cheek. "Tell me. I know you feel attraction for me, Archer. I know you still want to go back to your time and that the honorable part of you that I admire doesn't want to hurt me."

He sighed.

"I also know that there is more."

His resolve threatened to crack under her quiet pleas. "You should go."

"I should stay."

"You don't know what you're asking."

Violet brushed a lock of hair off his forehead. "I do. I'm asking you to trust me with your secrets. The secrets that give you nightmares and hold you apart from everyone."

She asked him to open his heart and let her in. His chest tightened until he felt as if he couldn't draw breath. "Violet."

"Please, Archer," she whispered against his lips. "I would know the man who holds my heart, before he takes it with him."

He heard the pain in her voice, and the certainty that he

would leave her. He never meant to hurt her. The one person in all the world he felt closest to, and he hurt her with his silence. God, he didn't want to share his shame. He felt sick even contemplating it.

After several long moments of silence, she settled back on her heels and looked at the center of his chest, tracing the open line of his shirt. "Perhaps you're right. I should go."

He'd never seen her look so defeated. "Stay," he whispered.

She shook her head and tried to step back.

He tightened his arms, holding her to his chest, unwilling to let her go even as he knew he should. But he needed her. Her laugh, her mischievous glances, the vibrant way she looked at life… He couldn't let her go looking as disappointed as she did, knowing he'd hurt her. His chest twisted in pain and his throat grew thick.

"It's my fault they're dead." The words were out before he knew he'd say them.

"Who?" she asked softly.

"My team. I could have… could have prevented their deaths… and…" His voice broke. "And I didn't." Archer untangled himself from her arms and crossed to the window. He didn't want to see her expression. Revulsion, horror, pity… it didn't matter. He'd seen all of it in the mirror plenty of times and couldn't face seeing it on someone else's expression. Especially someone he cared about. It's why he'd never told his sisters. He hated that he'd spoken at all, revealing the darkest part of his heart.

He heard Violet's soft footfalls as she crossed to stand behind him. "Your team in the military?"

"Yeah. They were my brothers. Men I trusted with my life. Men who…" He swallowed hard over the lump in his throat. "Men who foolishly trusted me with theirs."

She moved closer but thankfully didn't touch him. "What happened?"

"We had to evacuate someone to safety. There'd been reports

of insurgents—rebels trying to kill us and our target—in the surrounding hills, but we couldn't verify that. There were conflicting reports, and we didn't know who we could trust, so we trusted no one. We had to move the man and his family as fast as we could and set up a route to get them out, plus a diversion. At the last moment, one of our informants came to me, saying that the insurgents knew our route and had planted IEDs—hidden bombs—in the road." He remembered that moment clearly, even though much of the rest of that day was gone from his memories. The man was dirty and disheveled, eyes darting around, and shifting as if he couldn't stand still. He said the road was rigged but refused to say how he knew, or more importantly, how the rebels knew their route. With sketchy information, an unreliable source, and the need to get their target and his family out fast, he'd chosen not to trust the intel. It was the biggest mistake of his life.

"I didn't listen to him."

Violet moved to stand in front of him and put her hands on his chest.

He covered one of her hands with his but didn't meet her gaze. "He'd been right. I should have listened. I should have reported it to Church. He was my lieutenant, but he was also my best friend." He heard Church's cries in his nightmares every night. "The group in front hit an IED. We tried to go around, but they were smart. The rebels planted a second off the road, anticipating it. Kodiak, Church, and I were thrown clear, but the bastards weren't satisfied with the bombs. They started shooting anyone who survived." Pain throbbed in his leg as he remembered bleeding into the dirt, dragging Church behind a rock while Kodiak gave covering fire. "Church died in my arms. We needed to move but my wounds were bad, and I had lost a lot of blood. At some point, I'd passed out. The rebels must have thought I was dead. I… I don't know how I made it out of there. The only thing that I remember clearly is waking up in a hospital in Germany, bandaged like a mummy and hurting like hell. Kodiak lived long enough to tell our rescuers what had happened, but he died in transport to the hospital. Everyone else was dead. Everyone." Even their target and his family. He didn't tell Violet that. Some details were best left unsaid.

He laughed, though there was no humor in it. "You'd think I'd have learned. I should have known to trust my gut when the life of my best friend might have been in jeopardy, but I didn't."

"How could you have known?" she asked.

"Because it wasn't the first time I'd lost a best friend. When I was thirteen, my best friend Amanda and I did everything together. But then she started acting strange and keeping secrets. I finally got her to admit that she'd been talking to an older guy. She thought he liked her, but something seemed wrong about the whole situation, and when I tried to get her to stop talking to him she wouldn't listen. When I found out that she was supposed to meet him at school, I begged her not to, but she went anyway. It was the last time I saw her alive. If I'd just told someone about her meeting, maybe she wouldn't have gone. Maybe her parents would have kept her home." He rubbed a hand over his face. "They didn't find her body until after I'd joined the military." It took seven years to get that closure, and the details of her death left deep scars on his heart. And still, he hadn't learned from the experience.

"That's how Church and I became friends. He'd lost his sister to a former beau who wouldn't leave her alone."

Violet sniffed and he felt a tremor go through her body. "You blame yourself, yet none of us knows where a path might lead, Archer!" She fisted his shirt and shook him.

Archer finally looked at her, stunned to see tears staining her cheeks instead of the recrimination or pity that he expected. He wiped the tears away and cupped her neck in his hand. "What?"

"Even if you alerted someone to Amanda's rendezvous, she may have found another way to meet her beau. Had you reported the information that the man gave you to your team, to Church, he may have chosen to ignore the warning as you did.

They might both yet be dead, and instead of wondering what would happen if you'd acted, you'd be wondering what would have happened if you didn't act." She swiped more tears from her cheeks. "You must see that neither incident is your fault."

Weren't they? Would the outcome still be the same? He didn't know, and in that, Violet was right. "It hurts to know that I might have changed the outcome." He cleared his throat, trying to speak around the knot that lodged there. "I lost two people I loved, and I can't trust myself to make the right decision if I find myself in that situation again."

She made a pained sound and tried to wrap her arms around him.

He held her at bay. "Violet, you need a man who can protect you. I'm not that man." It killed him to say the words, but they needed to be said. When she didn't move, he released her and stepped back. "Do you understand now? Even if I stayed, I'm not the man you need."

She studied him, but he couldn't read her expression.

They stared at one another for a long moment. Finally, he forced himself to turn away and limped toward the bed. "Good-night, Violet."

He heard her huff and pad toward him. "Please," he said as he turned back toward her. It was the only word he managed before she pushed him back onto the bed.

Violet climbed up after him and straddled his waist. She leaned down until her face was inches from his. "Mr. Bennett, regardless of your determination to make me see you as unworthy, and regardless of your attempt to decide what is best for me, I shall have you know that it is *not* your decision to make. If I wish to see you as an honorable man who would do anything to protect those he loves, then I shall do so. Furthermore, if I want to give myself to you, then that is my choice."

God, she was glorious when she was angry. Her hair fell around them in a curtain of chocolate brown silk, and her heat pressed into him from her breasts to her core. His cock roared back to life at the feel of her body against his. Her plump pink lips were parted, begging for his kiss. "I—"

"Excellent. Now kiss me." Violet closed the scant inch between them and kissed him, blasting through his walls once more with ease.

Had he ever had any defenses with this woman?

He never thought he'd tell anyone the fears in his heart, Violet especially. He thought she was too young, too innocent to hear the horrors of war. But she hadn't turned away in disgust or fled. Instead, she *claimed* him. Archer felt a rush of desire so hot it felt as if his veins seared. He sat up and sank his hands into her hair, holding her head in place while he deepened the kiss.

Violet made a noise in the back of her throat and clung to him, matching the fire in his kiss. She stroked his tongue with hers and tugged at his shirt, pulling it up.

He broke the kiss long enough to rip the material over his head and fling it aside.

Violet shoved her wrapper off and pulled his mouth back to hers. "I want you, Archer. Now."

"Are you—"

"So help me, if you ask me if I'm sure, I will bite you," she growled.

He gave a dark chuckle. "Promise?"

Her eyes widened right before he flipped their positions, rolling her onto her back beneath him. He pressed his cock to her core, only the silk of her nightgown and his trousers between them, and kissed his way down her neck. "If at any time you want to stop…"

"I will tell you," she said, speaking over him, as she guided one of his hands to her breast.

Archer leaned down and sucked her nipple into his mouth, working the silk against her peak with his tongue.

She gasped and arched her hips.

He switched to the other breast while he reached for the hem of her nightgown. "Lift up," he murmured, scraping his teeth over her nipple.

Violet bit her lip to hold back her moan and lifted her hips.

He pulled the material up to reveal the most perfect breasts he'd ever seen. They filled his palms, and her nipples were dark pink from his ministrations. "Gorgeous," he whispered as he sucked one back into his mouth. Jesus, she tasted as good as she smelled.

She tugged the nightgown the rest of the way off until she was delightfully bare beneath him.

Archer had kissed her and touched her, he'd made her come on his tongue, but he'd never been granted the gift of seeing her beautiful body until now. He sat back enough to admire the pale satin skin beneath his hands. The way her hips curved, and her beautiful dark hair spread in waves around her on the bed. He stroked his hands over all of it, admiring each dip and curve, and followed the path with his mouth.

She shivered, eyes glazed with pleasure, as he kissed his way up the inside of her thigh.

"I want to taste you again, sweetheart, but you have to be quiet. Can you do that?"

She nodded, parting her thighs wider.

Archer lowered his head and nuzzled her curls. She smelled divine. He flicked his tongue through her folds, tasting that heady flavor that was all her.

Violet sucked in a breath but stayed quiet.

Moving her legs over his shoulders, he dipped his head and lapped at her folds. He worked her with his mouth, watching her face to learn what she liked best, then sucked her nub between his lips.

Violet slapped her hand over her mouth and let out a muffled cry, legs trembling.

He chuckled against her heat, then did it again, swirling his tongue around her. He pushed one finger into her tight depths and felt her clench around him.

"Please," she whimpered around her hand. "Please, Archer."

Yes. He wanted her to come on his tongue again, couldn't get enough of her, spread out beneath him, her slick heat filling his senses. He flicked her nub over and over with his tongue, working her with his finger until she curled up off the bed and grabbed his head to hold him in place.

Archer put his palm over her mouth just as she cried out in pleasure. She trembled and moaned against his hand as she came, then slowly sank back onto the bed with a pleasured sigh.

He kissed the inside of each thigh, moved up her body, and paused to suck her breasts once more. When he reached her mouth, she met him eagerly for a deep kiss. She was so perfect, so passionate.

Violet pressed her forehead to his and reached for the buttons on his trousers.

Archer covered her hands with one of his, but she batted it away and opened the flap with ease. Next went the tie on his drawers until her hand slipped beneath the fabric to cup his cock.

He moaned, rocking into her hand.

"Take your clothes off, Mr. Bennett," she murmured.

Archer stood and shed his clothes, taking the time to admire the naked woman spread out before him. Violet wanted him and he was done denying her. Denying himself.

He positioned her in the middle of the bed and climbed on top of her, settling back into the vee of her thighs. His cock slid through her wet heat, making his breath catch with how good it felt. He rocked his hips, reveling in the friction, while he pressed against her nub.

Violet sucked in a breath and wrapped her arms around his neck. "Archer," she whimpered. "I feel so good, but… empty."

He took her lips in a hard kiss, then gentled his mouth and nipped at her lower lip. "I can fill you, sweetheart. But if I do, there's no turning back from that. You won't be pure for the man you marry."

She searched his face. "You're the only man I want. To share this with, I mean."

In the light of the fire, he could just discern the darkening of her cheeks. What she offered was a precious gift. Not just her virginity, but her tender feelings for him. His heart swelled, pressing against his ribs. He wasn't the type of man to take the gift of virginity and discard the woman afterward. Violet meant something to him too. She'd broken past the barriers to touch the heart of the man beneath, and he welcomed her there. If he stayed here, if he never returned to his time, he'd marry her.

He'd told her that there was no coming back from this decision. He hadn't realized the same held true for him. Archer placed a soft kiss on her lips, memorizing this moment. "It might hurt at first."

She nodded.

He reached down to slide his fingers through her folds and brush his thumb over her nub. She bucked against his hand, trembling, and biting her lower lip. He rubbed her until she whimpered with need, then pressed his cock to her entrance.

"I'll go slow," he whispered.

Violet pulled his head down and kissed him, mashing her lips to his and muffling her sounds as he pushed into her.

Every hot inch was heaven. When he hit the narrowing of her channel, he stopped to let her take a full breath, then captured her mouth in a deep kiss and pushed through. Her muffled moan didn't sound pained.

"Okay?" he asked against her lips.

She nodded. "It pinched, but oh... don't... don't stop. I want you to make love to me, Archer."

He slowly withdrew, then sank back into her.

She wrapped her legs around his hips and shifted beneath him, drawing him deeper.

The pleasure was incredible, better than anything he'd felt before. He thrust into her, building a rhythm that sent chills down his spine. Violet held him tightly, hips meeting his every thrust, and moaned into his neck.

He lost himself in the sensations, letting her body soothe the parts of him left ragged and raw from being exposed. He would never be the same after suffering the losses of the people he loved most, but Violet's acceptance of him in spite of it made it easier to breathe. She'd shown him another way to view the events of the past. Maybe in time, his heart would heal.

Archer slipped a hand back between their bodies and rubbed her nub until her walls clamped down tight on his cock. "That's right, sweetheart. Come for me one more time."

Violet trembled, holding his gaze.

One more graze of his thumb, and she shattered. He couldn't hold back his own release. He pulled out of her body a second before he erupted, marking her as his. Slowly, he lowered himself to her side and pulled her close.

She turned to lay her head on his shoulder, touching her belly. "You didn't…"

"No." He didn't have a condom, so he did what he could. He just had to hope that he didn't get her pregnant. He tucked a lock of her hair behind her ear. It was so soft, one of the many things that he loved about her.

Violet rose up on one arm and kissed him. "I feel wonderful."

He chuckled and pulled her down on top of him. He didn't care about the mess they made, only that she felt so good in his arms. For the first time in over a year, Archer felt happy. He put all thoughts of the past out of his mind and held Violet close to his heart. She made him feel like he was capable of protecting her, and he'd do whatever was necessary to prove her right.

Chapter Thirteen

ALMACK'S WAS ONE of the most wondrous places in all of London, and Violet looked forward to the balls there immensely. The immense ballroom, with its brilliant chandeliers, carved medallions, blue velvet curtains, and sparkling mirrors, looked as grand as a palace hall, and tonight was filled with the creme of society in full dress. Lively music floated down from the band seated on the balcony, playing a country reel for the dancers paired on the floor. She felt the same excitement she'd had during her first Season, as if any moment something magical might happen.

At least it might, if one did not have Aunt Josephine tottering after them, chattering away about the punch and how unfortunate it was that the patronesses could not dispense something a bit more expensive considering the people in attendance.

"After all, one must be in good standing with them in order to even procure a voucher, let alone the tickets. But even the rack punch served to the masses at Vauxhall was superior."

Violet nodded or murmured agreement where appropriate, not really listening. Her aunt had the same complaint at every party, whether it be the Dowager of Leeds's dinner party or Lady Barlowe's annual ball.

"I do say that you ought to find a fine man here, Violet. *Someone* must be interested in the Rothden fortunes enough to consider you, eh?" Aunt Josephine chuckled. She swatted Violet's bare shoulders with her fan. "You're a fine-looking girl. Too bad about that dress and your temperament, but I suppose some things can't be helped. Now, do smile." She tapped the fan on the underside of Violet's chin. "Men find a smile more attractive than… whatever that look is."

Violet batted the fan away. "It's a scowl. One I reserve especially for horrid aunts who say terrible things." Her gown was beautiful, and she loved it. The aubergine silk and velvet overdress were accented with flowers embroidered in gold thread along the edges and sleeves. She wore a matching ribbon entwined with her curls and a hair comb engraved with flowers. Much lovelier than the yellow gauze dress Aunt Josephine had stuffed herself into and wore with a garish blue turban. The feather on it was long enough to stab whatever poor soul stood behind her in the punch line.

"This is precisely why I suggested to Gabriel that he accept the first offer made for your hand. However you managed to turn out this way after the hours of instruction in decorum I've provided, I shall never understand."

If she stomped on her aunt's foot in this crush of people, could she claim that it happened by accident? Would Gabriel believe that? No, likely not. He knew both of them too well. Indeed, she and Aunt Josephine regularly bickered, but the woman wasn't usually this dreadful. "It is a mystery," she agreed. "However, you need not concern yourself with my future, dear aunt. Despite my awful demeanor and poor taste in fashion, I'm certain someone will take pity on me. I shouldn't like to be dependent upon the kindness of my brother for the rest of my life." She pasted on her sweetest smile.

Josephine sniffed. "Your brother is the soul of kindness and generosity. You would do well to emulate him, girl."

Violet was the *essence* of generosity and kindness. One had only to ask those who knew her best, like Patience or Lily— though perhaps not Lord Musgrave. He undoubtedly did not hold her in high regard after their encounter at Gabriel's house party. She *did* need to apologize for that if she saw him, though it was unlikely he'd be at Almack's. She scanned the room, considering, and spotted a familiar face, which almost made her laugh with glee. "Oh look, is that Lady Parling? It appears she is going toward the *punch* line. Someone ought to tell her how poor the quality is."

Aunt Josephine's head snapped around so fast to look where she pointed that Violet winced in sympathetic pain. Her aunt seemed to not have felt a twinge, however.

"Indeed. Stay here, child. I won't be but a moment. I simply must ask Lady Parling about her daughter. That scoundrel Lord Twisden was after her, you know." She slapped her fan on the back of Violet's hand and bumped people out of the way with her girth as she pushed toward Lady Parling.

Violet shook her hand out, grinning. Now that her chaperone was otherwise engaged, she had time to—

"My dearest Violet, your ability to dispatch Josephine gives me no small amount of pride. Even I could do no better," a throaty voice said from behind.

She turned to find Zeph standing there, his silver-gray eyes glinting with amusement. He was taller than Gabriel by several inches, taller even than Christian, though similarly built in that muscular fashion she preferred. Like Archer.

At the thought of him, her belly clenched, and she scanned the room for him, but didn't see him amidst the crowd, though with as many people here, she was surprised that Zeph found her. "You look dashing tonight, Zeph. I think I prefer a black suit on you because it brings out your eyes." He wore a black tailcoat and knee breeches, with a snowy white cravat and dark gray waistcoat, looking as unearthly beautiful as a man could.

"Thank you, my sweet little flower. How beautiful you are tonight. You are ravishing in that gown, despite what old yellow buzzards might say."

"Thank you." Despite her own appreciation of her dress,

Aunt Josephine never failed to make her question herself, or her appearance.

"Bennett will be as slain by your beauty as the rest of us poor souls."

She didn't care a whit for slaying souls, but she hoped Zeph spoke true.

He lifted her hand to his lips and pressed a kiss there, then spun her out and pulled her back to his chest. "Would you allow me a dance?"

Violet laughed as her heart lightened, and he led her to the dance floor as a lively reel began to play.

"Where is your beau?" Zeph asked during a turn.

"Lord Mansfield?"

"Is Mansfield your beau then? I thought we were speaking of Bennett."

Violet couldn't help the blush that hit her cheeks at the thought of courting Archer properly and claiming him as her beau.

"Archer rode in the carriage with Gabriel and Lily tonight, and I have yet to see them. Aunt Josephine insisted that we arrive separately and spent the entirety of the ride lecturing me on my manners and listing out who I may and may not talk to."

"And where do I rate?"

"You are near the top of the list of gentlemen I ought not to speak with, ever."

Zeph's eyes twinkled with mischief. "Shall we scandalize her by dancing a second time later this evening?"

This is why she adored him. They were quite alike in temperament, which led to more than a few escapades. Poor Gabriel. The idea of flustering her aunt was too delightful to let go. "I think it is our duty, my lord."

As they came together again, he said, "Ah, there is your beau. Over by that column."

He directed her attention to their left, and as they turned in a circle, she spotted Archer. He looked exceptionally fine in his black suit so similar to Zeph's. But he wore a deep green waistcoat that she knew would match his eyes. He stood with his arms crossed over his chest, an unhappy frown on his face as he stared at them.

"It appears we may have made him jealous. What other trouble might we stir before the night is done, I wonder?" He winked at her.

Violet grinned. "Anything is possible."

"True enough. What is life without a little fun? Deadly dull, that's what."

She murmured her agreement as they parted to exchange partners in the dance, all the while watching Archer. He never took his eyes off her, and she could feel the connection between them. Yet even after a passionate night in his arms, he'd not promised her any future, never said he loved her, and she'd spent a good portion of the day wondering if she'd made a terrible decision in laying with him.

"You're worried," Zeph said.

"He doesn't want to stay," she said softly.

"Neither did Lily or Bellamy," he replied.

"But they fell in love with Gabriel and Christian and decided that love was worth the life they left behind. I don't think that will happen with Archer."

The music drew to a close, and she curtseyed to Zeph. He took her hand and led her from the dance floor. "You think he will leave so easily?"

"Even if he should fall in love with me, I doubt it would keep Archer from doing whatever he chooses. He is a soldier at heart. Once he decides to do something, it seems that even something like love wouldn't be enough to change his mind."

"Perhaps."

"I wish I knew what kept Lily and Bellamy here," she said. "What convinced them."

Zeph guided her through the crowd toward a corner of the room where fewer people mingled. "Quite simply, it was destiny."

"Well then, I wish I knew if it was Archer's destiny to stay."

He cocked his head. "You don't wish to know your own future?"

Violet clasped her hands together and mumbled. "I *do* know it. If he leaves, I'll turn into Aunt Josephine."

He put his hands on her shoulders, thumbs rubbing them gently. "Dearest, should that happen, you will be far more entertaining than she is and most welcome at anyone's home. But fear not, your beau may yet surprise you. I'm certain he would even dive into the icy depths of a lake to rescue you. How could he do less with his soul?"

"He might come to my aid were I in trouble. He's honorable, as are you and all my brother's friends. I have little doubt that any of you would try to rescue me. That doesn't mean he would stay with me, any more than it means that you would."

"True, but I am not the one in love with you, Violet."

"Neither is he."

He winked and tapped her nose. "Is he not?"

She growled at him under her breath, making him chuckle. "Men are impossible to understand."

"Before he comes to whisk you away to the dance floor, allow me to say this. When Lily and Bellamy both faced matters of the heart and the difficult decision to stay with the one they loved or leave, there were two paths before them, yes?"

She nodded.

"And both found happiness in the end. Allow Archer time to face his crossroads. When he does, if he doesn't make the correct decision, then do what you do best."

"What's that?"

"Go after what you want. Show him another path than the two he faces."

"What if he returns to the future without me?"

"Then I expect you to say goodbye before you go after him, of course. It would be rude to leave this century without a proper farewell."

Follow Archer to the future? Could she do that if he left? Not that the prospect wasn't exciting, but if he left her now, after the tender moments they'd shared, why would he suddenly change his mind simply because she arrived in his time? Her stomach flipped over in a most unpleasant way at the thought.

He raised her hand to his lips for a brief kiss. "Remember, dearest, any man would be delighted to have you for his wife."

He backed up as if to leave.

Something in the tone of his voice hinted at loneliness. Remembering their conversation from a few days ago about family, Violet tightened her hold on his hand. "What of you? Why are you not married?"

Zeph hesitated. Pain flickered in his eyes that always seemed so fathomless. "I outlived a wife once. I don't know that I could bear to lose another."

What? "But… Gabriel has known you since Eton and never mentioned that you had married. I've never seen you with a wife, and I've known you nearly as long."

He dropped a kiss on her forehead, a wealth of affection passing between them. "Be happy, dear Violet. Time passes too quickly to do anything less." Then he was gone, weaving through the crowd until he disappeared.

Why did he never answer her questions? She was just considering ways to pry the information out of him when a clean, woodsy scent hit her nose, and a husky voice spoke in her ear. *Archer.*

"Did you enjoy your dance, Violet?"

Was that jealousy she heard? How marvelous. His jaw was still clean-shaven, and he appeared relaxed. She admired his strength to look unconcerned about his scars when surrounded by dozens of people who thrived on the weaknesses of others. He was so handsome, in his fitted coat that clung to his shoulders and the dark green waistcoat that brought out his eyes. He also carried the cane she'd given him, which made her heart swoop.

"Zeph is a marvelous dancer," she said. "A turn about the floor with him is always enjoyable."

His brows lowered into a glower. "I noticed." Archer put his hand on her shoulder and anchored her in place as he closed the distance between them and lowered his head. His lips brushed the shell of her ear as he growled, "I had my mouth on you, last night, Violet. I tasted you. You're mine. Don't try to play upon my jealousy."

Her breath caught as he stepped back to a respectable distance. The interaction lasted only a few seconds. Long enough to make her knees weak and her heart gallop like a runaway horse. Her nipples hardened at that husky, dark tone and she felt an embarrassing bit of dampness between her thighs. She swallowed. "Zeph asked for a second dance later to fluster Aunt Josephine. He heard her being unkind to me and suggested it for a bit of mischief."

"What did she say to you?"

Heavens, that hard, angry voice was delicious. "She doesn't care for my gown or my manners."

Archer swept his gaze over her gown, then made a slow trail back up. "You are the most beautiful woman here, Violet. That dark purple dress makes your skin look flawless and your eyes glow. As for your manners, they're much better than mine. Or hers, for that matter. I heard that she slept through a dinner party last month."

She giggled at the reminder. "Indeed."

His mouth softened and he extended his hand. "I understand that a quadrille is to play next. Will you dance with me?"

Her heart soared. Not only did Archer come with his scars visible, but he also wanted to dance with her. She placed her hand in his and allowed him to lead her toward the dance floor. He handed his cane to Bellamy as they passed, and though his limp remained, it didn't seem to pain him.

Just before they took their places, Percy Mansfield stepped into view. He gave her a short bow but barely glanced at Archer.

"My dear, Lady Violet. I had hoped to claim this dance."

She felt Archer tense and step closer.

"Your pardon, Lord Mansfield, but this dance is promised to Mr. Bennett," she said.

He turned an assessing gaze on Archer, then nodded. "Then promise me the next? I have something to speak with you about. Something I hope should make you quite happy." He said, somehow making his words sound both an invitation and a taunt.

A quick glance at Archer, who looked coiled and ready to strike, and she stepped between the men. "Of course. If you'll excuse us? Thank you." She latched onto Archer's arm and pulled him to the rows of dancers lining up for the quadrille.

He gave Percy a final, hard glare, then took his spot. But when he stood across from her, his smile made her chest hitch.

Archer moved smoothly through the steps, not missing one. "You're quite graceful tonight, Mr. Bennett," she said as they came together.

"If I am, you are the only one to notice. Everyone else is looking at you. You are stunning, Violet," he murmured.

"Thank you." The way he looked at her made her feel as if she truly was the most beautiful woman in the room. Aunt Josephine's words from earlier faded away and she stood taller.

"I don't want you to dance with Mansfield."

"I must. I think he means to ask me for another outing, and I would prefer to decline when surrounded by people."

"Are you afraid of him?" There was an edge to Archer's tone, a warning that made her feel safe.

"No. However, I'm afraid that he might provoke me into a situation where I might not be... as well-mannered as I should."

He chuckled. "Afraid you might slap him?"

"Or worse," she admitted.

"There's that fire I admire."

How can I make him stay? She wished she knew the right words, or that the affection he felt for her was enough to change his mind about leaving. Perhaps that was selfish of her, but a future without Archer looked bleak.

When the dance ended, he tucked her hand into the crook of his arm and slowly led her off the dance floor. "I hope you found that as enjoyable as I did," he said.

"Yes, and I hope you might ask me for another."

"I'd like that."

"Lady Violet, I believe this dance is ours," Percy called as he approached.

Bellamy followed and offered Archer his cane. He took it with a nod of thanks. Then, ignoring Percy, he bowed once more to Violet. "Until later, Lady Violet."

She couldn't help but smile as she accepted Percy's arm and returned to the floor for another reel. The tempo was quite upbeat, not allowing for much conversation as they circled and spun this way and that.

Percy gasped for air as the dance ended but managed a bow. "That was a lively one," he managed between gasps.

Violet was a little out of breath herself. "Indeed. Thank you for the dance."

He caught her elbow before she could turn away. "If I may be so bold, I need to speak with you. Would you care for a cup of punch or tea?" He guided her toward the ballroom exit as he spoke.

"I shouldn't…"

"Don't be foolish. After an energetic dance, everyone needs a refreshment. Come." He all but dragged her to the tearoom set aside for refreshments.

Violet spotted Aunt Josephine with Lady Parling, their heads bent together, eyes equally wide as they spoke.

"Did you enjoy the gift I sent?" Percy asked.

Violet jerked to a stop. "*You* sent the gifts? But why?"

"Why send you a gift? Darling, I thought you knew how I felt. I intend to—"

"No, why send the gift without signing the note?"

His face scrunched in confusion. "I thought it would be obvious who sent it. After all, it's my understanding that you don't have any other suitors. Some say your brother is getting rather desperate."

Violet clenched her fists at her sides. *I will not slap him or stomp on his foot.* "That is quite impertinent," she ground out.

"Even so, I'm not wrong, am I? Anyway, why are you so upset that I sent a rose? I thought it would suit you. Regardless, I wish to speak to you about our future. I plan—"

A rose? She'd received more than that. "Only a rose? What about the vase of flowers or the poetry book?" she asked, interrupting him.

"What poetry book?"

Violet's stomach took a sudden dip as an unpleasant feeling settled in her belly. It felt like... dread. "The poetry book you sent two days past?"

He shook his head, looking confused.

If Percy hadn't sent the poetry or the vase of flowers, then who—?

"I'm afraid I must take credit for those," a familiar voice said from behind her.

Violet turned and then stumbled back a step. "Lord Musgrave."

Hugh Musgrave should have looked dashing with his dark blue velvet tailcoat and white breeches, brown hair, and dark eyes. He was strong and fit, though his nose had an angle to it that hadn't been there the last time she saw him, thanks to Gabriel. But there was a cruel twist to his lips that made her uneasy.

"Hello, darling. Have you missed me?" He looked over her shoulder at Percy. "We were quite intimate at her brother's house party last autumn. Did she tell you? No? Darling, I'm surprised."

Her mouth dropped open, and words failed her. Did he insinuate that she'd gone to his bed?

Percy gave a small cough. "Lady Violet said nothing. Though

I suppose that isn't surprising. Little wonder then that the earl is in a hurry to marry her off."

She gasped. "No, I never… I wouldn't!" Except that she had, with Archer. But never with Hugh Musgrave.

"Forgive me, my dear. I think I best leave you to sort out things with Musgrave." Percy's lip curled in distaste, then he nodded to Hugh and left.

Violet glared at the man standing before her, looking so smug for trying to ruin her again though this time at Almack's in front of dozens of people instead of simply at a country house party. "I wish Gabriel had been the one to shoot you in the arm," she growled. Instead, it had been their friend Seabright, who'd accidentally shot him on a hunt. At the time, she'd been afraid for Hugh. Now she wished Seabright had had better aim.

Hugh laughed. "Charming. My arm healed nicely. Better than my nose, as you can see. But I shall take that to your brother in good time. For now, I'm afraid I must insist that you join me for a walk. We have much to discuss. Did you like my gifts? I wanted only the best for my future wife, you know."

Archer had been right all along. Someone nefarious had sent the gifts and she'd dismissed his concerns. How she wished she had listened to him!

"You're mad," she sputtered. "I can't marry you."

Musgrave clamped a hand on her elbow, squeezing tight on the tender area at the back until she hissed in pain. "Oh, but I think you should allow me to change your mind. You owe me that. Come along quietly, darling."

"I won't go." She yanked her arm back, trying to break his hold, but he pressed harder until she whimpered.

"You will." He nodded across the room. "Look there."

Violet reluctantly turned to look. She spotted Aunt Josephine still in conversation with Lady Parling, her unnatural red curls gleaming in the candlelight. Behind her aunt, a gentleman in a fine tailcoat with a plain face sidled closer. Something glinted in his hand. He caught Violet's gaze, and at this distance, there didn't seem to be even a spark of life in his eyes. They were cold and flat. Dead.

The man held a thin blade, she realized, and he now stood directly behind Aunt Josephine. One quick move and he could plant the knife in her back. Violet sucked in a breath and started to tremble. As much as Aunt Josephine tutted and griped about Violet, she didn't want the woman to come to harm. Was this how Bellamy felt when Wainsright kidnapped her from the dress shop several weeks ago? What could she do?

"Come along, or my associate will cause a scene, and I shall take you anyway amid the confusion." Musgrave wrapped an arm around her waist and guided her toward the stairs. "Is your wrap nearby? It will be chilly in the carriage. I wouldn't want you to become ill."

She looked around wildly. Was there anyone she knew that could help? The faces all looked the same and a gray haze was beginning to cloud her vision. No. She couldn't go with Hugh. Maybe she could get away before they left the building?

"I know you're concerned for your aunt," he said. "Once we are in my carriage, my footman has instructions to alert my associate, and she will never know he was there."

"And if I don't come with you?" She knew the answer, but she had to hear him say it.

He ushered her down the stone steps to the main floor, weaving through the throng of people arriving for the ball. "I have another man waiting near your brother. I only wish time to talk, darling. Surely you can grant me that." He touched his nose with his free hand.

Violet had meant to apologize to him for the events last fall. If she did, would he let her go? "Only to talk?" She remembered Archer's tale of his dear friend, and how she'd been killed by a man who took her away. Was Musgrave capable of hurting or killing her?

Musgrave smiled down at her, and there was a softness about him that she hadn't expected. Was she overreacting? Maybe he didn't mean to hurt her…

"I know that I scared you last autumn when I tried to kiss you. You weren't prepared for that, and I realized my error. But I have not stopped thinking of you since. Please." He waved toward the front door of Almack's, which was open to allow the cool night air inside.

What choice did she have? She couldn't allow harm to come to Aunt Josephine or Gabriel. One last glance over her shoulder told her that no help was coming. Percy would walk away thinking she'd been ruined and not look back. Aunt Josephine, who should have been her chaperone, was too far in her drink to remember her charge. She hadn't even alerted anyone that she was leaving the ballroom when Percy wished to get some punch.

You're a ninny, Violet. A ninny who is in trouble. And now, because she had dismissed Archer's warnings, she found herself in a similar situation to the childhood friend he'd lost.

Archer, please notice that I'm gone and come find me. Please.

Trembling violently, she walked through the doors to where a line of carriages waited and prayed that Hugh Musgrave only wanted to talk. But the fervent gleam of delight in his eyes didn't bode well.

Several minutes earlier…

"YOU CAN'T LET her marry him, Archer," Bellamy said, as they watched Mansfield dance with Violet.

"She can marry whoever she chooses." But dammit, he didn't want her to marry Percy Mansfield. He could be the one sending Violet the secret gifts. Archer's gut curdled at the thought. Something about the situation felt too much like Amanda and her secret admirer so long ago. But he'd been a boy then and hadn't been trained as he was now. If Violet disappeared, he'd tear the world apart to find her. He couldn't let her light be snuffed out.

Not while he drew breath. Yet there was also a possibility that he was seeing shadows where there were none.

Violet had started him on the road to healing in every way. He could feel it. Perhaps it was time to let himself heal from what had happened to Amanda and realize that it really hadn't been his fault. Maybe it was time for him to stop fighting with his memories and regrets, and to step forward out of the darkness into the light.

"What if she chooses you?" Bellamy poked him in the side, disturbing his thoughts.

Violet was so pure, so beautiful, and special. She deserved a man of her own time, her own class. A man who could give her the life she was accustomed to. Not a broken warrior. "She's too young for me." He offered the same argument he'd been giving himself since his arrival, though it sounded thin even to his ears after the time he'd spent with Violet. When he woke this morning, she'd been gone from his bed. It shouldn't have bothered him. He could count on one hand the number of times a woman had stayed a full night in his bed, but with Violet, it was different. All his feelings, his needs, and even his senses were heightened around her. He felt more attuned to her than anyone in his life, even the members of his team. How could a woman that much a part of him be "too young"?

"You do realize that young women of this day often marry men far older? It's not unheard of for an eighteen-year-old to marry a man in his fifties in order to give him heirs. Violet is only thirteen years younger. That's not a terrible age gap."

"It's not a gap of age. It's a gap of experience. She's too innocent. I've seen too much. I've done things..." Things he could never admit to his sisters. Though, they were things he'd admitted to Violet in the dark of night when she was in his arms.

He ran a hand through his hair. God, she had him so twisted around that he couldn't even believe his own arguments. With one exception. "I can't make her happy." The words sounded like gravel coming out of his throat and pain pierced his chest.

"You may be older, but you certainly aren't wiser. Violet only has eyes for you. Maybe someone younger and less jaded by life is what you need, Arch. Someone to drag you out of your cave by your hair."

"Bellamy, you're supposed to be working toward a more formal tone," Lily said as she joined them. His middle sister looked radiant with her pregnancy. Her blue-green eyes seemed brighter in the light of hundreds of candles and the deep blue gown she wore made her skin glow. "And I think it was the male caveman who did the dragging by the hair."

Bells crossed her arms, her blonde curls dancing as she lifted a shoulder. "I didn't know how else to get the point across. Besides, I think a cavewoman is more than capable of showing the male he's being an idiot."

Cavemen and women? How had this conversation derailed into *that*? He would never understand his sisters. "My point is that Violet needs someone better suited to her."

Lily wrapped her arm around Archer in a side hug and leaned into him. "Who could be better suited than a man who sees her for the vibrant woman that she is, protects her as no one else could, and who loves her?"

"She needs a man she can count on. That's not me." He leaned a little harder on his cane as his leg began to throb. Even if he loved Violet, she deserved so much more. He didn't want to be the asshole that took her virginity and then left, crushing her feelings, but what else could he do? He couldn't provide for *himself* at the moment, so how could he take care of her?

"Do you hear yourself? You spent years as a SEAL. Do you expect us to believe that because of a leg injury that you can't kick someone's ass? Or find a way to use your skills to make money?"

"And that if Violet or one of us were in trouble, that you wouldn't do everything you could to rescue us?" Bellamy added.

"You know you would," Lily said.

Bells poked him in the chest. "Honestly, Archer, anyone who can make it through Hell Week or whatever they call it can survive a London Season."

He shook his head. "I just realized why I never won arguments when we were younger. I couldn't get a word in."

Lily laughed. "You couldn't win because you weren't right."

"And we were too cute to stay mad at." Bellamy looped her arm through Lily's and leaned into her sister, smiling at Archer, as if to remind him that nothing had really changed.

He gusted out a sigh. What could he say to that? "Fine. I'll think about what you said." With that, he turned to search for Violet, unable to let her out of his sight for long. Even if everyone else was right and he didn't need to be concerned for her safety, he was so drawn to her that he couldn't help but seek her out. The last dance had ended, and another begun while he and his sisters talked. She was no longer among the dancers on the dance floor. Where had she gone?

"We love you, Arch. We just want you to be happy," Bellamy said, bringing his attention back to her.

"Here. We want you to be happy, *here,* with us," Lily added. "We need to be a family again. It's been too long."

Archer pulled her into a hug, then wrapped an arm around Bellamy when she joined in. "I missed you both too."

Lily pressed a hand to her stomach, though her baby bump wasn't visible under the gown she wore. "Now, has anyone seen my husband? I want to dance a waltz with him before I turn into a whale and can't see my feet."

"He's there, talking to Christian and Zeph." Bellamy pointed to a spot over his left shoulder.

Archer spotted the men several feet away. All three were tall and built more powerfully than the men surrounding them, who looked softer. One fellow in particular caught his attention.

He was a few inches shorter than Gabriel, with brown hair, long sideburns, and a face that would blend in with the crowd: plain and forgettable.

The hair on the back of Archer's neck rose.

The man stood next to Gabriel. Closer than seemed normal,

even in this crowded ballroom. His arms were crossed over his chest as he scanned the crowd, looking more as if he was waiting for someone than like a man enjoying a ball at Almack's.

Their gazes met for half a second before the man continued his perusal and turned away. Something flashed in his hand.

Archer was moving before he acknowledged what he'd seen. The man had a knife palmed, and he'd been watching the doorway to the ballroom even as he kept Gabriel close.

He'd dealt with men like this before while on missions. Men paid to take down a target, even in a room full of people. The good ones could make it out in the chaos and disappear as if they'd never been there or were wholly forgettable men like this one who could take out the target and then stand by to watch the commotion that ensued because no one remembered their faces.

A trio of giggling girls crossed in front of Archer, their eyes lingering on him. He dodged them, squeezed between a bickering couple, and rushed toward the man. His sisters called his name as they followed, but he ignored them.

The man was disarmed before he knew Archer was there.

Archer pressed the knife to the man's groin and leaned into his space, lowering his voice to a dark whisper. "Who are you here for?"

Flat, brown eyes stared back at him without an ounce of fear. "Not you."

"Who paid you?"

A small smile flickered on the man's lips. "Not you."

Lily and Bellamy pushed through the crowd, just as Gabriel and the others noticed him. "Archer?" His gaze dropped to the glinting metal and then flicked up to the unknown man. Gabriel immediately positioned himself between the knife and his wife, shielding her.

Archer's respect for him rose a notch. He increased the pressure on the blade.

"What goes on here?" Christian asked.

"Saw this gentleman standing a little too close to you with his knife. I was just asking him what his business was."

Zeph squeezed in behind the man, blocking any escape. "Perhaps we should take this discussion to the antechamber. Somewhere a little more private so that we can hear the response."

Archer nodded and tucked the knife into his waistband. "Christian, will you stay with Bells and Lily?"

"Of course. Call if you have a need." He ushered the women a few feet away, leaning down to whisper to them, no doubt telling them what had transpired.

Where was Violet? Archer scanned the room again but didn't see her. Had she gone into the tearoom for refreshments? Was she with Aunt Josephine for once? As soon as they'd dealt with this man he needed to find her just to see for himself that she was safe.

Archer and Zeph walked the man from the room, while Gabriel followed. The gentlemen's anteroom was a small chamber off to the side, decorated in the same blues as the ballroom, but with comfortable chairs for sitting and smoking. Two men rose from their seats when they shoved the mystery man into the room, and quickly excused themselves, leaving the small space empty.

Zeph pushed him into one of the chairs and kept a hand clamped on his shoulder, holding him in place. Gabriel closed the door behind them and came to stand at his other side.

Archer took the opportunity to study the knife in the candlelight. It seemed well-made, with a simple leather handle. Dark brown speckles and worn spots on the leather hinted that the weapon had been used often. He kept it visible as he squatted until he was eye level with the man and waited.

Most people fidgeted as the silence drew out. Not this one. He stared back, steady and patient. Archer's gut said this man had spent his life in the shadows and had made peace with them. He was probably thinking about ways to get the knife back and use it to escape.

Time to switch tactics.

"I've known men like you," Archer said. "You take a job until completion, then move to the next, caring only about the money or the information given as payment. Your only loyalty is to yourself because you do not trust the men who hire you."

A flare of surprise went through the man's eyes that was quickly squashed, the cold mask of indifference sliding back into place. Archer smiled. "How much to give the name of your target and your employer?"

"What good is money if the man wants me dead?"

"That's nothing new though, is it?" Archer asked. "I imagine many of your employers would want evidence of their transactions permanently eliminated. You must be good at staying alive."

A small smile touched the man's lips. "And negotiating."

Now he was getting somewhere. "Your price?"

"Five hundred guineas. *Each.*"

"Five hundred for each answer to who your target is, and who hired you?" he clarified.

The man nodded.

Archer looked up at Gabriel and Zeph. Gabriel shook his head, declining the offer.

Zeph moved in front of the man. "Fifty guineas and I won't gut you like a fish, right here."

The man's cold gaze settled on Zeph.

Archer expected him to sputter at the absurd counteroffer and renegotiate. To his surprise, the man paled and nodded.

"Fifty."

"Total," Zeph said. He removed the money from inside his waistcoat.

The man swallowed. He tipped his head toward Gabriel. "Lord Rothden, though it might be called off."

"Is that what you were waiting for? A signal?" Archer asked.

"Aye." Sweat broke out on the man's brow and a trace of a Scottish accent tinged his word. "A footman would signal if the lass were agreeable. If not..." he flicked his fingers in a dismissive wave.

The lass...

Archer went cold all over. He surged forward, pressing his forearm to the man's throat. The chair tipped back on two legs but held under his weight. "Where's Violet Hawthorne?" he growled. The man tugged at Archer's arm, desperate to draw it away from his throat or his windpipe would be crushed.

"Archer." Gabriel stepped forward.

"There are only two young women that would need to be agreeable in regard to you, Gabriel, and Lily was with us." Archer didn't look away from the man's eyes as he held the knife up and nodded toward Zeph. "Tell me now or I'll give this to my friend here and watch as he slices the answer out of you."

Gabriel muttered a curse under his breath.

As Archer suspected, the man paled. A person at ease in the shadows was often immune to threats of harm. They'd seen and done enough harm to no longer be fazed by it. But something about Zeph made the man blanch and that tiny show of fear was a weakness he had no qualms exploiting.

"I would answer," Zeph advised the man. "You are not the only one capable of violence, as you can see."

Still clutching Archer's coat sleeve, the man said, "Aye. The younger Hawthorne."

"Agreeable in what way?"

When the man hesitated, he pushed harder, until the man gasped. He let up on the pressure enough for the man to breathe.

"She was to go with him. If she didn't, the footman would be around to give me and the other the signal."

Gabriel pushed Archer out of the way to grab the man's coat and lift him out of the chair. "What other? Speak or lose your tongue."

Archer wasn't surprised by Gabriel's sudden fury. He had just learned that he'd been a target, his sister was being pressured to go with someone, and that Lily might still potentially be in danger. If Gabriel hadn't acted, he would have. Still standing to the side, Zeph appeared relaxed with his arms crossed, but Archer could feel the tension radiating off his frame.

"The older woman. Red hair."

"Josephine," Archer muttered.

Gabriel swore, his knuckles turning white where they gripped the man. "Who paid you?"

"Didn't ask for a name," the man said.

It had to be Mansfield. "Did he have light brown hair and blue eyes, and appear to be about my age?"

The man's gaze darted to Zeph before he said, "Brown hair and eyes. Had a bump on his nose from where it'd been broken." He glanced at Gabriel. "Hates you."

"Musgrave," Gabriel and Zeph said in unison.

The name meant nothing to Archer, and he didn't remember hearing it in the time he'd been there. "Who's Musgrave?"

Hawthorne looked grim. "A friend once. He flirted with Violet last year at my house party. At first, she seemed to like him until they had a quarrel. Violet said he tried to kiss her, and when she refused, he pressed the issue. I forced him to leave."

Musgrave would have been humiliated in front of his peers. Now he'd retaliated. Coercing Violet to go with him by threatening her family. A man willing to hire someone to kill Gabriel out of spite was dangerous. They had to find Violet immediately.

He released the man and rose to his feet. "We have to find her."

Zeph tossed the coins into the man's lap and strode for the door.

Gabriel and Archer followed.

"Zeph, make sure the women and Aunt Josephine are safe. I'll go with Archer to find Violet." Gabriel clenched his fists, vibrating with anger as he spoke.

Archer's heart thudded in his ears, but he locked his emotions down tight. Violet needed all his focus. All his training. As they split up and searched every room on both floors, events of the past weeks slotted together. Percy Mansfield wanted Violet as his wife, but his actions didn't border on obsession. Archer had overlooked the simple fact that Violet's admirer knew her well. He'd followed her, chosen gifts, and intrigued her with the mystery of who sent them. Tempting her. Teasing her. Her admirer had fixated on her specifically. Archer knew all too well what a man like that was capable of. He'd never forget the pictures of Amanda's shallow grave.

Gabriel met him on the ground floor as they pushed outside and searched the people milling about, waiting to get in. No coaches were pulling away, and there was no sign of Violet.

"Where would he take her?" Archer asked.

"Musgrave has a home near Norwich, northeast of London. It's a day's ride on horseback. More by carriage," Gabriel said. He gripped the back of his neck and looked at the sky. When he met Archer's gaze, the lines on his forehead had deepened and anguish filled his eyes. "I trusted him. We were friends at Eton and for years after. I invited him to the house party. But even after I forced him out, I trusted him to be honorable."

"You couldn't have known that trust would turn to obsession," Archer said quietly. "None of that matters now. We must find her."

Gabriel nodded, straightening his shoulders.

Zeph burst out the door of Almack's. "Aunt Josephine is well. She had no idea she was being watched. Christian is gathering the ladies' cloaks to take them home."

Gabriel called for his carriage and the extra one that Violet and Josephine had ridden in.

"They'll be too slow," Archer said. "I need a horse."

"I can't ask you to go after her, Bennett," Gabriel said.

"I wasn't giving you a choice. I'm going."

"What's Carter doing here?" Zeph interrupted, pointing across the street.

Archer spotted a man wearing black breeches with a purple satin tailcoat and yellow waistcoat, his hat sitting at a rakish angle. The collector they'd tried to get the crystal from who'd disappeared and left them to fight off an attack in Hyde Park. His lip curled.

"Maybe he saw something." Zeph waved to the contact, drawing his attention.

Carter crossed the street, wearing a smug smile, and swinging his cane as if he hadn't a care in the world.

Archer wanted to punch him. He reined in that anger and locked it down.

When Carter joined them, he tipped his hat. "Gentlemen." He looked at Gabriel and nodded. "The Earl of Rothden, I presume?"

Gabriel nodded. "Huntington has spoken of you."

The dandy whipped a handkerchief edged in lace out of his pocket and dabbed at his temple. "It is quite warm tonight. Do you think it will be a sweltering summer?"

They didn't have time for this. Archer turned away, intent on borrowing someone's horse. He'd studied the maps of London and England in Gabriel's office shortly after his arrival. He had a fair idea of where to find the roads leading out of town and heading northeast, toward Norwich. If he found the right road, he felt sure he could catch up to Musgrave. He'd have put Violet in a coach if he meant to travel a good distance, which meant his pace would be slower.

Behind him, he heard Gabriel ask Carter about the incident and if he saw anything.

"I did," Carter said, sounding bored. "The woman was being forced into a carriage and didn't look pleased."

Archer spun at the man's words. "You saw Violet?"

"A stunning woman with dark hair, wearing the most delicious aubergine gown? She must have spent a fortune on it."

Gabriel sighed. "That's Violet."

"The carriage headed toward Grosvenor."

Grosvenor... he thought back to the map. Wasn't that...

Gabriel stepped forward. "Grosvenor? Are you sure? They

didn't drive toward Haymarket?"

Carter shook his head.

"Do you think Musgrave's trying to trick us into going the wrong way?" Gabriel muttered, more to himself than the rest of them. "Go toward Grosvenor then change directions and make for Norwich?"

Zeph frowned. "If he didn't take Violet to Norwich, where would he go?"

"It *must* be Norwich. It's the only place that makes sense."

"There is always Gretna Green," Carter stated.

Gabriel paled. "Impossible. Musgrave wouldn't risk it. He knows I'm a better rider. I would catch them before they ever made it across the border to Scotland."

"What's Gretna Green?" Archer asked.

"A town just over the Scottish border that allows couples to marry without their families' permission, which is required here and strictly enforced," Gabriel replied.

"Not if you were dead," Zeph said softly. "If Archer hadn't discovered our would-be assassin, I wonder if he truly would have backed off at the signal, or if his orders were to eliminate Gabriel regardless."

"How could I have misjudged the man so completely all these years?" Gabriel asked aloud, though he seemed to be speaking to himself.

Zeph laid a hand on his shoulder. "We'll find her."

But which road did they take? Scotland, or northeast of London? Two vastly different directions Musgrave might have taken Violet in.

Archer's heart skipped a beat, then began to pound.

Carter was more concerned with money and unique items than what happened to Violet. Could they trust what he said? And even if the coach did go toward Grosvenor, might Musgrave double back to take the road toward his home or continue on to Gretna Green?

A cold dread climbed up his throat, making it almost impossible to moisten his mouth. *No.* He couldn't be in this situation. Not again.

Amanda.

Church.

His team.

They'd counted on him, and he made the wrong decision, leading to their deaths. He couldn't do that again. He had to rescue Violet. But Jesus, what if he chose wrong? There wouldn't be time to turn around and go the other direction. Musgrave could force her to marry him, or worse. Far, far worse.

He'd seen it all in his years as a SEAL. He knew what sometimes happened to a beautiful young woman who displeased the man in control of her. He'd seen the aftermath. Violet needed him.

Two different directions and a man as trustworthy as a viper.

Somehow, he had to choose and hope he was right. Again.

CHAPTER FOURTEEN

VIOLET HUDDLED IN the corner of the carriage, staring wide-eyed at the man across from her, as they barreled away from Almack's. Hugh Musgrave, a man her brother had trusted as a good friend, a man she'd flirted and danced with—and briefly hoped for more from—had taken her against her will and threatened the people she loved. Her mind spun through every interaction with him that she could remember. From the time she'd been little when he'd barely given her a second glance, until the house party last autumn where she'd refused his kiss and he'd been forced to leave. She couldn't reconcile their last exchange with a man who still wanted to pursue her.

"Why?" The word slipped out, her voice shaky with fear.

Hugh removed his hat and gloves, set them on the seat beside him and ran a hand through his dark hair, smiling with a warmth she didn't understand. "Gabriel evicted me so unceremoniously that I didn't have a chance to explain myself. To apologize to you." His eyes took on a faraway look. "You were so lovely that evening in your pink shepherdess dress, looking as pure and innocent as a lamb." He focused on her once more and the intensity in her eyes made her press back into the cushion. "I admit, you left me feeling rather wolfish, my darling. For days, your beauty and wit had entranced me. How had I missed Gabriel's sister turning into the loveliest woman I'd ever seen?

Your flirtatious smiles, the way you tended me when I'd been shot... how could I not want to kiss you? In my haste, I didn't realize that you'd never been kissed, and I frightened you. For that, I'm deeply sorry."

He seemed so earnest. None of this made sense. "But why all of this if you only wanted to apologize? I thought you would be angry."

His gaze tracked slowly down her body. "I want more than to apologize. I haven't stopped thinking about you since that night in your garden, my darling. The image of your face turned up to mine as the moonlight bathed you like a goddess has haunted my dreams. I would give anything to take those moments back. To wait until you were ready for my kiss. I want to know the taste of your lips. Your skin. To breathe you in until you are part of my soul."

His darkly whispered words made her tremble and her chest feel too tight. She'd longed to hear words like this from him in the garden that night, but he'd startled her when he grabbed her arms roughly and pulled her to his chest. She'd seen something in his eyes that made her unsure of him, and what she wanted. Hearing them now, she wanted to get as far from him as possible. She itched to grab for the door handle. Could she leap from the carriage at this speed?

"You sent the gifts. W-why didn't you sign the notes?" She peered out the window at the dark street beyond, trying to determine where they were. If she could escape, there would be no harm to Gabriel and Aunt Josephine tonight. The shops looked familiar. Were they on Bond Street? If he only wanted to talk, as he'd said in Almack's, wouldn't he ask the driver to stay near the assembly hall? A cold ball formed in her stomach, the chill starting to spread through her limbs.

"You are a well-bred young lady. Society demands that you return them, and so you would." He leaned forward. "Did you like the flowers? The day that I saw you in that beautiful pink gown, I knew the rose would be perfect."

Ice slid down her spine. "You followed me?" Archer had warned her repeatedly, and like a fool, she'd refused to listen. The excitement and intrigue of someone sending mysterious notes overrode her good sense. The writer seemed to know her, and for once, it felt like someone saw her for the woman she was.

That feeling paled in comparison to the way she felt when Archer looked at her.

Hugh ducked his head. "I had to speak to you away from Gabriel. I followed, looking for an opportunity to approach you. But between your brother, your aunt, Mansfield, and that other gentleman who has been hovering about, I knew that the Season would be at an end before we could speak." He gave her a sharp look. "What were you doing with Percy Mansfield? Surely you weren't considering a match with the likes of him?"

"I… What do you mean? Do you know something about Lord Mansfield? Gabriel thought he might be a suitable match."

"And to think I looked so highly upon Rothden for years," he scoffed. "It is well known where Mansfield's business interests lie." He must have read the confusion on her face because he added, "He provides what we shall call…*inexpensive labor* to the West Indies."

She paled. "How do you know this?" Archer had been right not to trust Percy. *Archer.* Was Archer coming for her? Had he noticed that she was gone yet?

"Where money is involved, the law can easily be ignored. Mansfield is well known among my contacts on the docks. As long as the ships sail through ports where there is no law, men can still get rich. It's a repugnant practice."

"It's horrid." Thank God she hadn't felt anything for Percy. He'd met every one of her qualifications for a husband, and yet underneath, he was soulless. Anyone who could treat another man as only an animal had no heart to speak of. The very thought of what might have happened had Archer not appeared in their lives made her stomach turn.

Hugh took her hand in his. "Did you miss me, Violet? I know

things did not end well between us before, but did you wonder about me in the intervening months?"

"I did. I felt wretched for what happened." Not wretched enough to tender a flame for him, however.

He removed her glove, then pressed a kiss to the back of her hand. The feel of his lips on her skin made her flesh crawl. "I thought as much. I knew that we were destined to be together. Gabriel was wrong to throw me out the way he did. A gentleman of honor would have allowed me to explain. To offer for your hand as I wanted to. But he's changed. He's grown selfish, thinking only of his needs and desires. He cannot bear the thought of anyone being happy save for himself."

Violet slipped her hand from his as naturally as she could manage, while inside her heart hammered. Gabriel may be protective of her, but he did so out of love. The things that Hugh described were not true.

"Don't worry, darling. He will come around."

"Come around to what?" She looked out the window once more, not recognizing this area of London. Wherever he was taking her, it was not one of the fashionable areas she frequented, and that scared her.

"Our marriage. Once you are mine in body and name, he will realize that if he wants a continued relationship with you, he will have to apologize for his uncivil behavior to gain my favor."

"I cannot marry you," she whispered, limbs going numb.

He chuckled. "Of course you can. Your brother no longer has a say. Besides, a number of people saw you get into my carriage unattended by your chaperone. Your reputation is quite ruined. No man of quality will have you."

"W-where are you taking me?" She knew. Oh God, she knew. She had to escape.

"To Gretna Green, of course. Once we are well enough away from London, we will detour through the countryside long enough to confuse your brother. Then we will rejoin the main roads for faster travel. You will be mine in less than a fortnight."

He seemed so pleased with the idea, as if she would see this had all been some odd misunderstanding and fall happily into his arms now that he'd cleared the way for them to be together. Had it? *No.* He'd threatened Gabriel and Aunt Josephine's life in order to coerce her into the carriage.

"All I want is you, Violet. We were meant to be together. I know you feel it. We are alike in so many ways. Willing to take risks for what we want. And I want you, darling. Enough to risk your brother's wrath. I love you."

He was mad. The fervent gleam in his eyes… the way he looked at her like a hungry wolf and spoke about Gabriel as if her brother plotted to keep them apart these last months. She feared she couldn't reason with him, but she had to try once more. "Please, Lord Musgrave."

"Hugh," he interjected.

"Please, Hugh. Gabriel will be worried. If he's angry with you, he won't bless any arrangements we make." She would never marry him willingly. "Won't you take me back to Almack's?"

"No, darling. Your brother will be incensed no matter what happens. Let's finish what we planned and marry first. I promise, if he loves you as he says, he will reconsider his anger. Especially when you present him with a charming niece or nephew."

She shuddered. "And if we don't suit?"

He studied her. "Is this because you are afraid of the marriage bed? Don't worry darling, I shall be gentle." He reached for her. "Why don't you come sit with me? We have plenty of time until we stop for the night, and this will give you an opportunity to know your husband's kiss."

He wasn't listening to her. He hadn't listened that night in the garden when she hadn't wanted to kiss him. If he wouldn't listen when she said "no" to a kiss, he wouldn't listen to her on anything else that was important.

Hugh latched onto her hand and pulled her toward him.

Violet resisted. The carriage rolled at a fast pace now that they were in less a less populated part of the city. If she threw open the door and jumped, she could seriously injure herself. She didn't know where they were, and she didn't have any money to hire a hack. She'd be alone and defenseless in an unknown area of London. But if she attempted to escape when they stopped for the night, she'd be far from home, and there was no guarantee that anyone would help her. She had to flee now while she at least had a chance of getting help or Archer finding her.

Hugh scowled and tugged harder. "Don't be afraid, darling. I won't hurt you."

Violet let him pull her from the seat, then threw herself sideways at the door. She caught the handle and turned, putting her weight behind it to fling it open and jump.

A hard arm banded around her waist, yanking her back inside. Violet struggled and screamed. She fought and kicked and tried to bite any part of his body that came near.

Hugh plunged a hand into her hair, scattering some of her pins, and yanked her head back at an awkward angle.

She bowed her back, trying to relieve the strain on her neck and cried out at the pain.

He held her steady, reached out to grab the handle and slammed the door closed. Then he tossed her against the opposite seat and fumbled in the bag at his feet.

Violet launched herself at the door a second time, but he grabbed her and wrestled her down to the floor. She was pinned against the bottom seat cushion, breathing hard as he held her in place.

"I love that fire, darling, but that was a grave error. You could have hurt yourself." He yanked her hands behind her back, holding them in one hand. Coarse rope bit into her wrists.

Violet struggled to pull her hands away and bucked against him.

Hugh growled and leaned all his weight into her, cutting off her air as he crushed her against the seat.

She gasped and sagged forward until her head hit the back

cushion. "Don't do this," she whispered.

"You're being very foolish. I didn't want to bind you, but you leave me little choice. I'm going to take care of you, Violet. You will see. I will love you like no one else. All you have to do is have a little faith. I'll give you all of the children you want, and you will be happy. You're scared. I understand. But rest and think of all the joy we will have together." He picked her up and settled her on the seat. When he tried to bind her feet, she kicked at any part of him she could reach. He easily subdued her and soon, she was trussed up like a goose.

"There," he said as he took the seat opposite her, panting. "I know it isn't comfortable, but we shall be at an inn a few hours from now. I'll release you then. In the meantime, I suggest you consider how you wish to spend the next fortnight. If I have to bind you for the entire journey, I will. Nothing will stop me from claiming you."

"I don't want to marry you," she bit out.

He chuckled. "I don't believe you. I saw the way you looked at me at the house party. You are as much in love with me as I am with you."

She struggled to relieve the strain on her arms. "What happened to you, Hugh? You were always so polite, so honorable. Why are you forcing me to wed you when I know that there are many other women who would happily marry you. You're young, handsome, and you will come into an earldom soon. Why not take one of them?"

"They aren't you. Violet, the moment I truly saw you as a woman grown, the darkness in my heart lifted. You must know the years spent at Eton were dark, even if Gabriel never told you the details of what happened."

She nodded. How was she going to get away now? She had no weapon, no way to untie herself or cut the rope.

He rubbed a hand over the dark blue fabric on the seat beside his leg. "My father and uncle prepared me for two years prior to going to Eton. They instructed me how to be a proper servant to the prefect I would be assigned to, punishing me then as I would be at school later." He swallowed, and when he met her gaze, his eyes were haunted. "They were right, until Gabriel and Zeph came to my rescue. I shall never forget what they did for me, but it was too late. The darkness had long been in my heart. Then I saw you that day in the jewelry shop prior to the house party. Do you remember?"

Violet nodded. She didn't want to feel for Hugh, but his story made tears clog in her throat for the young man whose family should have been protected him instead of abusing him.

"It was if the dark clouds parted before the sun, shining down into my heart. When you smiled at me, the shadows were pushed back, and I could breathe for the first time in years."

She felt a tear trickle down her cheek. "What happened after Eton? Your father still lives. Did you return home?"

Hugh grinned, looking almost boyish. "No. Like you, I found happiness in doing what I wanted. My father has threatened to disown me a dozen times, but he won't. I'm his only heir, and he doesn't want to give the title to anyone else in the family. He's ailing though, so I hope that the title will soon be mine."

She couldn't judge him for wishing his father's death. Had she been through what he professed to, she might want to kill the man herself.

"Not to worry, darling. You will never have to meet him. We will stay away until it is time to claim what is mine. Now try to relax. We have a long journey ahead of us."

Violet huddled in the corner of the carriage seat and studied her captor from under her lashes. He confused her, angered her, scared her, and made her pity him. He'd revealed more in the last hour than he had the entire time she'd known him, and she wondered how much of this her brother knew.

With her hands tied behind her back and her feet bound, she couldn't escape. But he would have to untie her eventually. He couldn't throw her over his shoulder like a sack when they arrived at the inn and expect no one to notice. That would be her chance. No matter how much she pitied him, she had to take it.

She closed her eyes and thought of Archer. He'd been so handsome tonight at the ball. At least she'd been able to dance with him. Even if she never saw him again, she would cherish the memories he'd given her for the rest of her life.

No matter what happened, she'd never forget him. She loved him.

ARCHER URGED HIS borrowed horse through the darkened streets of London, Zeph keeping pace beside him. The horse's hooves pounded the dirt beneath him, matching the pounding of his heart and the uncertainty playing on a loop in his head. What if he was wrong and arrived too late? What if Musgrave's obsession overcame his sense and he hurt Violet? Gabriel and Christian both believed the man wouldn't harm her. What if they were wrong? Neither had believed the man capable of kidnapping either.

The decision of which route to choose had been agonizing. He didn't know Musgrave or what the man wanted from Violet. Marriage? Revenge? It was Zeph's words that ultimately guided him. The pale man had sent a runner for his horse and paid the boy to bring two more with him when he returned from the mews. As they waited, he said for Archer's ears only, "Violet knows you will come for her. Which direction did your heart go in?"

He had only to look inside himself to know.

Archer paced the walkway, as impatient as the other two men for the horses to be ready, he focused on his breathing and cleared his mind. He'd used the technique thousands of times in the military to focus his mind and prepare for a dangerous situation. This time, it also helped him drown out the pressing fear for Violet. She needed him, and in the space between one heartbeat and the next, he realized that he needed her too. She'd broken down his walls and taken hold of his heart. They were connected now, and Musgrave was taking her to Gretna Green. Archer was certain of it.

If the man felt even half of what Archer did for Violet, he'd want to marry her as soon as possible. He'd take her as far and as fast as he could to put distance between his pursuers, then disappear into the wilds and hide his tracks for the remainder of the journey.

They'd mounted the horses immediately after the boy arrived with them and made a plan. He and Zeph rode for Scotland and Gabriel went to Norwich, stopping only to have two of his men, Twisden and Granville, join him. They had taken up residence at Christian's townhouse and would watch his back in the event Archer was wrong and Musgrave had indeed headed for his home.

Though the hour was late, it seemed half of London was out. Archer and Zeph weaved through carriages and pedestrians as fast as they dared, though it slowed their progress.

"How far do you think we're behind them?" he asked Zeph.

"Musgrave would have had his carriage at the ready. I suspect he has close to an hour on us."

Archer swore. It had taken too damn long to get Musgrave's man to talk. Longer still to decide which route to take. He urged his horse faster as they left the crowded roads behind in favor of more rural land. The half-moon bathed the landscape in white light, the sky clear of all but a few wisps of clouds, and the road stretched out before them. Not a single coach rattled in the distance.

God, what if he was wrong? *No.* He couldn't be wrong.

"There are fresh tracks, but it's impossible to say if it was a carriage belonging to Musgrave," Zeph said.

"If you were making the trip from London in the dark of night, how far would you travel before stopping to rest the horses and consider taking another route?"

The cryptic man gave a low chuckle. "As far as I could. The excitement is in the fleeing. And the chase."

"He can't be too much farther ahead." *Please let us be in time.*

They passed through two more small towns before Archer spotted something dark moving in the distance. He could just make out the shape of a carriage as it was disappearing around a bend. "There!"

They galloped after the conveyance.

A faint shout rang out as they gained on the carriage.

Archer saw someone's head lean out the window. The person reached out, leveled their arm, and fired a shot.

Zeph snorted. "As if that fool could hit us firing from a bumpy carriage in the dark."

"How many shots will he have?" Archer didn't know much about antique pistols. Did they still use flintlocks in this time? Church would have known.

"Perhaps one more before reload."

A warning shot, then.

I'm coming for you, sweetheart.

They closed in. The driver urged the horses faster as Musgrave shouted orders from the window. This part of the road wound around the side of a low hill, and as the driver spurred the horses on, the carriage tilted hard to one side.

Archer's heart lodged in his throat. He spared a glance at the landscape and saw the ground slope away from the road down toward a lake.

The carriage teetered, but the driver kept it upright.

They were close enough to see the dark shape of luggage strapped to the roof and the edge of the curtain flapping in the wind as Musgrave leaned out and fired another shot.

Archer veered his horse back behind the coach, out of Musgrave's field of sight. Zeph rode beside him, focused on the opposite door.

"I'll distract him when you are close," Archer called to him.

Zeph nodded. "I'll get her. Take this." He withdrew a pistol from inside his waistcoat and held it out. Archer moved in close enough to grab the gun. He cocked the hammer, falling back enough to get a good view of Musgrave's door, and waited for Zeph to close the distance.

He reached the back of the carriage and gave Archer a nod.

Pistol in hand, Archer surged toward Musgrave's window.

Suddenly the carriage lurched right.

Zeph swore and reined his horse aside to avoid a collision. The driver stood on his platform, twisted around, and fired his own pistol. The shot went wide.

One of the horses neighed, bucking its head, and bumped the other, making the coach sway left.

The driver pulled the reins to veer back toward the center of the road just as the back wheel went off the edge of the incline. The carriage shuddered, then tilted to the left right as Musgrave leaned out his window to line up another shot. His weight unbalanced the coach and it tilted precariously.

Archer cried out just as the right wheels left the road and the vehicle tipped on its side. It crashed hard into the ground, sending dirt flying. The driver fell from his seat, the horses rolling over him in a tangle of legs and leather straps. The frightened animals regained their footing and began to drag the man as they tried to race away.

The carriage, carried by its own weight and momentum began to slide toward the lake. It slid down the slope, gaining speed before it hit a large rock protruding from the ground. With a loud crack and a sickening crunch, it flipped onto the roof and slipped into the lake upside down where it immediately began to sink.

No! "Violet!" Their horses slipped and slid down the hill after it. The lake was deep, swallowing up the carriage as the water rushed over it. This couldn't be happening. Not to the woman he loved. He'd just found Violet. He couldn't lose her. Not when he'd lost so many others. Not when he could save her.

Archer barely reined his horse in as he leapt from the saddle.

He shrugged off his jacket, watching for any movement, praying Violet was alive, and dove into the cold, dark water. He swam in quick, powerful strokes, reaching the vehicle just before the wheels went under. Taking a deep breath, he dove and felt for the door. The window was up on this side of the carriage. He pushed himself to the other side, surfaced for a breath of air, and dove back down.

The water was murky and pitch black. But this was what he'd been trained for as a SEAL; he had no fear or panic, his mind completely focused on his task. He felt the familiar battle-ready calm settle over him as he reached the carriage.

Archer found the window and pushed partway in. It was too small for his wide shoulders, allowing only his head and one arm through. He reached blindly inside, searching for Violet. He caught the edge of silk and pulled until he latched onto one of her limbs. Her arm, he realized as he found her elbow.

She didn't move at the contact.

Fuck.

Archer maneuvered her closer to the window. If he could get her out, he could still save her. An inch from the door, she jerked backward as if pulled from behind. Something moved inside.

Musgrave.

Archer reached for the knife in the special sheath at the small of his back that the tailor had sewn in. He pulled it free and stabbed at the dark shadow. The water resisted his strike, but Archer had trained for months in underwater combat and adjusted for it. He sliced at Musgrave, making the man jerk back, pulling Violet with him.

A dull thud sounded from the other side, as if Musgrave tried to open the carriage door, but he'd been under too long, and his movements grew sluggish.

Archer found Violet once more and pulled her through the small window as gently as he could, thankful for her size. She was so still in his arms. So cold. He used his knife to cut away parts of her dress that caught on the mangled carriage, then tucked her to his side and pulled her to the surface. Zeph was there, and helped Archer get her ashore.

"Musgrave?"

Archer nodded at the carriage and then laid Violet on her back. Her hands and feet were bound. "He fought me but ran out of air." She wasn't breathing.

Shit, shit, shit.

"You're not going to die, sweetheart," he said, thankful for the clear night sky and the light of the moon as he sliced through the ropes to free her and tossed them away, then set the knife aside. "I won't let you leave me." He gave her two breaths, then started chest compressions. Out of the corner of his eye, he saw Zeph slosh back in the water, heading for the carriage.

He knew Zeph and Musgrave had been friends once, but Archer didn't give a damn at the moment whether the man lived or died. Violet was his only concern.

He kept up the CPR another minute until she violently coughed and started to spit out water. He turned her on her side, murmuring words of encouragement, while his heart hammered in his ears.

She stopped vomiting and burst into tears.

Archer gathered her in his arms, holding her tightly. "I've got you, sweetheart. You're okay." He ran one hand through her hair, checking her head for injuries. There was a nasty bump on her temple and a shallow cut behind her ear. He'd check the rest of her for injuries soon. Right now, he needed to feel her alive and breathing in his arms.

"Y-y-you c-came," she whispered in a broken voice.

He pressed a kiss to her forehead. "I'll always come for you."

"But you're going to le—"

"*Shhh.* I'm not leaving you, Violet. When I found out you'd been taken, I lost my mind," he admitted, throat so tight he could barely get the words out. "And just now, when I saw the carriage crash into the lake, my world stopped."

She wrapped her arms around his neck, clinging to him as she cried. He hugged her closely.

"I've lost too many people, Violet. Amanda, my parents, my team… my best friend. I can't lose you too." His voice cracked with unshed tears, ones he'd swallowed back for years. He had so much pain and had denied it all. But now… "If I lose you, I won't survive it."

Violet pressed a kiss to the scar on his jaw. Her lips were cold, and she trembled in his arms, but he'd never felt anything sweeter.

She moved one arm enough to trail her fingers over his cheek.

He leaned into her touch and held her tighter.

"I love you, Archer Bennett," she whispered.

His heart cracked open, and he took a shaky breath. "Violet." Archer pressed his lips to hers, kissing her gently, and pouring everything he felt into the kiss. "I love you too," he said against her mouth, then kissed her again.

Archer held her until he heard Zeph splashing back toward the shore. In his arms was the unmoving body of Musgrave. He'd sustained several wounds, both from Archer's knife and the carriage accident. Blood seeped from his head, chest, and one hand.

"Is he dead?" Violet asked.

Zeph laid Musgrave on the shore. He stared at his friend, eyes stormy with emotion. "He lingers at the edge of death."

Violet's hand flew to her mouth and her words jumbled out in a rush. "Is it my fault? If I'd let him kiss me at the house party, maybe he wouldn't have done this. Or maybe if I'd been nicer to him. He—he suffered so much and being near me made him happy. I didn't understand. How could I? But if I hadn't lashed out at him, maybe… Maybe he would have found someone who could love him."

He understood her feelings. He'd carried the heavy burden of his team's deaths for over a year, and Amanda's long before that. He wasn't about to allow her to bear that same weight. Not when she didn't need to, as she'd so recently taught him. "It's not your fault," Archer murmured against her hair. "He made his own choices."

Tears streamed from her eyes once more. "I don't want him to die because of me." She buried her head in the crook of his neck, shaking as she wept.

Archer met Zeph's gaze. He knew the aching loss of losing the men you were closest to and didn't wish that on anyone. He set Violet on the ground beside him. He didn't want her to feel the guilt he felt every day, wondering if the outcome would have been different if only she'd made another choice. "Is his heart beating?"

Zeph put a hand on Musgrave's chest over his heart. But he didn't answer.

The hair on the back of Archer's neck prickled and goosebumps rose on his arms. The night air felt charged, like standing in the midst of a thunderstorm, waiting for lightning to strike.

"Can she ride?" Zeph asked.

"Probably a short distance. But she needs rest and dry clothes. Let me see what I can do for him. We don't have much time."

Zeph looked down at Musgrave. The moonlight reflected in his unusual silver eyes, and for a split second, they seemed to glow. With his pale hair and perfect features, he almost looked otherworldly. "I've got him. Get her to the horses."

"You sure you don't need my help?"

Zeph waved him away. "Take care of my little flower."

Archer found his coat and wrapped it around Violet's shoulders, then scooped her into his arms. He was halfway up the slope when he heard Musgrave sputter and cough.

He looked over his shoulder. Zeph knelt over Musgrave, pressing a hand to the man's chest, while he emptied the water from his lungs. "Looks like Musgrave will live, Sweetheart."

Violet lifted her head to see, then released a heavy sigh and settled back into his arms.

She didn't say anything, but then she didn't have to. Archer knew she'd wrestle with relief and guilt for a while, but at least she wouldn't have the man's death lingering in her heart.

By the time he had her settled on his horse and had retrieved Zeph's mount, the man had carried Musgrave up to the road.

Zeph lifted Musgrave into the saddle with an ease that surprised Archer. Not many men could lift deadweight like that. He was stronger than he appeared.

"There's an inn up the road. We can get some food and with a bit of luck, a couple of rooms," Zeph said.

Archer swung up behind Violet, adjusted her in his arms, and took the reins. His priority right now was getting Violet warm and fed and finding her a place to rest. Nothing else mattered. "Lead the way."

CHAPTER FIFTEEN

T HE INN ONLY had one room to rent, but seeing their wet, straggly appearances and the two wounded people in their party, the innkeeper opened a back room and made a pallet on the floor. Fortunately, Zeph had money and compensated the man for the rooms and some food for them.

Archer had never seen the cryptic man act so serious as he carried Musgrave into the back room and lay him down. He wore a sardonic smile so often that the sight of worry on his face was almost jarring.

Violet tried to help, but Zeph waved her off. "He is my responsibility this night. Rest." Then he directed the innkeeper to show Archer and "his wife" to their room.

He tucked Violet close to his side and urged her upstairs. The innkeeper returned a short time later with some stew and a hunk of bread, as well as a pot of warm water and some cloth to wash up with. It wasn't a hot bath, but it was damn better than nothing.

The moment the man left, Archer locked the door behind him, then stripped Violet out of her sodden clothes. He laid them over a chair to dry, then bathed her with the cloth until her pale skin warmed to a healthy pink and between that and the roaring fire in the hearth, she no longer shivered.

"You don't have to wash me and feed me as a babe," she

murmured, cheeks pink as she sat naked before him.

Archer tugged the quilt off the bed and wrapped it around her. "I like caring for you." He removed his own clothes and used the last of the water to clean as much of the lake water from his skin as he could. Taking care of his woman, seeing to her needs, was a new experience that he found immensely satisfying. During his years in the service, he hadn't thought much about having a wife and kids. As one of his instructors once told him, if the Navy had wanted him to have a wife, they would have issued him one.

He'd expected to stay in until retirement, even if that meant teaching new recruits or new SEALs for those last few years. He'd figured he had time to decide what he wanted after that, and if there was a woman along the way, so be it. The IED had changed all that and made finding a woman to share his life with seem that much more unlikely.

Time travel hadn't really been part of his plan either, but here he was, bare ass naked in an inn in the middle of nowhere in the nineteenth century with a woman thirteen years younger than him and feeling happier than he had in a decade. He hadn't seen that curve ball coming, but he'd hit it and somehow, made it through to home base.

Home.

Yeah, being with Violet kinda felt like that. Like being home. With his sisters here, he had his family back too. Staying meant that he wouldn't find Amada's killer, but somehow, he thought she would understand and in the end, would want him to be happy. He'd just have to trust that justice would catch up to the man. If he was even still alive. Either way, putting Amanda's killer behind bars wouldn't bring her back.

Leaving Violet would destroy what was left of his heart.

Archer watched her as she ate her fill of the stew and bread. She was so damn beautiful. She could have any man she wanted.

Violet set the bowl aside and brushed her fingers off. She twisted the quilt in her hands and looked at her lap. "Archer?"

"Yeah, sweetheart?"

"Did you mean what you said?" Her voice was rough from coughing up water.

"That I love you?"

Her breath hitched and she met his gaze. "Yes. Did you mean that?"

He crossed to stand in front of her and cupped her cheek in his palm. "I do. I love you, Violet. You're aggravating, you're a little wild, and your heart is as beautiful as you are, but I've never loved anyone more."

She leaned into his palm. "Are you staying?"

Archer scooped her into his arms and set her in the middle of the bed. He tucked her under the sheets and spread the quilt back over the bed, then climbed in beside her. She turned in his arms and stroked his back, hands wandering lower. He caught one hand, holding it to his side. He couldn't let her distract him yet. "Violet, you know I don't have the means to give you the life you're used to. Not yet. Would you still want me to stay even if you had to give all of that up?"

She pressed a kiss to his lips. "Yes."

He read the certainty on her face. Her eyes shone in the candlelight, and she traced her free hand over his shoulder and down his arm. "I will find something. There has to be some way to put my skills to use in this time. Then, when I have the money, I'll marry you."

Violet pinched his arm.

"What was that for?"

"If you wish to marry me, you will do the proper thing and ask me, not simply tell me what I will do. And if you think that I will sit around waiting for you to make however much money you think you need to marry me, then I assure you that you are mistaken."

"Is that so?" He couldn't hide his grin. He'd never loved anyone more than this woman.

She nuzzled his neck. "Yes, that is so. You've already ruined me. Besides, the longer that you take to ask me to marry you, the longer it will be until we can live as husband and wife, making love at night, and kissing whenever we wish."

Damn, she had a valid point. In this society, she couldn't live with him even if he had a place to live until they were married. Archer sat back and pulled her up until she sat before him. Taking her left hand in his, he raised it to his lips and pressed a lingering kiss on her palm. "Violet Hawthorne, I don't have a ring, or any money." He glanced down at himself. "Or any clothes. But will you marry me?"

She burst into giggles and hugged him tight. "Yes, Archer Bennett. I will marry you. When we're dressed."

He snorted and kissed her, tangling their tongues together. He laid her back down on the bed and tugged the quilt over them, wrapping her in his arms.

"You're so handsome," she said, pushing a strand of hair out of his face. She traced the scar on his jaw down his neck. "I shall never tire of looking at you. I love your body and the strength of your muscles. You make me feel treasured whenever you take me in your arms."

"You *are* treasured," he said.

"Show me."

Archer groaned and rested his forehead against hers. "You nearly drowned tonight, sweetheart. You need rest."

"I need *you*. I need to feel more than fear, and cold, and pain. Please, Archer." She slid her hand down his chest and wrapped it around his cock. "Show me."

Her plea slayed him. Archer rolled her onto her back and caged her beneath his body. Violet gasped and undulated her hips, rocking her core against his hardening cock. He slid through her folds and barely held back a moan of pleasure. He flexed his hips and pressed harder against her heat.

"Yes," she breathed.

He kissed his way down her body, taking time to tease her breasts with his tongue, then continued down between her parted thighs. Her arousal perfumed the air, and he breathed her in, then put his mouth on her. He took his time, licking through her folds and sucking her nub, pleasuring her until she came. She trembled against his lips, fingers clutching his hair to hold him where she wanted him. He felt her come down from the peak and worked her into another.

Violet arched her back as the climax took her, breathy little moans spilling from her lips. He'd never heard anything so beautiful.

"Archer," she whispered, tugging him up.

He moved up her body, pausing to lick and suck her pretty nipples, and slowly slid into her warm depths. Archer made love to Violet, eyes locked with hers, letting her see how much she affected him. How much he loved her. When he was close, he rubbed circles on her nub with his thumb until she came. He barely remembered to pull out before he spilled his seed, claiming her as his. Then he tucked her into his arms and held her close.

He'd almost lost her tonight. If it weren't for his training, she might have drowned in that carriage. He hadn't been able to save Amanda, Church, or his team, but he'd saved the woman he loved, and that went a long way toward healing those wounds. Amanda and Church, the rest of the guys, they'd always be part of him, but they would want him to be happy. He knew it, because if the situation were reversed and he was the one who'd died, he knew he would want them to move past the darkness and find their own happiness.

As Violet dozed in his arms and he felt sleep tugging him under, he said a final word of thanks to the people he'd lost, including his parents. He kissed Violet's temple and then gave in to sleep.

THE FOLLOWING MORNING, after a short breakfast, Archer helped Violet up onto his horse. They were returning to London immediately so that Lily, Bellamy, and Christian wouldn't worry.

Zeph led two horses out of the barn. "I paid the barkeep for this one." He patted a dapple-gray horse on the flank. The horse nudged him with its nose and flicked its tail. Zeph grinned. "I think she likes me." He winked at them. "I'm heading east to find Gabriel. With luck, we will return to London late tonight or tomorrow morning."

"What of Musgrave?"

Zeph looked past him toward the inn. "He will ride with me. He hasn't spoken since the accident, and I sense deep guilt and sadness in him."

"Do you think he'll come after Violet again?" He felt her tense beside him.

"No. I will make certain of it before we part."

"How?" she asked.

"We've been friends for a long time. I can reach him as no one else can, even in his present state of mind. He will listen to me. Trust me, my sweet."

Violet nodded and the tension bled from her shoulders. "Thank you."

Archer handed the reins to Violet, then moved closer to Zeph. Something about last night had been bothering him. "You didn't answer my question last night about whether Musgrave had a pulse. Even if he did, you got him breathing faster than I could have with CPR. How did you do it?" Not to mention the ease with which he lifted a full-grown man who was deadweight into the saddle.

A smile played at the edges of Zeph's lips and his eyes sparkled. His white hair blew in the breeze when he adjusted the brim of his hat. "It is of no consequence. Time was of the essence to revive him, so I worked quickly."

Could anyone work that quickly? Archer remembered the feeling of a gathering storm in those last few moments before he'd taken Violet up the hill to where the horses waited. He'd seen some weird shit during his time overseas. Things that often defied explanation. Something told him he'd just seen another. "You must have a magic touch."

Zeph laughed. "You give me too much credit. It's not as if I brought the man back from the dead, is it?"

Did he? No. That was crazy. The man was mysterious to the point of esoteric, but he was not someone who could bring the dead back to life. Still, it was also unlikely that Musgrave would have responded to the CPR so fast. "If I asked you to tell me exactly what happened, would you?"

"Ask me and see."

"Tell me what happened with Musgrave last night."

"No." Zeph clapped him on the shoulder as he strode past. "See you in a few hours."

Archer swore and shook his head, unable to hold back a chuckle. Had he really expected anything different?

Zeph pressed a kiss to Violet's forehead when she leaned over to hug him, then strode inside the inn, presumably to retrieve Musgrave.

Archer had mixed feelings about the other man, but as long as he didn't come after Violet again, it didn't matter what he thought. He mounted the horse behind her and then settled her onto his lap. She felt so good in his arms. "Let's get you home."

"I am desperate for a bath and clean clothes."

He kissed her, savoring her taste, then urged the horse onto the road back to London.

THE MOMENT THEY arrived at Gabriel's townhouse in London, Lily had thrown open the door and rushed down the steps to envelop Violet in a warm hug. She'd cried tears of laughter while begging to know what had happened. Bellamy and Christian had run out shortly after to hug them and usher them inside for tea and cakes.

Violet told them about Musgrave's appearance at Almack's and how he'd coerced her to leave, then his plans to take her to Gretna Green. She struggled with whether to reveal any of the secrets he'd shared, but in the end, said only that he'd been lost within his mind and the dark parts of his heart when he'd concocted his plans.

Archer gave a brief version of the rescue, leaving out that she'd almost drowned and that he'd made love to her again.

After that, she'd taken a delightful bath and put on clean clothes in time for a small dinner. They'd avoided any further conversation of the events from last night, for which Violet was immensely grateful. She wasn't ready to think more about Hugh Musgrave, but a part of her truly pitied him.

The five of them were now gathered in the drawing room for tea and dessert. The sun had set, and Lily and Bellamy chatted quietly about another young woman Bellamy had met at Almack's last night who was in dire need of her services for a more flattering wardrobe. Violet held the latest issue of Ackerman's, not really looking at the pages as she turned them. Were Gabriel and Zeph okay? Would they return soon? She heard that Owen Granville, one of the other men from Eton, had traveled with Gabriel toward Hugh's country estate, in case he'd taken her there. Hopefully they hadn't ridden all the way to Norwich before Zeph intercepted them.

Movement by the window caught her eye and she looked up to see Christian walking toward Archer. They spoke quietly, then Christian withdrew the small, jeweled egg clock from his pocket. Her heart seized in panic at the sight of it. Had he repaired the clock? Archer said he would stay, but that was when the clock was broken, and they thought it would never be repaired. If Christian were able to find the crystal and the clock could time travel again, would Archer reconsider? Would he leave?

She surged off the chaise and flew across the room, ready to do anything, say anything to make him stay.

"...Carter at Almack's. He gave me this." Christian removed

a tiny crystal from his pocket. It was a shard of white with small veins of aqua blue.

Violet had never seen anything like it. "You can't," she cried, grabbing the clock out of Christian's hand. She hid it behind her back, as if Archer couldn't see it, and glared at him. "You said you would stay. You made me a promise."

The room fell silent except for the ticking of the clock in the hall. It seemed loud, like each tick reverberated around her.

"This is his chance to return home, Violet," Christian said. He looked at Lily, then at Bellamy and his blue eyes clouded with pain. "For all of them. We can't force them to stay. They must stay because they want to."

"Maybe it won't even work," she said. "Maybe it's the wrong crystal. What do we even know about Carter? He could have sold you a fake, and you would be getting their hopes up for nothing. Well, I won't let you do it. I'll… I'll throw it in the fire first."

"Violet!" Gabriel's voice boomed from the door.

She spun to see her brother storm into the room. His eyes were wild with emotion, reflecting the fear she and Christian both felt.

"Give me the clock," he demanded. He held out his hand.

Violet squeezed her eyes closed and gripped the jeweled egg. She didn't want to give it to him, but Christian was right. Archer would resent her if she forced him to stay, and whatever love they had would wither and die. She prayed that he loved her as much as he professed. As much as she loved him. She opened her eyes, then slowly set the clock in Gabriel's palm.

Gabriel handed the clock to Christian, then faced Lily. He didn't say a word, just clasped his hands behind his back, and waited.

Lily smiled and went to him, wrapping her arms around his waist. "I've faced this decision once, remember? I had the clock and chose not to use it."

"It wouldn't have worked," he said in a gruff voice.

"True, but I didn't know that at the time. I'm staying, my

love. You can't get rid of me that easily. You're my husband, and you're damn well going to take care of this baby with me."

Gabriel let out an inarticulate noise and hugged her tightly. He whispered something into her hair and Lily glowed with love, pressing a kiss to his lips.

Violet saw Bellamy at Christian's side. She held the crystal up to the light, then passed it back with a smile and wrapped her arms around his waist. It seemed she was staying too. Would Archer also make that decision?

She blinked away her tears and tried to still her racing heart. When she finally found the courage to face him, the look he gave her stole her breath. He crossed the short space between them, not limping in the slightest, cupped her face and kissed her. It was a rough, deep, passionate kiss. Terribly inappropriate for the company they were with, but Violet didn't care. Archer claimed her with that kiss. There, before everyone, he told her with his mouth that she was his.

Gabriel noisily cleared his throat.

He sucked her lower lip as he broke the kiss and stared down into her eyes. "I'm not going anywhere, sweetheart," he whispered. "Throw that clock in the fucking fire if you want. Nothing will take me from your side."

Violet melted against him. The tears broke free once more, flowing down her face as her heart burst with happiness. They'd each lost people they loved. Archer had lost his friends and his parents. She'd lost her father, and then her mother when the woman couldn't cope with the loss and now spent her days in a cloud of opium or a bottle of laudanum. Through the clock, they'd found each other, and together, they'd finally let their hearts begin to heal.

Christian pulled a tool from his pocket and opened the clock face. He set the crystal inside and fiddled with the mechanics. Then he closed the clock and set the time to just before twelve.

"I know just where to put that," Lily said. "I found it in a desk that once belonged to you, in a hidden compartment at the back of a drawer."

Christian smiled. "I know the spot."

"It was in a black velvet jewelry box," Lily added. "I found it by accident and took it home to repair it for my boss in thanks for giving me a job. I had no idea it would bring us all here."

"How else would you get home?" Zeph asked. He lounged against the door frame with a cup of tea in his hand.

Violet hadn't heard him enter and suspected that was just how he liked it.

He winked at her over the rim of his china cup. She realized then that it was painted with tiny purple violets in a pattern she'd never seen before. Where had he found that? Surely he didn't bring his own teacups with him wherever he went.

She shook her head at her silly thought. No doubt he got it from one of their servants in the kitchen below, after he'd turned his horse over to a footman.

Lily smiled at him. "We *are* home, aren't we?" She looked at her siblings. "It's what I wanted. I think it's what Mom and Dad would have wanted."

Archer and Bellamy agreed.

Zeph wandered into the room to talk to Christian and Bellamy, while Lily studied the little egg once more.

Gabriel pulled Violet into a hug. "I'm happy for you, Vi. Tell me, does he meet your list of qualifications? I have it on my desk upstairs if we need to review it once again."

She laughed and gave him a light shove. "No, I don't think he meets any of them. I realized that none of those things mattered. What I wanted most was the kind of love that you and Lily have, and that's what I found."

He kissed her temple. "Good." Then he turned to Archer, piercing him with a steady look. "I believe you have something to ask me, Bennett?"

"I do. I'm going to marry Violet, and I'd like your blessing." Archer wrapped his arm around her waist, holding her against him.

"You don't want to ask me for my permission?" He leaned in as he spoke, closing the scant space between them in an almost threatening manner.

"No. I'm marrying her anyway." Archer held his ground, not looking the least bit intimidated by her brother.

Violet nearly swooned. Seeing him meet her brother with such confidence was heady.

A flicker of a smile crossed Gabriel's lips. "You are perfect for her aren't you? There's no one else I would consider for her hand, Bennett. I know you will love and care for her more than any other."

Archer nodded and they shook hands.

"Come by my study tomorrow, and we'll go over the details." Gabriel clapped a hand on his shoulder and then went to find Lily.

"I don't know how marriages work here, but I'm guessing there's no drive through wedding chapel with Elvis nearby."

Violet blinked. "What's an Elvis?"

"Never mind. I meant that I'm pretty sure that you can't marry immediately. Like tomorrow or something."

She smiled, her heart warming as she realized that he was anxious to solidify their union. "No, it will take a few weeks for the banns to be read. After that, we can marry whenever we wish. I believe that Bellamy and Christian are hoping to marry next month."

"What kind of wedding do you want, Violet? Summer? Fall? Big with all of your friends and family?" He shifted from foot to foot, looking a bit nervous.

Violet pressed a kiss to his jaw, then whispered in his ear, "I want to be your wife as soon as possible, Archer Bennett. That way I won't have to sneak into your bed."

He kissed her long and sweetly and with so much tenderness. "How about I sneak into yours tonight?"

She grinned. "As long as we're together, it doesn't matter which."

Archer pulled her closer and kissed her again. "Sweetheart, we'll never be apart. Destiny… fate, whatever you want to call it, brought me to you."

"That must mean we're meant to be together."

"Even if it doesn't, you're mine. No one will take you from me."

"Then you're mine also," she said.

"I am. I love you, Violet. I'll spend eternity showing you."

Archer smiled at her, and it was the most beautiful thing she'd even seen. This warrior had barged into her life and won her heart. He'd shown her his scars and saw her own. Now she planned to give him as much happiness as he could hold. Archer Bennett deserved all that and more.

EPILOGUE

Christmas, 1814
Hawthorne Hall
Marston, England

BIG, FLUFFY SNOWFLAKES fell outside, blanketing the garden and green beyond in white. The windows were frosted around the edges and a cool draft seeped in despite the heavy dark blue drapes that hung on either side. A fire crackled merrily in the hearth, giving much-needed warmth to the drawing room, and pine boughs hanging on the mantle scented the air.

Violet loved Christmas at Hawthorne Hall. Some of her best memories were here, when her papa had been alive, and her mother still glowed with happiness. Much had changed since those long-ago days, but some things were far better. Warm arms wrapped around her, pulling her back against a solid chest. She breathed in Archer's clean, woodsy scent, and snuggled into his embrace.

"Thinking of a frolic in the snow before dinner?" he asked, his low voice brushing her ear.

Violet shivered with awareness. "I had, but I confess that I am considering frolicking in a different place now."

He gave a dark chuckle. "I could be tempted to oblige you. Where did you have in mind?" His hand on her stomach slid lower on her belly and across to her hip.

Anywhere she could strip his clothes off in privacy. Violet turned in his arms and met his lips in a fierce kiss. He pulled her closer and slanted his mouth over hers.

In the months since he'd decided to stay, the fire that burned between them seemed to only grow hotter. They couldn't keep their hands from one another, and she instigated their lovemaking as often as he did. They'd married a week after the last banns were read in the small chapel in Marston village down the road. It meant leaving London before the Season was officially over, but Violet was more than willing to do so if it meant she and Archer could finally be husband and wife.

Gabriel had given a generous dowry of both money and a small estate several hours away. The money was enough for them to live on quite happily, but Archer still wanted to make his own way here, and Violet loved him all the more for it. They hadn't yet moved into their home either. In truth, Violet wasn't ready to leave, and she suspected that Archer wasn't either. He and Lily had become quite close, and Violet loved her sister-in-law dearly. Living with Gabriel, Lily, and baby Jacob was wonderful, and she hadn't once felt like a burden to them, as she'd feared.

"I just rang for tea," Lily said as she entered the drawing room. "Although it appears I might be early."

Archer and Violet broke apart and he brushed his knuckles over her cheek before stepping away to see Lily. She held little Jacob, and in seconds, Archer had lifted the boy into his arms and tucked him close.

Lily laughed as Violet joined her. "I think Archer is going to spoil him."

Violet grinned as her husband made faces at the baby. "He'll be a wonderful father."

Lily linked their arms together. "Any news about that to share?" she asked hopefully.

"Not yet." She looked forward to motherhood, but she

wasn't disappointed to not be pregnant. It gave her and Archer more time together. "With Jacob, and soon Bellamy and Christian's baby, we shall have plenty of practice when the time comes."

"Indeed. Let's have tea."

They turned just as Reginald and a footman entered carrying trays loaded with tea, sandwiches, and sweet cakes. Gabriel and the rest of their party followed. Bellamy and Christian were visiting, as were Owen Granville and George Twisden.

Reginald was Gabriel's steward, although he frequently took the jobs assigned to the butler. Violet always suspected that it was so he could be within earshot of Gabriel at any given moment. The man hovered worse than a mother at a ball. No one else quite annoyed Gabriel like her and Reginald, and it had become an entertaining pastime to see who could annoy him more.

"Thank you, Reginald," Gabriel said as the steward placed one of the trays on the sideboard. The footman set the tray of tea beside it, bowed, and quit the room.

"Is there anything else you require, my lord?" Reginald asked.

"No. Yes. Take some time to spend with your family. You don't need to hover over me the entirety of Christmas."

"I never hover, my lord."

Gabriel eyed him. "What would you prefer to call it?"

A corner of Reginald's lip curled. "Entertainment, my lord."

Gabriel looked confused, but Violet burst into giggles.

"Lord Lael should arrive shortly. When he does, please show him in and make sure his room is prepared."

Reginald gave a short bow and left the room.

Violet went to Gabriel and hugged him.

He wrapped his arm around her and sighed. "That man is a menace."

She grinned. "That's why I adore him."

"It is a wonder that I let either of you live here." Despite his grousing, he pressed a kiss to her temple. "Add in Zeph, and I shall go mad before the New Year."

That reminded her of a conversation she'd had months ago. She'd meant to ask Gabriel and forgotten until this moment. "Why didn't you tell me that Zeph was married once and outlived his wife? I felt terrible asking him and bringing up that pain."

Gabriel pursed his lips.

"You didn't know." That surprised her. Gabriel, Christian, and Zeph were the closest of their group of friends from Eton.

Gabriel shook his head. "There are a great many things that I do not know about Zeph. I feel as if I could know him the whole of my life and never truly *know* him. I'm not sure that anyone does or if anyone ever will."

Violet frowned. How sad that no one knew much about him. Perhaps he wanted it that way, but every man should have someone they could confide in. She would be that person whether he liked it or not. Decision made, she followed Gabriel over to the chaise and joined their guests for tea.

LATER THAT EVENING after dinner, they gathered once again in the drawing room for desserts, games, and music. Archer leaned against the mantle and watched his wife play the pianoforte, while the others gathered around her to sing. It was his first Christmas with family since he was eighteen, and he couldn't remember the last one. He knew it had been with his parents, but not much more than that. He shipped out six months later with the Navy and never looked back.

He'd been deployed for most of the Christmases after, and the few that he hadn't been, he hadn't wanted to go home. By then his parents were gone, his sisters were struggling, and he couldn't bring himself to face any of it. He'd missed so much.

Archer rubbed his left thigh. It still pained him, but he no longer needed the cane. His external wounds from the attack had healed as much as they could. The wounds in his heart were also healing, though slowly. The nightmares came less often and didn't hold him in the grip they once had. He attributed most of that to Violet and this family and knew that those he lost would be happy for him.

He felt someone at his side and looked up to see Zeph there. "Lael."

The man nodded in greeting. "Happy Christmas, Bennett."

"Happy Christmas. I'm glad you could join us." It was true. Zeph was as much his family now as Gabriel and Christian.

"Where else would I be?"

"Making mischief with my wife somewhere."

Zeph laughed. "I fear she is the instigator."

Archer snorted. "She would say the same of you."

"Undoubtedly." That unusual silver gaze focused on him. Zeph looked more serious than normal tonight. "Do you miss your time?"

"No." It was a question he'd asked himself several times before, and the answer remained the same. His heart was with Violet and this family. "I'm glad for the work that I did, and if it hadn't been for my training, Violet would have died. But I don't miss the war, or seeing the evil that can permeate a man's heart. After the attack, I really struggled to reacclimate to a normal life. I'd seen and done such terrible things. I felt as if I couldn't even talk to a normal person, because the scars on my soul were too deep. Coming here, meeting Violet, and seeing my sisters again, forced me to learn to how to live instead of slowly dying." Shit, he hadn't meant to share so much.

"There will always be wars," Zeph replied. "We may be at peace for the moment since Napoleon abdicated, but it will not last. If not him, then another will rise up. It is the way of mankind."

Archer nodded. He'd seen far too much of it.

"And just as there will be another leader, there will always be soldiers in need of an anchor to hold them steady when the seas seem like they will never be calm again. Even now, men are returning broken from war. Men in need of their own anchor."

"Violet is my anchor," Archer replied.

"Who will be theirs?" Zeph's piercing gaze seemed to speak to him, and an idea began forming in Archer's mind.

"Are you suggesting that I find a way to help them?"

Zeph shrugged one shoulder. "Only you can answer that."

The idea had merit, but he wasn't sure if he could help them. He'd barely helped himself. Still, the thought took root. Maybe, if they returned to London for the Season, he could find a way to help them and support his family at the same time.

Lily broke away from the rest of the group and danced toward them. When she reached them, she planted a kiss on Archer's cheek, then took Zeph's hand. "I've asked Violet to play a few dance tunes. Join us?"

He grinned. "How can I deny my hostess?"

"You cannot. Come on, Arch, you, too." She tugged Zeph toward the center of the room where Gabriel and Christian began to move furniture out of the way. Reginald nearly tripped on his feet running from the doorway to help them.

"How would you know I needed assistance if you weren't hovering?" Gabriel groused.

"Excellent timing," the steward replied before he moved a chair out of the way.

Archer watched their interaction for a moment more, then sought out his wife. Violet turned a few pages of music, searching for something. When she looked up, their eyes locked, and the room faded until he could see only her.

Violet's love shone light into the shadows of his heart, drawing him like a moth. In a fortnight, she'd become everything to him, and in the months that followed, he'd known a love he hadn't believed existed.

Maybe it was fate, or something more. But somehow, he and his sisters had been taken by destiny, and the love they found brought them together again. If their parents were looking down this Christmas, he hoped they would be pleased with their children. Life hadn't turned out the way any of them had expected, but it had never been sweeter.

Archer crossed the room to take his wife in his arms. His future was right here in the past, with a love that would last for eternity.

THE END

Dear Reader,

Thank you so much for joining me on this journey back to the Regency era with the Bennett family. When I first conceived of this trilogy I had no idea how vibrant the characters were or how wonderful their stories would be. I fell in love with these couples as each story unfolded, met some fascinating side characters that are begging for their own stories, and learned a lot about the time period. I truly hope that you love them as much as I do.

If you haven't read the other books in this trilogy, then I encourage you to read Lily and Gabriel's story in *The Earl's Timely Wallflower*, and Bellamy and Christian's story in *Tempting the Reclusive Earl*. There's also a connected story featuring the side character Owen Granville in the *Night of Lyons* anthology.

Speaking of connected stories, I'm developing a series featuring Carter from this *Taken by Destiny* trilogy. The dandy collector is not at all who he appears to be and has a long history with Percy Mansfield. Stay tuned for more! And to keep up to date on all my new releases, please sign up for my newsletter at aurrorastjames.com/newsletter.

I know that your time is precious, and it means so much to me that you opted to spend some time reading one of my books when you could have done so many other things instead. I hope this story provided you with a few hours of entertainment that swept you away into a world of love, excitement, and romance!

Best wishes,
Aurrora St. James

About the Author

Aurrora St. James has been writing romance since she was a teen. Fortunately for the world, those stories will never see the light of day. Now, she loves writing sexy, paranormal romances featuring tough and sometimes dark heroes, women who find their inner strength, and a touch of humor added in for spice. In particular, she enjoys writing both Medieval and Regency romances that whisk readers into the beautiful landscapes of history, where love can overcome anything.

When she's not writing, you'll find her reading, drinking coffee, making her own journals, or watching old B, C, and D-movies. She lives in the Florida jungle with her husband, a slightly crazy dog, and a cat that thinks he's a brontosaurus.

Social Media:
Website: www.aurrorastjames.com
Facebook: facebook.com / AurroraStJamesAuthor
Instagram: instagram.com / aurrorastjames
Pinterest: pinterest.com / ladyaurrora
Bookbub: bookbub.com / authors / aurrora-st-james
Amazon: amazon.com / Aurrora-St.-James / e / B00E46VJD8
Goodreads: goodreads.com / AurroraStJames